D1624613

Truelove & Homegrown Tomatoes

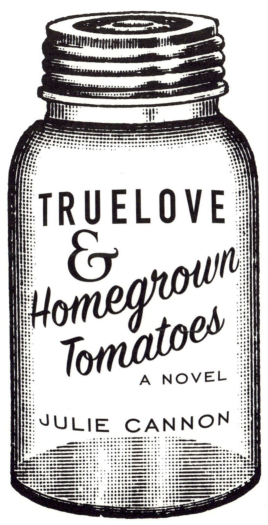

TRUELOVE
&
Homegrown Tomatoes

A NOVEL

JULIE CANNON

HILL STREET PRESS ᴅ ATHENS, GEORGIA

ADULT SERVICES

A HILL STREET PRESS BOOK

Published in the United States of America by Hill Street Press LLC
191 East Broad Street, Suite 209   Athens, Georgia 30601-2848 USA
706-613-7200   info@hillstreetpress.com   www.hillstreetpress.com

Hill Street Press is committed to preserving the written word. Every effort is
made to print books on acid-free paper with a significant amount of post-
consumer recycled content.

This is a work of fiction. All names, characters, places, and situations are either
products of the author's imagination or are used fictitiously. No reference to any
real person, living or deceased, is intended nor should be inferred, and any simi-
larity is entirely coincidental. The author states that although this novel is set in
an actual town, along an actual river, it is nevertheless a fictional work and the
source of inspiration is her respect and affection for the farming folk of rural
Georgia, and their devotion to the land, and reverence for God.

Library of Congress Cataloging-in-Publication Data

Truelove & homegrown tomatoes : a novel / Julie Cannon
        p.   cm.
    ISBN 1-892514-87-7 (alk. paper)
    1. Widows—Fiction. 2. Georgia—Fiction. 3. Loneliness—Fiction.
    4. Tomato growers—Fiction. I. Title: Truelove and homegrown tomatoes.
    II. Title: True love & home grown tomatoes. III. Title.
    PS3603.A55 T78 2001
    813'.6—dc21   2001016830

ISBN# 1-892514-87-7

10   9   8   7   6   5   4   3   2   1

First printing

FOR MY TRUELOVE, TOM,
without whose inspiration and support,
this book would never have been written

CONTENTS

PREFACE

The Lore of the Tomato, or Love-Apple

Like most Southerners, tomatoes have always been a part of my life. I grew up on homegrown tomatoes and waited expectantly each summer for that zingy burst of flavor from the season's first tomato. From June through September, they were devoured fresh from the garden. We ate them alongside snap-beans, squash, and new-potatoes, between slices of white bread with salt and mayonnaise, chopped and stewed with butterbeans and corn in succotash, and out-of-hand in the garden. The remainder of the year, those same specimens found their way out of Mason jars and freezer bags and onto our table.

I never questioned their origin. I figured tomatoes were placed here by God and enjoyed since the beginning of time. But it wasn't long before I realized that our innocent sun-kissed tomatoes had a dark, lusty, and turbulent past.

It was early in the writing of this novel, while hunkered down in the gardening aisle of my local library thumbing through books, that I came across a story which held me spellbound. It was fantastic. It wasn't fiction. It was all about tomatoes. I whipped out my library card and then I hurried home to finish reading it.

Once upon a time, in the 1500s, when conquistadors brought back loot from Mexico and Central America, they returned to Europe with an unusual round, red fruit which the native Nahua people called *tomatl.*

Our forefathers examined the fruit suspiciously and called it a "wolf peach" when they discovered it was a member of the deadly nightshade plant family. In fact, everything except the fruit *is* toxic, containing dangerous alkaloids, and causing severe digestive upset when ingested. "We only have them for curiosity in our Gardens, and for the amorous aspect or beauty of the fruit," wrote Englishman John Parkinson in 1629. He called the tomatl the "great apple of love," because it was a shapely, scarlet, sensual-looking fruit. Plus, the tomato was thought to be an aphrodisiac because it resembled the human heart, which according to the ancients was the seat of love.

Love apples made the return journey across the Atlantic with settlers from Europe. Thomas Jefferson wrote that they were grown as ornamental plants in gardens across the state of Virginia by the 1780s. Still, suspicion lingered, and the tomato was a forbidden fruit, feared by virtuous maidens. Still, it was reputed to be deadly. The tomato was condemned from the pulpit and marked with the skull and cross bones by the doctors.

Colonel Robert Gibbon Johnson gets the credit for the tomato's emancipation. In 1820, this brave, eccentric gentleman stood on the courthouse steps of Salem, New Jersey, beside a basket of tomatoes and said: "The time will come when this luscious, golden apple, rich in nutritive value, a delight to the eye, a joy to the palate, whether fried, baked, or eaten raw, will form the foundation of a great garden industry, and will be recognized, eaten, and enjoyed as an edible food. And to help speed that enlightened day, to help dispel the tall tales, the fantastic fables that you have been hearing about the thing, to show you that it is not poisonous, that it will not strike you dead, I am going to eat one right now!"

He chose a tomato as a crowd of two thousand curious onlookers waited to watch him die. He bit into the juicy red fruit, seeds sliding down his chin. He ate another and another. At first the crowd was silent and then, amazed to see him still on his feet, they began shouting and cheering. Colonel Johnson's contented slurping was heard around the country, and by 1835 the tomato was regularly appearing in markets across the land.

Today, the spicy, provocative, sultry, vine-ripened Love-Apple whispers the hints of its dangerous reputation and unsavory past from the backyard gardens of everyday folks. Nothing else has the homegrown tomato's mass appeal and without a doubt, it is the most popular fleshy fruit and will remain an American institution. If there is any controversy now about the tomato, it is which of the over 3,000 varieties to grow and then, how to prepare them.

Truelove & Homegrown Tomatoes

PROLOGUE

My Aunt Imogene sprinkled manure tea on her roses, and on her tomatoes, too. She said that was why Calvary Baptist always asked her to bring the pulpit flowers for Easter, and it was also the reason Uncle Silas married her. When she was sixteen she had the biggest Beefsteak tomatoes at the Bartow County Fair, and he was in charge of distributing awards. Uncle Silas got to her, pinned a blue ribbon on her dress, and said he sure would like to taste one of those tomatoes on a biscuit.

Over the years he tasted plenty of Imo's tomatoes, along with her squash, watermelon, cucumbers, butterbeans, and anything else that would grow in dirt, too. She called the garden her little bit of Heaven on Earth and she worked that rectangle of Euharlee the way God does a sunset. In her flower garden, Imo had hydrangeas, zinnias, sunflowers, and blue flag irises taller than I was. Some of the dahlias got so big she had to make slingshots to hold their heads up.

One time, we were all outside on a nice spring day. Jeanette and I were helping Imo gather flowers to take to her list of shut-ins. She was happy, humming along and tenderly snipping stems to the tune of "Bringing In the Sheaves."

"Would you look at this lily, Loutishie?" Imo said. She held up a bright yellow flower, twirling it around and gazing at it with such joy in her eyes. "Put a big smile on Miss Terhune's face, I imagine." She asked me to lay it gently on an old bed sheet alongside the garden.

Finally we had that sheet full of flowers. "I reckon this will do it," Imo said, gathering the corners of the sheet, walking backward and tugging it toward the house. Halfway there, she bumped into my uncle who was standing with his head bowed, his cap in his hands.

What did this mean? Something was wrong if Imo went by the look on his face. Uncle Silas turned his Feed 'n' Seed cap over and over in his hands, and I watched him looking from the garden to Imo's face. After a while he said, "I reckon this here flower patch is the only place to put it."

I remember the next moment like it was yesterday.

"Put what?" Imo asked, bed sheet poised in mid-air and a smile frozen on her face.

"We need to add another chicken house. For the money," he said. He wiped his shirt cuff across his forehead and cleared his throat.

Jeanette elbowed me in the ribs. I knew she was scared; I was, too. We could not imagine what was going through Imo's mind. Maybe she was so stunned and hurt that she couldn't find any words. Perhaps she was about to drop dead from sadness. Anyway, we could not fathom her silence. What we did know was that the money from one more chicken house couldn't have equaled the joy and delight those flowers brought her.

However, Imo never uttered one word of protest and that night we all sat down together for supper—pork chops, crowder peas, tomatoes, and biscuits.

"There sorghum?" Uncle Silas asked tentatively, peering around a clump of Queen Anne's lace spilling out of a Mason jar.

Imo rose to fetch the sorghum jar and the iced tea, too. In a couple of minutes, he aimed a knifeload of hot crowder peas and sorghum into her mouth. She smiled and fed him a morsel of 'mater biscuit.

I came to believe that true love was not blind—Imo knew perfectly well that her flowers would soon be gone. She chose to believe only the best about Uncle Silas. This is not to say that doing that was always easy, but when people have true love, they will endure a lot and suffer long.

Even now, ten years later, when I'm out on my condo's deck in suburban Atlanta, sliding my barrel garden of Better Boy tomatoes around, from sun puddle to sun puddle, trying to come as close to full-sun as I can manage, I see those two during the last four months of Uncle Silas's life. Imo sitting beside him, patting his hand and smiling bravely as her world spins out of control.

It was my world, too. My grandmother was born and raised right there on the farm. She had Imo when she was nineteen, and it took her until she was forty-five to have another child—one that lived. When Imo was just sixteen, she married Uncle Silas, and he became the son my grandmother never had. He moved in there and took up farming with my granddaddy.

Imo and Uncle Silas tried to have children of their own, but they never did, and then, ten years into their marriage, my grandmother got pregnant with my mother. It was really hard for a woman of her age and health to have a baby, so Imo was the one who raised my mother, and after my mother died, unmarried, in childbirth at age twenty-four, Imo raised *me*, Loutishie. I started calling her I-mo when I learned to talk, and she encouraged that; I guess out of deference to and respect for her sister.

Motherhood, I heard someone say once, is not an occupation automatically embraced by a woman when she gives birth. Mother is a title that is earned. When I look at photographs of me and Imo taken in my childhood, I can see how deeply she loves me. She often tells me that she couldn't have ordered a daughter that would be more perfect.

I was three when Imo and Uncle Silas adopted Jeanette. She was six years old and had bounced from foster home to foster home. Jeanette immediately called Imo mama. "Mama, mama, mama," she rolled it around on her tongue and cried it out in her sleep.

Of course, I knew that we were not the typical family, but

I realize now we had everything a person could ask for. Our lives were full of assurance and love.

I loved to be outside at dusk, chasing the lemon-green pulses of lightning bugs with Jeanette, while Imo and Uncle Silas sat in the glider holding hands. Imo didn't mind when we rifled through her Mason jars in the barn to find a home for our catch. I loved running out over the vast fields of the farm, which stretched across 300 acres of prime Georgia land and butted up against the majestic Etowah river. I loved the *feel* of the four of us: together around the supper table, hip-to-hip in the church pew on Sunday, walking single-file along the edge of the cornfield to check Uncle Silas's crop, piling into the cab of his pickup for a trip to Dairy Queen—a continual banquet of security and companionship.

I was thirteen years old that terrible afternoon in late October when our world as I knew and loved it turned upside down. I was walking with my Uncle Silas along the banks of the Etowah.

"Been a long dry spell, hasn't it gal?" he said, picking up a stone and skipping it across the water. He beckoned me over and lowered his voice even though we were the only ones around. "I guess Imo told you I'm sick."

"Uh uh, she didn't." I wondered if his arthritis was acting up.

"Dr. Bonnart said there's cancer." He skipped another stone and didn't look at me.

Cancer. I bent my head. So that was what all the hush-hush whispering and the phone calls were about. That was why all those folks at church were hugging him so hard. I fumbled for words.

"They can cure it now, you know," I managed to say, even though I couldn't swallow. I had stopped breathing.

He didn't explain what kind of cancer. Or where. And neither did Imo when I asked her that night. Jeanette told me that it was in his private parts, called the prostate, and that since he'd waited so long to go to Dr. Bonnart, it had already spread to his lymph nodes and was all over his body.

"How come nobody told me?" I whined.

"Didn't tell me neither," Jeanette said, "I heard some people talking about him down at the Buywise."

It was the beginning of December when he really had to slow down. He had gotten a lot skinnier, if that was possible, and he didn't have much energy.

Flocks of neighbors and church people started coming by with food and cards that had sunsets printed on them. They stationed themselves all around the den with serious faces and their own cancer stories.

I could tell how uncomfortable Uncle Silas was with all those people milling about the house. I saw it in his eyes whenever I walked by his bedroom door.

In February, he lay in a hospital bed, finally too weak to protest not being at home. He looked so unlike himself in a light blue gown with oxygen tubes running from the backs of his hands. There were flowers and cards lining the heater and his food-service tray.

He kept pressing the pump that slipped morphine into his blood stream, and the backs of his hands were covered in needle bruises. They were shaking, so I slipped off my sweater and laid it over them, careful of all those jutting tubes.

"I reckon things are all right at the house?" he asked.

I nodded, keeping the tears at bay by blinking a lot and thinking of a funny knock-knock joke I'd heard at school.

"I want you girls to take care of your mother," he said. "Promise me." Sick as he was and supposed to be resting to conserve strength, he kept right on.

"I promise," I said. Turning my head, I saw tough old Jeanette had dribbles of black mascara on the tops of her cheeks.

"Me too," she whispered.

I heard the door knob turn and nurses shoes squeaking across the floor. "Well, well, Mr. Lavender. And how are we today?" The nurse chirped as she lifted his chart and tapped it with a pen. "Let's check those vitals!"

She put the blood pressure cup around his pathetic biceps. Imo came in at that moment; she kissed Uncle Silas's cheek and laid a big stack of mail on his tray. Turning to speak to me and Jeanette, her shoulders drooped. "Girls, go wait out in the hall."

I heard the murmur of a serious conversation between

Imo and the nurse. I knew when I saw Imo's face coming out of that hospital room that Uncle Silas wouldn't be with us much longer.

ONE

The Dead of Winter

*"You don't have to look any further than your
compost heap if you want to be comforted.
If you need reassurance. You've got this stinking,
rotting heap of decay, and then out of that springs
sturdy, green, new plant shoots. Somebody shout
Amen! Yes, they push up through this putrid
mixture, this decomposition. Just like the
fulfillment of the gospel's promise that says
there will be life after death."*
— REVEREND LEMUEL PEDDIGREW
of Calvary Baptist, offering comfort to the bereaved

*I*t was the day of Silas's funeral—a freezing February
morning at Calvary Baptist. Patches of leftover snow
were turning to orange sludge on the roadsides.
Imogene Lavender felt like Rosie, the robot-maid on *The
Jetsons* cartoon Lou liked so much. This couldn't be her life
that was happening. Somebody somewhere was pressing
buttons to make her speak and wave at appropriate times.

Standing outside the church, Imo saw the folks she'd

known all her life; but today they were strangers, wearing expressions she didn't recognize.

"I sure will," she said when they squeezed her hand and said to let them know what they could do for her.

Perhaps the one operating her by remote control was her dear friend Martha, the Reverend Lemuel Peddigrew's wife. She was standing beside Imo, greeting folks and directing them inside to get warm, answering their questions and giving out comforting words like, "I know Imogene appreciates that," and, "She's holding up real good."

"Let's get you inside now, the service is about to start," Martha said. They settled on the cool front pew and a peaty smell rose up from Imo's corsage.

A herd of clip-clopping heels echoed on the hardwood of the vestibule and made them both turn and look over their shoulders. Here came the rest of the Garden Club girls, some with husbands to lean on.

It almost made her cry, but Imo steeled herself and gave them a neat wave. Martha had pressed a packet of tissues into Imo's pocket, but they were still smooth and dry. She would make sure they stayed that way, because Silas said she should laugh at his funeral for all the good times they'd had.

Toward the end, when Silas knew the cancer was winning, he took on the job of trying to cheer her up, for God's sake. Now, if he could, he'd probably sit up in his casket, turn to point his finger right at her and say, "Don't you cry, Imogene. Things aren't that bad."

But they were. This was terrible, sitting here at his funeral, listening to somber chords of organ music.

Imo watched Jeanette out of the corner of her eye. Rail thin. In a slinky black dress that dipped way too low to be seen in anywhere, much less at her father's funeral. Eyeliner and rouge and lips so wet you could see your reflection in them. Imogene bowed her head; the girl looked like a common tart.

Sitting on her other side was Loutishie, her Lou, with skinned knuckles, wearing a sweet cardigan over a modest cotton dress. Now, that girl was crying enough for all of them. Splotchy cheeks and swollen eyelids and a lap full of soggy toilet paper.

Imo made it through the eulogies and opened her hymn-book. She could just barely glimpse Silas's face when they stood up. He certainly looked peaceful.

The last of the service crawled by. During Reverend Peddigrew's sermon about being ready to meet your Maker, she leafed through the hymnal to distract herself.

She planned to get home fast after they put him in the ground and send Martha away so she could think.

How did that ditty go? "Better to have loved and lost than never loved at all?" Something like that. But she didn't know if it was true after all.

This whole episode in her life was worse than she'd ever imagined. The big gaudy mums and heart shapes of hot-house roses lining the front of the pulpit were in the same places where she'd put vases of poppies when she married Silas forty-eight years ago.

Lou held Imo's hand as they left Calvary. Jeanette sashayed ahead of them like a movie star heading to her limo.

"Wow," Jeanette spoke for the first time all day, "we get to ride in *that?*"

The hearse was long and gleaming, gun-metal gray that matched the casket, with a velvety interior that Jeanette stroked when she sat down.

The gravel scrunched as the hearse pulled out, leading a string of headlights burning in the gray haze. No one said a word as they traveled the small narrow roads that stitched the back side of the county together. Here and there, an old dilapidated out-building stood, tucked into the pine trees like the cows who watched the cars go by. They turned up the last hill, creeping along a dirt road that the rain had gutted years ago. The hearse shuddered to a stop. Silas's grave was in the family cemetery—a high, rocky spot between a stand of pines and an empty alfalfa pasture.

"Let me help you, ma'am." The driver opened Imo's door and held out his white gloved hand.

"Wasn't that a nice service?" Martha squeezed her arm when they were standing near the freshly mounded earth. "He looked so natural up there. Real peaceful."

"Natural," Imo repeated as the casket was lowered. She caught bits and pieces of the final prayer and heard a shovelful of earth hit Silas.

"And you. You're holding up good, Imogene." Martha pressed another rectangle of tissue into her palm.

Imo stood there silently watching Jeanette's face. Oh Lordy, was she really lighting up a cigarette? Heat rushed up Imo's chest and neck, settled in her cheeks. She couldn't reach over and pinch the girl at the grave side, or yank that nasty cigarette out of her fingers with their long red nails, could she?

Well, what did anything matter anymore anyway? Imo held a hand over her heart. How could she manage her own life now, not to mention Jeanette's? For some reason all she could think of was the Bible verse about "Let the dead bury their dead." I am the dead, she reasoned.

Imo came home to a house that no longer had Silas Lavender in it, yet did. When Martha was gone, she took the phone off the hook and put away two spiral sliced hams, four cakes, three chess pies and unlimited foods in Tupperware and tinfoil. She stood in the kitchen and looked at Jeanette and Lou, seated around a table loaded with flower arrangements.

"There's some of Betty Neal's potato salad in here, Jeannette," Imo said, standing in front of the refrigerator. "We didn't have a chance to have any lunch, did we?"

"I'm not hungry," Jeanette snapped.

"It's your favorite . . ." Imo's voice broke off. She closed the refrigerator door. Then she turned to Lou. "How about a ham sandwich, Lou?" She opened the refrigerator door again and pulled out ham, mustard, mayonnaise, and cheese, lined them up on the counter. "I do believe there's a congealed salad in here, too." Imo made three sandwiches, despite Jeanette's refusal, and placed one in front of her with a tall glass of tea.

After Imo washed up, she went and sat down in the den. Her head felt stuffed with cotton and her heart was so heavy that it actually ached. All of her best years were gone. What was there left? She prayed for courage and for wisdom to move ahead.

Imo decided to go outside and let the cold air clear her head. She walked into the yard, feeling she was floating in a dream past the stark leafless trees and the tractor shed, her black pumps punching holes in the ground. She found herself standing at the edge of the garden. Nothing but dry, brown stalks in a hard frozen ground. A barren wasteland of dormant furrows covered with clumps of stubborn snow that looked like tombstones. Dead of winter was the perfect description.

Imo walked the perimeter of the garden, oblivious to the cold. In her mind's eye she still saw Silas, lying there dead, his face frozen in a half-smile. She felt her heart, hanging lifeless in her chest. She didn't know how she would survive in this cold, empty world without him.

No matter what people said about Silas being happy now and in a better place, Imo was not comforted. They'd even had the gumption to say *I know you're relieved that all this is over.* She paused at the compost pile to gather the courage to walk back into that house. She took a deep breath and gave herself no choice.

She stopped by the girls' room. Lou was huddled up on her bed with the dog and when Imo pushed the door open she flinched and yanked the covers over him.

"Hey, sugar foot." Imo patted Lou's thin shoulder and sank down on the edge of the bed. "Bingo miss you today?"

"Yes ma'am," Lou said, tentatively peeling back a corner of the quilt while she searched Imo's face. "I'm just letting him stay inside with me a little while. He was so sad."

"Well, good. Where's Jeannette?"

"Bathtub." Lou stared at the wall and petted Bingo's side as Imo rose to turn off the lights. "Wait," she called when Imo was back out in the hall, "can he please stay inside tonight?"

"You know how Jeanette feels about him."

"Pretty please?"

"Well, for a while longer," Imo said. Her face was sore from all the big brave smiles she had worn for everybody lately.

She put off going to bed. She worked a spell at straightening the mountain of mail and then turned on the television set. She sat in front of it without really seeing what was on. When the screen turned blank she looked at the kitchen clock. 3:00 A.M.

With a sigh, she made her way down the hall, peeping in at Lou and Jeanette on her way to bed. Lou was asleep in her funeral clothes with that smelly dog nestled in beside her. She strode over to grab his collar and put him out, but then a thought stopped her. What did it matter anymore? She didn't care if the whole herd of cows, the chickens, and the barn cats went ahead and set up housekeeping inside.

Finally, in her own room, Imo stood in front of the

dresser, gripping the handles of her underwear drawer. Dead. The word echoed around their bedroom. She knew one thing: It was worse to be this sad and lonely than to be dead. Every now and then you heard about a mate dying of pure grief soon after their true love was gone, and now she understood it down in the depths of her soul.

By force of habit she slipped into her flannel nightgown and lay down stiffly on her back. Maybe she could somehow will herself to die.

Jeanette probably wouldn't care one way or the other if Imo kicked the bucket. Actually, she'd be glad, because then she'd get the car and she could drive it wherever and whenever she pleased. And sweet little Lou was still young enough to bounce back. Maybe Martha would be hurt for awhile, losing her best friend, and some of the old folks she took care of would notice, but on the whole, things would go right on if she went ahead and died.

The fact was that ever since Silas took his last breath she had sensed the Grim Reaper trailing her, a dark specter creeping along at her heels, waiting for her to give up the ghost. Her body was still good enough, but her broken heart was leaking its pain into her bones. She'd done her duty—stayed on just long enough for Silas to have a proper send-off.

She took a deep breath, her mind fixed on an image of herself on the other side. With Silas. There would be none of the prostate cancer hanging over them like a black cloud. Her eyes filled with hot tears. The first ones that she had let escape since they learned the cancer had spread too far.

They teetered on her eye rims and spilled over her cheeks and filled the corners of her mouth with salt.

Now she'd gone and lost it, at least as far as the tears. Why not just go on and let go?

She did. A huge painful sob tore out of her chest and left her gasping and hiccoughing herself into sleep.

❦❦❦

Loutishie's Notebook

After Uncle Silas's funeral, I remember looking out the window and seeing Imo, walking around the garden. Good, I thought. Nothing like the garden to salve her heart. But the way she was muttering to herself made me wonder. Then she paused at the edge of the compost heap and it looked like she was blessing it out. That was when I realized how hard things were going to be around here.

The garden used to make her happy. Even in the dead of winter, she would pore over her garden catalogs, order her seeds, and draw up a garden plan. In years past she put in her English peas at the end of February, and although there were still the icy blows of wind and frosts, from that moment on, the garden became a growing place and the promise of life was there.

I had seen her get excited talking about her compost pile. "Lou, this is black gold to a gardener," Imo told me once when I was little. I was holding my nose and peering into her smelly heap. She picked up a fistful of dark, rich crumbly black compost that had once been a mound of corn cobs, egg shells, chicken manure, rotted vegetables, coffee grounds, pine needles, and Kudzu vines, among other things.

Toward the beginning of that same summer, when I was following Imo around the garden, she stopped and pointed at the edge of the dirt. "Look, Lou." As I stepped closer, I noticed a corn cob, only half-decomposed, jutting up and out from underneath a butter bean plant which was loaded with blooms. In fact, there were bits and pieces of stuff I recognized from the compost pile just about everywhere in the dirt of our garden. "Life springs from death," she reminded me every time we were cleaning up the supper table. "Don't throw out a thing, Lou. We'll put it in the compost heap."

From that spring on, I thought there was something almost spiritual about composting. It put me in mind of the promise that we heard from the pulpit Sunday after Sunday—that there would be life after death.

"Please God," I breathed, pressing my mouth against the cold window pane, watching Imo. "Let her see right up through the clouds into Heaven. Let her have just one glimpse of Uncle Silas all happy and free now."

I knew Uncle Silas was up there because on one of our last visits to see him in the hospital, he held Imo's cheeks and made her look at him. "We'll see each other again," he said, and she nodded her head. I knew he was talking about in heaven.

Normally, she was a real cheerful person with the kind of face that said *isn't this a great world and aren't we all so happy to be alive?* But she came in from the garden that day of his funeral, and there wasn't a glimmer of hope left in her eyes.

Looking back, I think I believed that if only she would start her garden, it would pull her back into life. I have a vivid memory of the month that followed. Daily I checked the south-facing windowsill where she used to start her tomato seeds indoors. Nothing but dust. Then I expectantly trotted outside to the cold-frame and peered in. A barren wasteland.

She might not even realize it's time to start her tomato seeds, I reasoned. Come to think of it, I hadn't even seen a single one of her garden catalogs out. She didn't seem to notice much of anything.

"Imo," I said, trying to find some shred of my fingernails left to bite on, "when you going to start the tomatoes?"

"Hmm?" said Imo, gazing off into space. "Sure is warm in here, isn't it?" She sighed and pressed her hands together. That was when I realized she wasn't connecting with reality anymore.

When March slipped by I prayed that God would illumine Imo's mind so that she would remember to start the garden. Next, I dug out old garden catalogs and placed them in the kitchen, the bathroom, and on her bedside table.

Then I imagined her outside in the sunshine where her heart would mend—digging and weeding and working the compost into the dirt so deep she felt the pulse of the Earth. I even imagined her smiling at the promise of harvest.

TWO

A Garden Plan

*"Don't you tell me you just need a little more time
before you get out. It's been too long already. Truth
be told, Imogene, you need to get out and get your
mind on other things. Plan on coming to this
Wednesday night's potluck and prayer meeting,
the girls will be so tickled to see you."*
— MARTHA PEDDIGREW
long-time friend of Imo coaxing her back out into life

*N*ight number twenty-eight without Silas and
Imo was not dead yet. Instead, she lived her
days underneath a cloud of profound grief.
Inside she was an intense mix of despair and futility. At
times she just didn't see how she was going to put one foot
in front of the other.

The rest of the household stood by and watched help-
lessly as the maniacal grief threatened to do Imo in.
Jeanette was a worry. Imo felt that she could not connect
with her at all. She had always been a difficult child, sassy
right from the beginning. Silas called her spirited. Hard-

headed was the word Imo used. When she was smaller, you could tell her to get her hair out of her face or not to pick at a scab, and that girl would do all in her power to be contrary. Imo could understand why she'd been in three different foster homes by the time she was five. Now that Silas was gone, she didn't know if she could handle Jeanette.

As she lay there in bed, envisioning the days ahead, her pulse was flying like she'd just run ten miles. It was 4:00 A.M., and sleep was as elusive as ever. The house creaked and groaned with the gradual warming of Euharlee; a full moon sent in slants of shine through the thin shades. Bingo wailed. A bull bellowed from the back pasture. Imo took a deep breath.

Well, at least little Loutishie was doing all right. Lou was made right out of the Euharlee soil, hardy as a honeysuckle vine. Strong and earthy, at home in the garden or out in the barn, she was a quiet and respectful child.

But lately, everything Imo said to Jeanette was met with a blank stare or rolling eyes. Perhaps this was a natural part of being a teenager, although Imo didn't remember being so sullen and disrespectful when she was sixteen. Why, she was *married* at sixteen!

What would be good at the moment, she reasoned, was to escape into one of her best memories and just stay there awhile.

Squeezing her eyes shut tight, Imogene searched her soul to find Silas. First, she willed herself to see his profile against the murky gray shadow of the wall; the curve of his nose, his lips, and his chin resting on the covers. Once that was in place, she conjured up the warmth of his flesh, and the pulse of his blood, and smelled his earthy scent. Heaven.

She had squandered moments like that when he was alive. Had not treasured each infinitesimal shred of him. During the first years of their marriage, she was too young and silly to cherish the moments they had together. And after they'd been married for a while, she was so used to everything she wasn't living in the moment anymore.

In the very beginning, even chores were fun, as long as they were together. It was like playing house. She made gingham curtains for their tiny kitchen, and spent hours cooking his favorite pies, and he brought home flats of pansies for the yard. In the evenings, she cleaned the garden soil out from under her nails, put on her red lipstick, and, eager to please, dressed in one of her new house dresses. They laughed and talked about their busy day and recited memories until they became private poetry between the two of them.

For a wedding trip they drove off to Gatlinburg, Tennessee, holding hands and dressed in stiff, unfamiliar clothes, while their friends waved from the back steps of Calvary's social hall. She'd never even been out of Georgia before and when they crossed the state line, she felt so worldly.

He pulled up at the Desoto Hotel where they would spend two nights. Already nervous about the coming darkness, she looked out the passenger window into some pine trees and told Silas how exhausted she was. "I'll probably fall right to sleep." He laughed and squeezed her thigh like she was the funniest thing on earth. She chewed her lip and tried to remember what her friend Ruth had said the night before the wedding when they were sitting together up on Imo's bed looking at a new silky pink negligee. Ruth seemed to know all about what a married couple did.

"It'll hurt the first time," Ruth told her, "I mean, that's what they say. But then it's heavenly. You just move in the opposite direction of him and gyrate your hips."

"What do you mean?" Imo asked, hugging her arms against the fear of the unknown. She was terrified of disappointing Silas.

"It'll come natural. You don't even need to worry." Ruth laughed a know-it-all, "hah, hah."

Of course it would come natural, she reasoned to herself as she shivered on the tile floor of the tiny hotel bathroom, tugging the frothy hem of the negligee down as far as it would go. Anyway, she tried to reassure herself, it *was* natural; the farm animals did it, the birds and the bees did it. Her own Mama had to have done it, and every human being out there in the world was the result of it. "Lord help me," she breathed and pushed open the door.

"You're beautiful," Silas gasped, grabbing her white wrist and pulling her down onto the bed and crushing her in his arms, "I want you." He growled and ripped the new negligee off with his teeth.

"I love you, Mrs. Lavender," he whispered into her neck afterwards; stroking her arms, her neck, and between her breasts where the perspiration glistened. It looked like she had made him happy.

Later on, while she was alone and thinking it over, she understood. What he wanted was beyond fleshly lust, the satisfying of desires; although they had that. What they both wanted, what they couldn't live without, was pure love that transcended the physical stuff. Love as true as the sun coming up every morning. Two joined souls traveling through this celestial body called Earth.

They *had* had true love, she acknowledged to herself in the lonely darkness, and though fitful sleep came, she woke several times to stretch a searching arm or leg over between the icy sheets, in search of Silas's warmth.

Well, bad as these nights were, what she really hated were the mornings, because they meant a whole day to get through. If she didn't hop right out of bed and get herself busy the moment she woke up, the memories just about killed her.

One flooded in this morning with the sunrise. In sharp excruciating focus, it spread its colors over her as she lay in bed. She was crossing the perimeter from asleep to awake and she could see herself from a dreamer's out-of-body perspective.

In this one, which was two years ago, before they knew about the cancer, she was sitting on the lowered tailgate of the pickup, shucking a mountain of sweet corn in the truck bed and tossing the naked ears onto an old bed sheet below her feet.

"I've got to get this cut off and in the freezer before it goes bad," she said to Silas. He was standing on the front steps, motioning for her to come inside and sit with him.

He chuckled all the way out to her and right in broad daylight pinched her fanny. "I had something a little more fun in mind," he said. She snorted and returned to the corn.

"Let it go, my comely bride (he'd called her that since their wedding day) and enjoy the best of life for which the first was made!"

"Old fool," she hissed, "you be quiet out here." There had been a couple of teenagers from church helping out at the farm that day and Jeanette and Lou were playing around the pecan tree.

Imo sat up in bed and rubbed her eyes to purge the memory. She patted the flat bed beside her in deference to Silas. This was one of the memories that hurt her the most. She hated the fact that she couldn't go back and leave the corn just sitting there to be with Silas. Over the years, she had messed up a lot.

Funny, but now she even missed his snoring. She'd give anything to have him sawing logs beside her right this minute. Twenty-five years ago, when she was going through the change of life, she put a tennis ball into an old sock and safety pinned it to the back of his pajama top to keep him off his back. It turned out that he could snore just as well on his side or stomach, and so she lay there and looked as hard and as mean at him as she could manage.

She got out of bed, wrapped in a shroud of self-contempt

and padded barefoot to the kitchen. The girls were still asleep, and she sat down at the breakfast table. For a moment she forgot what she had come into the kitchen to do.

She wouldn't make coffee, she decided. Because indulging in the ritual they had shared together lessened her mourning. Maybe she wouldn't get dressed either. Just stay in her robe. Why bother going through the motions? Just let herself go to seed. She could drive to Hembree's grocery in her robe and pick up some TV dinners and one of those big bags of plastic utensils and Styrofoam cups. Virtually eliminate the need to cook and wash up.

Here it was midnight again and she had made it through one more interminable day. But the problem was that doing nothing had left her mind a fecund field of grief. All day long she'd wallowed in sorrow, so that the minute she stretched out in bed, even the sleeping pill and the fiercest concentration were to no avail.

She swiped away tears with the shoulder of her nightgown. The terrible thing was that there was no evidence that this was going to let up.

Be patient, my foot. Everybody said to let Time be the great healer. So far, Time had let her down. She didn't have time for Time to work. She was getting old now. Oldness that started when Silas left her. Her bones were snapping and creaking, the joints turning to dust. She'd grown a neck like a turkey and her face was dropping the same as her bosom.

Imo lay in bed, gripping the edge of the quilt so hard her

knuckles turned white. "Well, Silas, you are dead," she whispered over to his side of the bed, "and don't take this the wrong way, because I am glad you are not suffering anymore, but I am almost *mad* at you. How dare you go on and leave me down here!" She sat bolt upright in the dark.

She could not tolerate this one minute longer. This house *was* Silas. For that matter, this whole town was Silas. He remained a specter, a stubborn silhouette on the edge of Imo's existence. And he would, too, as long as she remained here.

Sometime around three A.M., she rolled out of the covers and pulled her nice London Fog over her nightgown. She grabbed her purse and car keys and crept out to the Impala.

She reckoned Bingo was in Lou's bed again since the shed was so quiet. Idling the car for a minute to collect her thoughts, Imo considered which way to go. Cruising through the parking lot of the Wal-Mart for a Pepsi, she decided to head west out of Euharlee. She drove for a solid hour right up to the Alabama line. A whole new state would be a good start.

She was driving along fine until she started thinking of what would go on at her house in the morning with her gone. Lou would fry herself an egg and take care of Bingo's breakfast like always. Jeanette; who knows? Usually a Diet Coke and a cigarette around noon.

Imo pulled over to the shoulder of the highway. Her conscience might get the better of her. A good Christian woman would just turn the car around and head on home to tend to her responsibilities.

She rubbed her eyes. *Keep going, Imo. Probably you are just exhausted, and you are not thinking clearly.*

Oh, surely the girls would have sense enough to call one of the church ladies for a hand, and they would make out fine in this world. Better than with herself hanging around, in the sorry state she was in. Holding onto this thought, she crept back out on the highway and accelerated up to fifty. If she stopped now to worry over them, she'd never have a bit of peace.

She cracked the window a bit for some air and turned on the radio. It was that awful stuff Jeanette listened to. She moved the dial to a station with country favorites and cruised along, watching the sky which was a real pretty milky gray tinged with pink.

Surely, she reasoned, a sixty-four-year-old widow-woman deserved to come and go as she pleased. She pulled into a filling station to use the ladies room.

The sullen girl behind the cash register handed her a key on a big wooden paddle. She decided to buy some crackers from her when she brought the key back.

I've got to do this, she thought, as she lined the toilet with two thicknesses of paper and then hovered over it anyway.

It was nasty in the bathroom, with some of the ugliest things written inside the stall. Folks these days had turned perfectly good words into cuss words, and she could only guess at what some of them meant. She washed her hands and blinked at some crudely drawn pictures of private parts which were etched into the wall above the sink.

She walked out of the little bathroom and stood staring into the murky shape of some pine trees backlit by the moon. If it weren't for those two girls, she'd just crawl off into the woods like an old tom cat and lay down and die right now.

What had come over her? How could she leave the girls in this filthy world with no moral compass to guide them?

Imo laughed nervously as she spun the Impala in a 180 degree turn. She could be home by lunchtime, and the girls would never know!

On April Fool's Day, she'd been back three days. She went outside after lunch to sit in the glider, and the sun licked right through her cotton shirt. The jonquils were blooming as if not a thing in the world had changed. Barn swallows were calling out "wit-wit," and Bingo had a bounce in his step.

She used to love early spring. Longer days full of lemony-yellow sun meant it was time to get the garden in. Spring always came so sudden. Every year it surprised her. She was usually too impatient to wait until the soil warmed up before she lifted her shovel. But this year she felt apathetic and wouldn't even have thought too hard about the garden if she hadn't run across stacks and stacks of old seed catalogs everywhere she turned. She'd even carried one outside to leaf through today, but instead, had set it beside her to rest her tea glass on.

She glanced around at the shaggy yellow heads of dandelions popping up everywhere. Pollen had coated everything with a thick silken layer of yellow, like cake flour. It was so thick beneath the pecan tree that the Impala had left tracks in it. Thrift and vinca carpeted the lawn and wisteria hung in cascades from the trees—clumps of biblical grapes.

After being on the road, she could appreciate the beauty and safety of this place. No ugliness out there in the world could get to her here. When she got home, she had decided she would just focus on the things necessary for their existence. She picked up her tea, which had sweated so much that it stuck to the cover of the catalog. A piece of notebook paper fluttered out and drifted down right onto her toes.

It was a penciled diagram of a garden plan. A much thought-out, lovingly erased, and redrawn sketch ringed in the coffee cup circles of deep concentration.

The limas and snap-beans and collards were at the upper end, the okra and black-eye peas and green peppers in the middle, and the cucumbers and squash at the lower end. Running the length of the garden, on one side, were three rows of sweet corn. On the other side, were tomatoes, her personal favorite. The whole thing was encircled by marigolds. She peered hard at it. It definitely wasn't last year's layout.

The county agent advised a four year rotation for tomatoes as a precautionary measure against disease, so this diagram must have been drawn a while back.

A tingle made its way down her spine as she realized it was from exactly four years ago.

Of course, it was usually earlier than this, mid-March, when she got the tomato seeds going indoors, to give them time to grow before she put them out in the garden during the second week of May after the last possible chance of a freeze. She panicked a little—March was long gone now. Then a still, small voice inside reassured her that plenty of people seeded their tomatoes directly into their cold frame to get a jump on the season. That would give her a little over a month, and surely they would be tall enough in time to be set out.

As she made her way out to the tool shed, her thoughts turned to divine inspiration. Probably God had waited so long to get her out here because He was developing her patience at the same time He was refocusing her. She opened the door and waited until her eyes adjusted to the darkness inside.

Other women had vanities lined with precious fragrances and jewels, but Imogene Lavender had her garden tools. She saw the wheelbarrow, lopping shears, rake, hoe, shovel, seeder, pick, and lime spreader. Everything was right where she'd left it last year.

In her other life.

A pair of flowered gloves with the ghost of her hands still shaping them hung beside an old straw hat. She slipped them on and bent down to touch the tiller. Silas had been so proud of this machine. "Six horse-power model with a reverse gear and steel tines on a powered horizontal shaft," he told her when she'd asked if they could afford it. Imo plucked the key off a nail in the wall. She did not see anywhere on the machine that read, "Men Only." Certainly, with the Lord's hand so clearly nearby, she could manage it by herself. She drew a deep breath and wrestled the cumbersome thing out onto the grass.

The feel of the earth tumbling and churning and the smell of the soil were medicine for her, and she tilled for five healing hours. It was not quite dark when she cleaned the dried roots and caked dirt from the tines and put it back in the shed. Exhausted with the pleasure of physical labor, she watched darkness fall beyond the open window while she fixed supper.

The next morning she got her tomato seeds into the cold frame and she made a trip to the Feed 'n Seed for lime and fertilizer.

Even if she wasn't happier, she was at least distracted. She planned to just zero in on the garden and lose herself there. Calvary just held too many fresh and unpleasant memories.

Anyway it seemed like the Lord spoke to her better outside in the garden with her hands in the dirt than inside the church with them wrapped around a hymnal. She was meant to garden, formed by the Lord God Almighty to work the earth; gifted with the knack of knowing how to coax big beautiful vegetables up out of the dirt.

Martha called her every day around lunchtime.

"You need to get out, Imogene," she would say. "Back into the bosom of your church family."

"Oh," Imo would say and wave her hand, "I just need a little more time."

Eventually she said she would go, just to hush Martha

up. Maybe it would be good, in a way, to go back to Calvary. Because, although she felt God's blessing on her out in the garden, it was scaring her a bit, too. The reason for that was that sometimes she got so busy working in the dirt that she didn't think of Silas for minutes at a time.

As if he'd never even existed! She would scold herself. When these times happened, instead of being glad for the distraction, she would fear the prospect of senile dementia coming on her and erasing him completely.

Loutishie's Notebook

The worst part of life after Uncle Silas was seeing Imo's vacant eyes and hearing the way she went around with this continual sigh. Like she was trying to breathe the life out of herself quicker.

Imo was falling apart, and it felt like the world was unraveling whenever I heard her crying into her pillow at night.

Poor Imo. She splashed cold water on her face and dusted it with loose powder every morning before she came into the kitchen.

"Morning, girls," she said, starting the water boiling for grits. Her powder didn't hide much.

I peered out through sleepy eyes at Jeanette who was popping open a Diet Coke. "Morning," I said.

"Over the hump day," Imo said. She asked Jeanette how school was going. Jeanette answered her with a shrug.

"I reckon we'll go to potluck and prayer meeting tonight." Imo slapped some ham into the skillet.

"Not going," Jeanette said.

I looked over and scowled at her. This was the first time since Uncle Silas's funeral that Imo had even mentioned going out anywhere other than the mailbox. Some days I just wanted to punch Jeanette, knock some sense into her. I gave her a knowing look when Imo went down the hall.

"You better go, Jeanette," I whispered to her sullen face, "or I'll tell Imo you snuck off again last night."

We reached Calvary just in time for the potluck supper.

"Imogene's here!" Martha screamed, galloping over to take the bowl of creamed corn and the basket of biscuits from Imo's hand and set them on the table. A clump of ladies jammed around her, patting her and talking all at once.

The good thing about Wednesday nights at Calvary was that everyone was more relaxed. Reverend Peddigrew wore checkered shirts and plain pants instead of his silken robe, the sermon was shorter, and little kids stayed in the sanctuary and climbed around on their parents' knees. There was no choir, just the Reverend standing out on the steps in front of the altar rail and moving his arms while we sang hymns without the piano.

Jeanette slid into the back pew when it was time for the preaching. I sat down beside her. Right behind Miss Mattie Hembree. We believed she was at least 100 years old. Wisps of silver hair were pulled back into a puny bun which sat above a neck as wrinkled as an elephant's leg.

Miss Mattie's head in front of me was making tiny jerking movements. I stared at her pearl ear-bobs which were trembling while she searched for the right page in the hymnbook. Then I allowed my eyes to glance up a few rows to Imo. My heart did a complete break. There was this unidentifiable feeling when I saw her there without Uncle Silas. There was something so final about being at Calvary on a Wednesday night without Uncle Silas there. He was dead and life was marching on without him.

I could hear the blend of voices, young and old, crooning out a hymn all around me, but I could also feel a silence closing in. A tightness began in my stomach and worked its way up to my chest. There was a knot in my throat the size of a peach pit.

I knew the Reverend was a firm believer that whatever happened was the will of God. He said that God had His reasons for everything. But Uncle Silas's dying was senseless to me. We were having a fine, sweet life until he died and left this hole in it. **Look what it's doing to Imo!** I wanted to shout. **She's given up on life!**

We rode home silently, the absence of Uncle Silas riding on my shoulders like a horsehair shirt. Things still being so fragile with Imo, I didn't say a word to her about my feelings. Instead, I beat a path outside, and taking my usual approach to pain, held a pity-party all by myself.

I lay down in the dark, nestled in a patch of cool grass at the edge of the garden. I reached a hand out and absentmindedly patted the dirt. The garden was tilled! I won't lie, my heart was still throbbing like a blister that needs to pop, but as I lay on my stomach and stared at the neat rows of dirt, I was encouraged.

Late, but she **had** gotten around to it. I rifled my fingers through the soil a while, then I flew out to the cold-frame and saw her tomato seedlings, along with lettuce, kale, beets and turnips. What was the most comforting was the knowledge that Imo wasn't planning on dying anymore.

T H R E E

Support Systems

"They say, hon', that when you look good, you feel good. Emotional baggage can sap a woman's beauty potential. And that's a scientifically proven fact."

— WANDA PARNELL

beautician and owner of the Kuntry Kut 'n' Kurl,
convincing Imo of the benefits of a makeover

*I*mo awoke to a pretty Saturday morning in early May. It was the first really warm morning of spring, about the perfect temperature for setting out tomato seedlings.

She stood at the sink washing breakfast dishes, looking out beyond the hayfield to the blue sky. The daffodils came and went so early this spring she hadn't had a chance to enjoy them; but now the irises were at their peak, and everywhere she looked, they were standing tall and proud on such thick sturdy stalks.

So beautiful out there and such perfect weather for a picnic! Not too hot, not too cold. Maybe she should try and do something fun today. Something that wasn't necessary to survival. Surviving, those first months, had been all she could manage. But look at her! She had gotten that garden started and her tomato seedlings were right on schedule.

She finished the last dish and opened the cabinet underneath the sink to hang up her rubber gloves. Her gaze fell upon the morgue of left-handed gloves under there. She always wore out the right-handed ones first, or else they got poked by a fork or a knife when she was washing up, so that they were useless. The sight of those left-over gloves clutched at her heart. They were like her—incomplete and useless without a mate. The real craziness was her even thinking she could have fun by herself. Everybody knew a picnic by yourself was pitiful.

Her soul was hurting now like a rotten tooth as she picked up the phone and cradled the receiver. "Martha?" Her voice probably sounded too needy.

"Oh, hey, Imogene." Martha was out of breath and there was barking in the background. "I was just outside helping Lemuel in the garden."

"I'll call back later when you're done with . . ."

"Now listen, don't you hang up. I was ready to stop anyway. I've been meaning to call you about the next Garden Club meeting. Do you have it on your calendar?"

"Yes," Imo said, her voice breaking. Now she'd done it. Lost her composure right in front of Martha, and now she'd be on prayer chains all over Euharlee. If there was one thing Imo hated, it was having everybody know her business, and

Martha was famous for calling in all "prayer needs" quick as lightning. But she was also the best listener Imo knew. She held onto the receiver feeling weak and pitiful.

Martha said, "I'm coming right on over there, hon'. You don't sound good."

Imo went outside to wait in the glider. She fished her watch out of her pocket. Eleven o'clock. Lou wandered outside with Bingo close on her heels. "Jeanette chase you two out of the house?"

"Nope, she's not here," Lou said over her shoulder.

"What?" Imo cried.

"Oh. Uhm . . . I mean . . . I don't know where Jeanette is." Lou disappeared quickly beyond the forsythia.

"What do you mean she's not here?" Imo clasped her hands together. "Come here, child," she called. When Lou was back, Imo looked straight into her eyes. "Is there something I should know?" she asked, patting Bingo, trying to stay calm.

"She's been gone all night," Lou blurted, then twirled on her heel and skipped off.

Imo bit her tongue. She hugged Bingo's smelly neck. Maybe she shouldn't try to be a mother, maybe she just didn't have it in her. Just be Jeanette's friend. You know, watch movies together and giggle about boys. After all, when the doctors diagnosed fibroid tumors in her uterus, something the modern medicine of 1951 couldn't fix, she decided it wasn't God's will for her to bear children and be a mother.

Silas had been better than her at it. In all the years of caring for foster children, he excelled at chasing away the boogeyman and telling nighttime stories. He could patch up a skinned knee and kiss the pain away as good as any doctor. He had deserved a complete woman who could bear him his very own seed, but he never made her feel bad about her affliction.

"Imogene? Yoo-hoo, you back here?"

She nearly jumped out of the glider. She'd been so lost in thought she hadn't heard Martha's car.

"Where is everybody?" Martha sank down next to Imo.

"I imagine Lou's down at the river bottoms."

"Jeanette?"

"Jeanette didn't come home last night." Imo's voice broke. "I just don't know what to do with her."

"Now, dear." Martha draped her arm over Imo's shoulder. "Is that what's bothering you? How old is that girl, anyway?"

"She's sixteen."

"Well, the teenagers in the flock do stray sometimes," Martha said. "But she'll come back. When she does, why don't you sit her down and have a little talk with her?"

"She won't listen to me. Silas was always the one that had a way with that child." Tears dribbled down Imo's face.

Martha pressed Imo's head down on her shoulder and patted. "There, there, now. Let it all out. The Lord's catching all them tears in a great big bucket. Come to think of it, I didn't see you shedding a single tear at the funeral. You need to cry."

"I suppose," Imo managed.

"You know what?" Martha slapped her thigh. "You really shouldn't have to take care of this place and those two girls all by yourself. What you need is a man."

"I hired Wayne Jackson, Martha. He comes every day, and he can help right up to the end of September."

Martha wrinkled up her nose. "I didn't mean a hired man. I meant a man to lean on. To love on."

Imo sat bolt upright. Crazy talk! How in the world did their conversation get around to this? Oh, she was pathetic, so obviously lost without Silas it must be written all over her life.

Now Martha was saying how Silas would want her to find another man and be happy. That was going too far! Maybe she should try and change the subject. She should tell Mrs. Know-it-all here that this was really none of her business; that if someone gives their heart to a person and that person dies, then their heart is buried with them and can't be resurrected.

"Now, don't you think a thing about it, Imogene. It won't be moving too fast after Silas. Lemuel sees this type of thing all the time."

"What type of thing?" Imo eyed Martha.

"You know, when he does funerals. The ones who enter a new relationship the soonest are the ones who had the best marriages. He says, if you feel the loss of a spouse really deeply, you cannot *bear* the thought of being alone."

"Martha, I am not alone."

"You may as well be. . . Buy yourself a Winnebago. Or go on one of those AARP tours to Europe. Club Med has singles weekends you see all the time on TV." Martha looked like she was going to keep on all day and all night. "It won't mean you've forgotten Silas. You just need somebody to fill up that hole in your heart." Martha used her preacher's voice. "It will actually be a compliment to him!"

Imo cleared her throat, wishing she could think of the right thing to say to get Martha to cut this nonsense out. Only three months ago, Silas had been sitting right there where Martha was now. She was saved when a car pulled around to the back of the house and rolled to a stop.

The fur along Bingo's spine raised up, and he left the space between Imo's ankles and lunged at the wheels of a low, black Camaro with dark windows. Jeanette slid out and ran inside.

"Who do you reckon?" Imo whispered.

"Go see." Martha nudged her. "Hurry. Before they get away." Imo leapt up, ran over and tapped on the driver's window. It rolled down an inch and she could see a dark man behind the wheel. The more she studied him, she decided he was from one of those foreign lands where they worship cows. The smell wafting out from the car's interior was a faraway one, laced with exotic spices she could not name. The man's eyes were big as muscadines.

Imo's imagination ran wild. She knew it was her Christian duty to believe the best about somebody till she had the facts to think otherwise. Maybe this man was just giving Jeanette a ride home; the father of one of her girl-friends. She ought to invite him inside for some tea.

"I'm Imogene Lavender," she said through the crack in the window. Had she lost her mind? Here she was, asking a stranger in, and a foreigner at that. "Jeanette's mother. Please, won't you come in and have some tea?"

She smiled at him. He smiled back tentatively. Straight white teeth. He was wearing a Dairy Queen smock and hat.

"Got to go work," he said, in broken English, jabbing a finger at a plastic badge on his chest. Then he accelerated so fast that he left two ruts in the yard.

Imo was stunned.

"What in tarnation?" Martha came huffing and puffing up to her, eyebrows nearly meeting her hairline. "Who was it?"

"I don't know."

"What?"

"He didn't introduce himself."

"Young people today." Martha shook her head. "Anyway, I had the perfect idea while you were talking to whoever that was."

"What, Martha?" said Imo. "Excuse me, but I've got to have a little talk with my daughter."

"Well, let's go on in the house then. I'll call The Kut 'n' Kurl and make you an appointment!" Martha cried, heading toward the back door.

"I am tempted to yank that girl's hair right out of her head!" Imo climbed the steps with her hands clenched.

"Now calm down, Imogene," said Martha, "that would cause more harm than good. What you need is a new look."

"I have to keep in mind," Imo said under her breath, "that a person's genes will come out." She stood in the kitchen, looking bewildered. "Still, you'd think all those years we took her to Sunday school would count for something . . ."

Martha was talking into the telephone. She held a palm over the receiver. "Can you make it on Monday morning?" she asked Imo, who was walking towards the girls' room.

"Let me in, Jeanette," Imo called, jiggling the door knob. "I need to speak to you."

Jeanette unlocked the knob and opened the door a crack, peering out.

Imo put her hands on her hips and wedged the door open wider with her knee. "Who was that man?" she said, "And where have you been all night?"

Jeanette sighed and rolled her eyes. "Why should you care?" she said and slammed the door.

"Open up that door, young lady, and look at me when I speak to you!" Imo snapped.

"Leave her be," said Martha, bustling down the hallway. "Bide your time. She'll come around. Listen, Wanda's got you down for Monday at ten."

"I just don't want things to get too far," Imo said, her voice rising. She ran a hand through her hair and slumped against the wall.

"Well, now. You just talk to Wanda about it while she's

fixing you up, Imogene. She was a wild teenager if there ever was one. And now look, she's got her own business."

When Martha was gone, Imo sat down to think a spell. She felt worn out and hopeless. She was scared to think of the future. Lots of girls turned out to be dope fiends. Girls with God-fearing parents. Just look at Pastor Ramsay's daughter, Lydia. Now that man laid down the law, and still she turned out bad.

She'd never stopped to think about it till now, to realize just how many of the younger generation she'd known of who went bad. It seemed their parents' love and guidance didn't amount to a hill of beans. Selma's son was in the prison, and the Johnson girls were lazy trailer trash, and Lord knows how many others weren't fit for society.

Loutishie's Notebook

One day in May, Imo ran down to the bottoms to get me. "It's time to put the tomato seedlings into the garden, Lou."

We walked to the cold frame and I watched her slice into the flats with her trowel like it was a rich chocolate sheet cake. She cut the soil into three inch blocks around each tiny plant. The delicate root hairs and tender white ends were showing.

"Lou, run water into those holes we dug real good before we set them in," Imo said, "then run in the shed and get me that old box full of stakes."

"The stakes?"

"Yessum."

"Stake them when they're no bigger than this?" I peered down at the tiny things and laughed.

"Well, you don't need to tie them up yet, of course. Just set the stakes in. Because if we wait till the tomatoes need them to put them in, it will hurt their roots."

When we finished, Imo looked satisfied and went over to Martha's. Bingo and I ran down to the bottoms and trotted along the bank, stopping to admire the honeysuckle. We traipsed along feeling very accomplished because the tomatoes were in the ground at long last, and it had been two nights running now that Imo hadn't cried herself to sleep.

As we got back up toward the house, I spotted Jeanette. She was all dressed up in tight jeans and a pink shiny top, walking in circles underneath the empty shed.

"Where's the car at?" she said, race-walking out to meet me.

"Imo had to go see Martha."

"Well, when's she getting back?"

"I don't know," I said. "You need to go somewhere?"

"Yeah," she spat out. "I need to get the hell out of here." She stomped over to the glider and huffed down.

I followed her. "Where?"

"Why do you care?" she asked.

"Because I can call Martha's for you."

"Don't bother. She don't give a shit about me," Jeanette hissed, smoke from her cigarette curling up through the oaks and sweet gums. Then she said how Uncle Silas was the only one who had ever really loved her. I could tell she had thought about this a lot and that she really believed it. I think that was the first time I sensed how lost Jeanette felt without Uncle Silas around.

I wanted to shout "That's crazy! Of course she cares. She loves you!" but I guess Imo was so caught up in her own grief that she didn't realize Jeanette wasn't getting enough attention.

Martha was the one who understood that Imo needed attention. She needed a lot of support right after Uncle Silas passed away, and then a push. A not so gentle push, either, to get her back out and into the land of the living. Martha also believed that one needed to go after things. While she confessed a strong faith in the fact that the Lord supplied all your needs, she also declared that a person had to do all in their power to help Him along. She loved to say, "You can't kneel at the foot of your unmade bed and moan and pray, 'Oh, Lord, please make this bed!'"

FOUR

Wet Feet

MANURE TEA
Put some well-aged manure in a burlap sack and tie it closed. (You have to age it so it won't burn the plants). Hang it over the side of a barrel. Let the rain fill it up, or if the rain doesn't cooperate, use well, pond, lake, or river water. Let the water run over and through the bag of manure. It is best if you allow it to soak three to four days, (steeping like tea). Agitate the barrel a few times each day. When it is ready, dip a bucket in and take some of the "tea" to your tomato plants. Pour it in a circle about four feet around the plant.
— IMO'S GARDENING NOTEBOOK

anda tilted Imogene's face up and peered hard at her. They were inside a mint-green camper-trailer parked in Wanda's yard. A sign out front, shaped like a hand mirror read: "Kuntry Kut 'n' Kurl." The air was full of perfume and hair spray. Imo sat in the styling chair, twisting her hands together in her lap and thinking *what in the world am I doing in here? How on Earth do I let Martha talk me into these things?*

"It's the first step to a new life." Wanda filled up a tray on wheels with rollers and spritzer bottles. "When you said okay, I said to myself, I said, I cannot wait to see the new you!"

"Nothing fussy," Imo said. "Nothing real fancy. Something I can manage all by myself at home."

"I'm the beauty professional here," Wanda said to Imo's reflection in the mirror. Wanda's hair was frosted and flipped up on the ends. She wore a short denim skirt with a pair of high-heeled mules that tilted her perpetually forward so that her breasts seemed to lead her everywhere. She snapped her gum and bopped along to a tune on the radio. "Like we said, you need more than a new hairdo."

Imo studied herself in the mirror; she saw bags underneath her eyes and furrows along her forehead.

Wanda patted her shoulder. "You look like you've had a rough time. Sister said Jeanette is giving you fits."

"Yes."

"Hard age." Wanda laughed. "I was sixteen once, you know." She met Imo's eyes in the mirror.

Imo didn't feel like giving her the details.

"Anyhow," Wanda said, scrunching handfuls of Imo's hair in her hands, "We all seem to make it through being teenagers. I figured you were just having a hard time getting over Silas."

Imo bit her tongue. Probably she would never get over

the man she'd shared forty-eight years of her life with. She had every right to run out of there at that comment, but it dawned on her that Wanda wasn't one to look back and reflect. She was on husband number four.

"Don't turn into one of those old women whose idea of a hot date is a box of chocolates and a trashy novel," Wanda said, smiling and shaking her head.

"I don't have time to read," Imo snapped.

"Touchy, touchy. Now, first we'll do something with that hair."

"Just shape it up a bit, dear. Silas loves it like this."

"He loved it. Past tense. Now, you just relax, hon', and let me handle this. I'm trained at working with your face shape and your hair type."

Wanda twirled Imo around in the chair. "You are a walking period piece. Straight out of the *Ladies Home Journal* of 1970." She folded her arms and looked hard at Imo. "You need fullness at the sides, sugar. This style you got, if you can call it that, is accentuating your long face." She fished a comb out of a glass jar. "I'll cut it, do a body wave, and while we're at the chemicals, we're going to conceal this gray."

Two hours later, Imo sat on the edge of the chair while Wanda arranged hand mirrors so that she could see the sides and back.

"Voilà!" Wanda cried. "The magic of mousse!"

Imo looked at herself. Her close-capped helmet of wiry gray with the pin curl in front of each ear was transformed into a softly shining dark brown page boy.

"What do you think? I think it's shaved twenty years off. That would make you about forty-five. Now for the makeup. You are definitely an autumn."

"Hold on, let's don't go hog-wild," Imogene said. A new hairdo was one thing, but she'd never thought much about makeup, besides red lipstick for Sundays and the grocery store.

She poked out her lip and sat there. Wanda crossed her arms and leaned against the counter.

A standoff.

Wanda lowered her voice. "Look, don't get all mad. Let's just try something. Okay?"

Imo said okay, and she had to admit it felt good to be fussed over. She closed her eyes.

Wanda patted on a foundation in porcelain beige. She smoothed on blush and copper- colored eye shadow.

"Don't ever, ever, match your eyeshadow to your clothes, darlin'. That's a beauty don't. I'm going to give you testers of this stuff in your color family."

"Now this is truly gratifying," said Wanda. "Like restoring a beautiful antique." Wanda did a drum roll on the sink. "Ta-da! The new Imogene Lavender. I should've done before and after photos. I could get rich from the publicity."

Imo looked in the mirror at all angles. The transformation was truly remarkable.

"Speechless, huh, babe? Didn't know that gorgeous creature was trapped in there, did you?"

Imo touched her hair and face as if it belonged to a china doll. "I just wish Silas could see me."

"Uh uh, no tears, dear." Wanda shook her head. "That will ruin your makeup. Anyway, maybe he can see you, and he wouldn't want you to spoil this. He'd want you happy."

Okay, so she was doing this for Silas. She could accept that. Now she would get herself on home and tend to the garden. The Better Boys were needing the extra support of their stakes now. The speed of spindly tomato seedlings metamorphosizing into tall, stout-stemmed plants with leaves bigger than your hand was simply amazing.

On Sunday morning Imo entered the cool vestibule of Calvary Baptist. She paused outside of her Sunday school room. Placing a palm over her pumping heart, she drew a deep breath and pushed open the door.

Twelve heads turned to welcome her, and there was silence as she walked to her chair. Her class consisted of five widows, four with husbands in various stages of advancing age, and three Unclaimed Blessings, their name for the women who had never married.

Bifocals were removed, and faces peered closer. The Sunday school lesson was all but forgotten.

"Imogene?"

"Hello, Geneva, Viola," Imo said. She sat down humbly and placed her Bible on her lap. She was not going to let Pride trip her up.

"Positively radiant."

"Who did it?"

"I need to make me an appointment!"

"You look so young! The Lord's wrought a miracle."

". . . yes, I was able to manage the whole sha-bang by my-self this morning," Imo said. "Well, actually, Lou helped me blow dry the back. And Wanda let me carry a little cardboard face home with me that had the makeup directions on it."

She trembled before she spoke the next words. "Martha and Wanda think I should find a new man."

Imo said all of this so matter-of-factly that when she ac-tually got the words out there, it was like flipping a switch on inside of her. The whole idea of hunting a man wasn't nearly as scandalous to her anymore.

Actually this same phenomenon had happened to her a good bit in her life. A thing would be as obscure and for-eign to her as the Chinese language, but once she said the words, that thing took on a life of its own and marched for-ward like it had always been her idea.

"Pickings are slim out there," warned Hazel Strickland, who was sitting next to Imo. She sipped her little styrofoam cup of coffee. "I read in the paper that there are ten times as many women as there are men for folks over age sixty, and those men that are out there have more than likely still got themselves a living wife." Hazel was one of the Unclaimed Blessings and had no business raining on Imo's parade.

That only fueled Imo's fire, "Well, I'll just have to be a real go-getter then," she said, her voice rising over the group's ex-cited chatter.

When they got home from church, Imo changed into her gardening clothes. Lou watched her fasten on her straw hat.

"Come help me tie up the tomatoes, Lou."

"Yes ma'am."

"Run get that clump of my old nylons out of my bed-room."

Imo watched her go. Poor child. She wasn't handling Imo's new look very well.

Lou followed Imo outside and they stood at the edge of the garden. "Alrighty, let's get down to business," Imo said. She studied Lou's face. "You just watch me for a while, and then I'll let you do some. Understand?" She patted the child's shoulder.

"Yes." Lou's knuckles were white as she clutched the ny-lons.

Carefully, Imo tied the first tomato to a stake. "You've got to mind these flower clusters," she advised Lou. "Keep them away from the stake as best you can or it will crowd our tomatoes." She tied the hose tightly to the stake and then swathed it loosely around the main stem, fastening it with a square knot. "Now, mind their arms, too," she warned, "they can snap so easily."

"Okay."

"We'll have to re-tie them every week or so." Imo petted one of the plants. "About time to put down mulch, now that the days are staying warm. Tomatoes like their heads in the sun and their feet in the shade."

"You make them sound like they're human." Lou put her hands on her hips. "Hey! I know. We could sell 'em. If you got ten cents a tomato we'd be rich!"

Imo wiped a drip of sweat from her nose. "Why would we want to do that, child?"

"So we'd get some money. So we could go to the movies. We never go to the movies." Lou gave her a sideways look.

"Well, we've got the TV to look at, Lou," Imo said, holding Lou's shoulders. "Besides, we've got enough money from your uncle's Social Security checks, and it wouldn't be very neighborly to make people pay."

That was yesterday afternoon. Today Imo settled herself onto a plush chair inside the Southside Grille, across from Wanda. She was hoping that the change of scenery would take her mind off Lou's sad face. The Southside Grille was a trendy silver diner on wheels in the heart of Atlanta's Buckhead with cloth napkins, crystal salt and pepper shakers, and a menu thick as a novel.

"That guy over there by the jukebox has his eye on you," Wanda said.

"Oh, he does not." Imo cast her eyes downward. If he was looking their way he probably had his eye on Wanda, who was in a body hugging purple dress and great big hoop earrings. Her hair was teased up into what Lou called a country-music-star-do.

"Oh, yes he does. Admit it. You are one fabulous babe now."

Imo glanced back and caught him looking at them. Maybe he *was* looking at her. It really was hard for her to change her self-perception from the old Imo to the new. But let's face it, she was in the dating market now.

"Wanda," she whispered, "I honestly don't know where to start looking for men."

"What about at Calvary?"

"There are only two single men my age or older, and neither one will do."

"Picky, picky." Wanda smiled and wagged a cherry red nail at her. "You could at least get your feet wet there."

"Frank Binnard: seventy-two, terrible breath and fussy as a wet hen. Henry Oakes: sixty- nine, five feet tall and about 300 pounds," she said, arranging her napkin in her lap.

"Seriously," Wanda laughed, "why not go for the younger ones then? After all, women live longer."

"They're all claimed past forty, and really Wanda, I don't think I can go any younger than that."

Wanda smiled. "Let's work on a criteria list, then, and we'll know who it is you're after."

"You ladies need anything else?" The waiter hovered over them to pick up their plates. "Some coffee and dessert?"

"Two coffees," said Wanda. "And how about some of that lemon pie."

"Coming right up." He scribbled on his pad. He was thirty-ish and handsome in a beach bum kind of way, but not at all Imo's type. Even before she met Silas, when she'd considered any type of man, she preferred the dark, bookish look. He slid his pencil behind his ear. "Cream and sugar?"

"Yes." Wanda dug in her bag for a pen. "Hey, can we use some of your paper?"

He tore off three sheets of his order pad. "Shopping list? You ladies must be headed over to Phipps Plaza."

Wanda shook her head and snuffed out her cigarette. "Man hunt."

"Really?" He grinned.

"You bet. For my friend here. She makes the best fresh coconut cake in the state of Georgia."

"Is that right?" He played along, probably hoping for a big tip. Imo wished Wanda didn't have to let strangers in on their business.

"You don't happen to be single, do you?" Wanda flirted with him. Imo gave her a *shut-up* look.

"Yes ma'am, at the moment, I am."

"Well, get a load of this lady," Wanda said, "newly on the market and she owns her own home. Cooks, gardens . . ."

Imo kicked Wanda hard underneath the table.

"Table three's getting antsy," the manager said to their waiter.

"Excuse me, ladies. Back with dessert in a second." The waiter went off with his pad.

"For starters, I'd say reasonably good health," Wanda wrote down a one and circled it. "I don't think you want to lose another one."

"No, I don't," Imo said. This sounded a lot like the conversations at the cattle auction barn back home.

"Let's add financially stable. Homeowner. Okay?" Wanda was on number two. "Or you could get him to sign a prenup. With my second husband, when we split, he tried to get the house I got from my first husband."

Imo lowered her voice. "This seems so calculating, Wanda. Love is more like . . ."

"Listen, hon', love is optional. We're talking companionship here. Now, number three: No criminal record. Number four, kind to animals and children. Number five, country boy." Wanda reached over and grabbed Imogene's hand. "Listen, are hair and teeth optional?"

"Yes, yes," Imo was playing along while the waiter set down their coffee and pie, praying that Wanda would keep her mouth shut this time. "The hard part will be finding him, Wanda," she said.

"Alaska? That's where the man-woman ratio is in our favor." Wanda tipped cream into her coffee.

"No. I thought we agreed on Southern," said Imo.

Wanda sighed. "Okay, Florida then; it's senior city down there."

"I want to stay put. For the girls," Imo said.

"Well, all right then. On to Plan B. Let's see . . ." Wanda lit another cigarette, took three rapid puffs and pursed her lips. "I've got it! The frozen foods section at the Kroger! That's where you're going to find your single men! Your widowers, bachelors. Everybody's got to eat and men love those Hungry Man dinners." She crossed her arms and sighed. "I am brilliant."

"You mean go down to the grocery and spy on shoppers? I certainly will not!" Imo whispered.

"You won't be spying. You'll be shopping. Push a buggy, and when you see your prey just get right up beside him and fondle a single-serving frozen meal, sigh, and say something like, 'It's so hard to cook for just one, isn't it?' Then he'll look up in amazement at your beauty . . ."

"My prey? Wanda, that sounds terrible. In my day, the men did the pursuing." Imo lifted her chin.

"Your day is gone. You have to be aggressive now. Don't let life pull you along, Imo, make it happen!" Wanda had roused herself up so much she was shaking.

Imo closed her eyes and gulped the last of her coffee.

"You'd be better off going on a Wednesday. Isn't that senior citizens day?" Wanda maneuvered her car onto Peachtree Street, toward Lenox Mall.

"Yes."

"That's settled then. Now let's go find a really sexy dress for you to wear."

"Nothing very fancy for a grocery trip. I've got a dress I made last Easter."

Wanda smiled. "Forget your Sunday school frock, you need a dress that asks."

Imo found it hard to believe that Wanda was Martha's sister. Wanda was speeding. Maybe everything about Wanda was too fast for Imo's taste. Well, she supposed she could try this thing. Pretend she was an actress. One thing she was not going to do was to look like a floozy.

"You want to make the sale, you got to ask for the order. That's what they say," Wanda said. "I should start a new business with this. Combining the beauty industry with the love one. Wanda's Make-over and Match-up Service. First I reveal a woman's true beauty potential using my cosmetology degree, and then I hook her up to some man who fits her credentials. Two no-fail businesses . . ."

"You better wait and see how your first client makes out," said Imo.

❧ ❧ ❧

Loutishie's Notebook

Imo lost weight after Uncle Silas died. But she still looked like herself, wearing everyday cotton house-dresses or pant-suits, sensible Keds Grasshopper shoes and the exact hairdo all the other ladies at church have.

Her beauty regimen was face powder and bright red lipstick called Cherries Jubilee; and on Saturday nights she washed, rolled, and set her hair fresh for church.

That was good, because it was steady. You could depend on Imo to at least look like herself, even if she was acting strange.

Then one Saturday afternoon, when Jeanette and I were sitting on the sofa watching Candid Camera re-runs, Imo walked through the den and she looked just like one of those women in the J.C. Penney catalogs. Her hair was pure brown, flipped under with bangs and she had on blush and eye shadow and this dramatic lipstick that was the color of red Georgia clay. She had on a ritzy flowered dress.

"Wow!" Jeanette marveled. "Get a load of Mama."

I had to admit it was nothing short of a miracle. Imo seemed kind of shy about it, though. She said "Hi, girls," without making eye contact, and she flew into the kitchen and started pulling out pots and pans to cook supper. Like she was trying to prove it was really her.

We watched Imo a while, as she stood over a pot of crackling fat, turning the chicken. "You really look hot!" Jeanette yelled.

Imo gave a little "hmph." She measured out a cup of rice. All business.

"I hate it," I whispered to Jeanette.

"That's why you're such a bumpkin," she answered, "a dirt-scratching little country bumpkin, whose idea of fashion is over-alls."

"I'm telling," I hissed.

She stuck out her tongue and waggled it at me. That got me mad. Here I was helping Imo out in the house and in the garden, and the only things Jeanette cared about were if her thighs looked fat or her hair didn't do right. "Maybe you're so mean because you're still feeling sick like you did this morning!" I glared at her.

"You're feeling sick, baby?" Imo's eyebrows flew up, and she ran over to press the back of her hand onto Jeanette's forehead.

"Leave me alone," Jeanette spat and twisted away. "I'm fine."

Imo said, "Just worried, hon'."

It started raining heavily that night, pounding down so hard that puddles sat on top of the garden. The water wasn't percolating through our hard clay soil.

On the second day of solid rain, Imo was almost frantic. I was glad to see she was still the same Imo on the inside. "Tomatoes hate to get their feet wet," she said to me.

"What?"

"Their roots need good drainage. When God cursed the soil, He started with Euharlee," Imo said. "I am going to work in compost." She worked in the garden till her arms gave out.

The funny thing was that the very next day, the rain stopped, and it did not fall again for three weeks. Euharlee was so dry that Calvary Baptist started holding prayer vigils for rain. One evening, I followed a concerned Imo around the parched garden. Bingo walked between us, his tongue lolling out. "This is real serious," she said, bending down to scratch in the dusty soil near a wilted squash plant.

"It is dry," I admitted. "Why don't you run the sprinkler out here?" I asked.

"Watering tomatoes must be done with great care, Lou," Imo said, stopping to squeeze my forearm and looking into my eyes.

"Oh," I said, trying to sound like I understood.

"Rain's the best drink, but you just cannot depend on the rain." Imo looked wistful. "I've been putting well water on the garden, but it's so cold I have to let it warm up. Takes all day."

"Why?" I asked.

"Water that cold will shock my plants," she said. She had a twinkle in her eye. I knew it pleased her to impart wisdom. Get her going on a garden subject and you had just better be prepared for an earful.

"Tomatoes love their manure tea," she said, herding me to a barrel she kept for that purpose.

Imo peered in and sent me to the bottoms with two buckets to haul more river water, which we poured into that barrel until it was full, letting it run through a burlap sack filled with manure. She gripped the edge and agitated fiercely. Then we lugged buckets of it to the garden.

One evening soon after we managed that dry spell, Imo and I were strolling around the garden. "Would you look at how good the tomatoes are coming along, Lou! The best ever, I do believe," she said, with her eyes shining.

FIVE

Pulling Suckers

"My secret is to pinch suckers off when they're still teeny-tiny. Less than an inch. That way, the poor tomato plant won't bleed. Tomatoes are a lot like people. When you wait too long to pinch off their suckers, they get stressed out and sickly. Their energy is just plum wasted."

— TERESA LUCKASAVAGE
county agent, discussing pruning methods
at a Garden Club gathering

*I*mo got up early on Wednesday to think about what she was getting herself into. Jeanette was asleep, and Lou was off somewhere with Bingo.

She could use the solitude to stew about the flashy dress hanging on the back of her bedroom door. It was made of a stylish fabric of red hibiscus flowers, with a flirty full skirt. Imo worried that it was too young for her, but the salesgirl and Wanda both said it was perfect.

Plus, Wanda sure seemed confident about her searching for a suitor in the supermarket.

Let people laugh and point at me, she thought. That couldn't be as bad as this lonely feeling that she lived with. After all, one of these days Jeanette and Lou would get married and move off, and then where would Imo be? She felt her pulse accelerating, so she pressed a palm against her heart and hurried outside. There was nothing like the garden to calm her nerves.

Imo sat down between the butterbeans and the cucumbers. She took a deep calming breath full of the peppery smell of marigolds. She felt better. It was amazing how much stronger she was lately.

Was it having a purpose, she wondered, and all its possibilities, that was easing her burdens and pushing her along now? Making the loneliness easier to bear? She stuck her fingers out and touched a banana pepper. The bushes were loaded. Everything out here was just exploding! Burdened down with blooms and fruits.

Imo parked the Impala and adjusted the rearview mirror to check her lipstick. She had on the dress, a string of red beads, suntan pantyhose, and white sandals she'd worn only once before.

Plunking her hand bag into the seat of a buggy, she glided to a card table set with doughnut holes and coffee. Kroger had this out each senior citizens' day, and she took her time here, selecting three powdered sugar holes.

She strolled slowly along, until she came to a little island cooler of cut-flower bouquets; mostly mums and shasta daisies with baby's breath wrapped in cellophane. The Garden Club ladies always laughed at them. A clump of hothouse posies for $5.95!

Imo was beginning to feel like an actress as she wheeled to the deli case. What always amazed her here were the bowls of things like three bean salad and cole slaw with prices you wouldn't believe. But she thought the laziest thing of all was the prepared macaroni and cheese—$4.99 a pound when you could make it in five minutes with a 69¢ box and a stick of margarine.

There were some nice-looking eclairs in the pastry case, but she resisted the temptation and headed for her favorite section: produce.

She thumped a watermelon and went so far as to weigh some snap beans and then empty them back into their bin.

"Mrs. Lavender, is that you?" Mr. Arnold, the produce manager, was not a bad-looking man and he knew his vegetables. But he was married.

"It's me," she chirped. "Don't your zucchinis look good today?" She scooped up a few as props. She squeezed a yellow squash.

Looking back at her, Mr. Arnold tripped over a rubber floor mat. "You look so . . . so different. I mean . . uh. . great and . . uh . . . I mean you looked great before too, but, . . . uh. . ."

"Thank you, Mr. Arnold." She saved him, then turned down the health-food aisle. A song about paving Paradise blared over the PA system.

As it turned out, there were quite a few things she actually needed. She scanned the rows of crackers and picked up her usual saltines.

My, there were so many choices these days, it was a wonder anybody ever got out of here. Now, at the Clover Farm Grocery in Euharlee, the items they carried were probably about one twentieth of the ones in the Kroger, but you could get all you really needed and save yourself time, too. The only time that the extra twenty-three miles you drove into Cauthen to get here was worth it was when you needed something out of the ordinary, like those Oriental pea pods or wrapping paper.

When Imogene finished aisle nine, she turned to the frozen foods. There were two aisles of eight-foot high shelves with clear glass doors and perpendicular to that, one large thirty-foot long waist-high bin.

The frozen foods section crawled with people. She lost herself among them and circled to find the Hungry Man dinners.

There was a good five feet of them and she parked herself at the end of aisle ten, beside a cardboard ice cream cone display. From this vantage point she could see the whole section. She grabbed a box of ice-cream cones and pretended to read the nutrition panel.

What now? As it turned out, there was not one single gentleman in sight. Be patient. She had to realize that Rome wasn't built in a day. Still, she could be home working in the garden.

It was mid-morning before she spied the first single gentleman leaning over the prepared meals. He had a tower of Swanson dinners in his buggy. He had no hair and walked with a cane, but he was at least worth practicing on. She rolled up beside him.

"It's such a drag cooking for one, isn't it?" She shocked herself by sounding like Wanda.

The man looked up and cupped his ear. He leaned in closer, "What'd you say?"

"I said it's not easy fixing for just one is it? I mean, that's why you're buying these Swanson dinners, right? You're a single man, having meals alone?"

"Meals alone? Heck no, my Ruby ain't cooked a decent meal in forty-seven years!" He knocked at the base of the freezer with his cane.

Lord bless poor Ruby. At least Silas had never gotten fussy, even at the end, when he'd been eaten-up with cancer.

Imo reminded herself that there were lots of fish in the sea. She certainly didn't have to take the first one that came along. She cruised the wine and spirits aisle.

Using cooking sherry for her beef burgundy at New Years was not a sin because the alcohol part evaporated during cooking. She wondered if eating rum balls didn't count either.

A tall distinguished-looking man lingered at the burgundys. Sixty, maybe. Pretty well preserved.

Imo put some cocktail twizzlers in her buggy and grabbed a jar of olives. She sidled close to him. He smelled good.

"Excuse me," he said, "I'm in your way."

Imo's heart swelled with promise. She was forced to examine the shelf of wine as he moved away. He headed toward frozen foods. She decided to hesitate a respectable time before she surged after him.

Patting her hair, and taking a deep breath, she moved in. He held a box of Weight Watchers eclairs in his left hand. No wedding ring.

"You don't see any chess pie around here, do you?" she spoke to the back of his khaki suit.

He looked up at her and her knees turned to jelly. Beautiful blue eyes and all of his hair, and a superman cleft in his chin.

It really didn't matter if he looked prettier than her. Take peacocks; males were hundreds of times flashier. She also decided to ignore the gold chain at his wrist.

All Silas had ever owned in the way of jewelry was his wedding band, two pairs of cuff links, and one nice tie tack for weddings and funerals.

"No, I certainly don't, hon'. Maybe in the deli, and if you don't have any luck there, try that little bakery on Fargo."

He called her hon'! This was going to be easy, after all. She searched desperately for something witty to say back. "Yes, that bakery is a really good place to get bread," she said.

"Ooo, yes, darling, and such exquisite eclairs," he said, "but I can't even get within smelling distance. Watching my waist, you know." He smiled with the prettiest white teeth, and patted his tummy. "But if I don't watch my figure, who will?"

Oh, she wanted to squeeze him right now and end this search.

"I see you watch what you eat," he said and touched a box of All Bran in her buggy.

Was he coming on to her?

"Oh, go on," she laughed. It was her dress, she decided. Whatever it was, she had to keep this thing happening. Should she be coy now? Or should she do this modern thing some more?

She glanced at the other shoppers nearby. She couldn't just ask for his phone number right here in public like some brazen hussy. She needed a little more conversation and some background on him. If she could just think of some telling questions to ask. Maybe, where do you go to church? No, too serious.

She looked over at him. He was smiling at someone behind her.

A thirty-ish boy in tight jeans flung something into the older man's buggy. Was this his son? It was okay if he'd been married before, maybe they could help one another over the memories.

"Some angel food cake for my angel," the boy said as he pinched her dream-boat's cheek. Imo watched their intimate conversation with her mouth open until she noticed her feet were throbbing.

It was the sandals. Worn only once to last year's Easter service, they were beginning to pinch her toes. Dear Lord, this was misery. Shouldn't she just give up and run home and slip into her house-shoes? In her mind's eye, she saw Martha's serious face. One more try.

She adjusted her stockings and drew a deep breath.

Soon there was a new flock of shoppers, and her well-trained eyes sifted through for prospects. One emaciated man in a wheelchair, with an afghan over his knees, pushed along by a black nurse. Money, thought Imo, but poor health. Companionship, but likely fussy.

A gigantic pair of cardboard scissors in bright, metallic red hung above the central freezer. Twirling slowly in the air conditioner's current for the past hour, they made her dizzy. She gripped the handlebars of her buggy and closed her eyes. Just for a minute, she figured, until she regained her bearings.

The buggy rolled slowly forward and Imo followed it along, her eyes closed and her lips blue with cold. Without warning a scene ensued that Imo could not piece together even later, when she was back at home.

"Fossil down on aisle nine," a strange voice boomed out over the intercom.

The whole Kroger stopped. People crowded around her as she lay on the floor. "Call Mr. Arnold in produce," someone said, "he knows how to handle the seniors."

A bag boy led Mr. Arnold toward her. "She's disoriented or something," he said. "Maybe she hit her head. Man, Wednesdays are getting pretty freaky around here. Last week, all six of us bag boys were wandering around the parking lot, following the fossils who didn't remember where they parked their Dodges. Man, this chick here is really out of it!"

Imo intended to speak to the manager about this impudent young man, but what could she say? "I was loitering in the frozen foods? Looking for a man?"

Mr. Arnold pulled her to her feet, but they hurt so much she could only hobble.

"I know this woman," he said to the bag boy, "I'll handle this." Mr. Arnold looked at the five items in her buggy, and she knew he wondered what she'd been doing since she wheeled through produce over an hour ago. He didn't say a word, though, just steadied her by the elbow.

"Got to get these sandals off," she pleaded, and he waited against a shelf while she slid them off and flung them into the buggy. She left her buggy and leaned on Mr. Arnold all the way across the parking lot.

"We'll get you home, Mrs. Lavender," he said. The asphalt was blistering hot on her feet and when they reached the Impala she rolled off her panty hose before she climbed in. Mr. Arnold stood there with his eyes bulging, twisting his apron, like he thought she might take everything off. "You okay to drive home? Do you know where you live?" He wrung his hands.

"Of course I do!" she snapped, pulling the door shut and tossing her handbag into the back seat. She was not sure she could show her face in the Kroger again. Alaska was beginning to sound mighty good to her.

She sped home, then hobbled around the house, mentally calculating the chores that needed doing. A pile of laundry, supper to make, and countless hours of dusting, mopping, and scrubbing.

Exactly what I should have been doing, she fussed at herself. Instead of listening to Wanda.

Actually, eating Whitman's Samplers and reading silly paperback romances didn't seem that bad right now. Or perhaps it was time for an old woman to turn to the senior's ministry at the church, the Keenagers, and go riding on bus trips to the Tennessee Aquarium or to an art museum in Atlanta. What good did it do to go out looking for some stranger, when you had people who needed you right here?

Plus, she could just spend her time in the garden. It had never let her down, and it was really thriving this year.

Loutishie's Notebook

One afternoon in early June, Imo slung gravel as she turned the Impala past our mailbox and zipped into the shed. She limped inside, barefooted, wearing that fancy new dress. She sank down into the La-Z-Boy. "Will you fetch me the Epsom salts and the blue plastic bucket on the back porch, Lou?" Imo said, rubbing her feet.

Her eyes told me something troubled her, but I didn't dare ask what.

"It's time to pinch the suckers," Imo said that night after we'd finished supper. She marched out to the garden. I followed her. "Lou, I have one rule that I follow to help me get the most tomatoes out of my plants," she said, her voice rising as she flexed her thumb and forefinger. "You get on up here and stay close so I can teach you."

She eyed a row of tomato plants. "It's called double-stemming. You only let the first sucker, these are tiny shoots which develop in the crotch formed between the leaf and the stem, grow." She narrowed her eyes. "When you do that, you end up with two stems per plant, and that's a whole lot easier to stake." Imo ran her hands over a multitude of suckers. "Plus, they'll make earlier, and they'll make more!"

I nodded my head. To my aunt, the immense satisfaction of giving away a mess of collards or a sack of tomatoes could not be equaled. Her goal was abundance.

"Now, if you let those suckers be, each one will grow into a stem," she snorted. "Then they'll split and split and split again, until you end up with a sprawling, non-productive tomato plant."

I got a mental image of each extra sucker becoming a full-fledged stem itself, which in turn sent off suckers forking wildly, ad infinitum.

"Pay close attention, Lou," she told me, eyeing the tomato plants like they were in eminent danger. "We've got to remove every excess sucker before it's too late." With a sigh, she shook her head. "The sooner we get rid of them, the sooner the ones we are encouraging can get their growth."

I caught her pinching off some of the yellow blooms, too. "What are you doing?" I cried. "Don't those turn into tomatoes?"

We'd been studying blooms in Ag Econ and I knew the little yellow flowers turned into fruits once they were pollinated.

"All these many blooms are draining the plant's vigor," she told me, "so I pluck a good number to force energy into the rest of them."

SIX

Ripe and Ready

*"You may enjoy indulging yourself with certain
memories of you and Silas. But the bad thing
about doing that is that each time they retreat, they
suck away a part of you with them. Plus, you can't
hug memories, no matter how warm they are.
The time is ripe for you to get back out there
and find that man!"*

— RELUCTANT SUB-CONSCIOUS THERAPIST OF
IMOGENE LAVENDER
admonishing her as she lay in bed

*J*mo stood at the stove, stirring a pot of collards and peering into the stove every so often to check on her pies. She wished she had thought of taking care of Calvary's shut-ins earlier.

What in the world had come over her? She couldn't remember, but the pain of the Kroger incident was fading, and all this cooking and visiting was a gracious plenty to keep her mind off things.

She checked the pies. Browning nicely. Twin top crusts of gently rolling buttery perfection. She stirred the collards.

Imo mopped her brow. What a pleasure to work so hard! She started to take the pies out, but a knock at the back door distracted her.

"Hello, Wanda," Imo said, avoiding her eyes. "Come on in out of this heat."

Wanda stepped in. She wore a denim dress so short Imo wondered how she could sit down without showing her rump. Her hair was all swept over into a pony tail behind her right ear. She sucked in a breath when she saw Imo. "What has happened to you? No makeup, wearing that drab old rag! You're a mess!" She set down her handbag and grabbed the sides of Imo's head. "We have got to tend to those roots."

Imo bit her tongue. "I have been too busy in my garden to worry about it," she managed. "Besides, I'm thinking of going natural again."

"That's silly," Wanda said.

"I *am* busy," said Imo, indignant. "Things have just piled up around here. Why, this afternoon I've got to carry the Impala into town to get the oil changed."

"That's why men were invented," said Wanda, laughing. "We can get my ex number two to come out here and do it for you. He owes me one."

"I don't know, dear. I think I'll just carry it where I always do. I'm going to get him to put some air in my tires and check my antifreeze, too."

"It's summer. You don't need antifreeze. And, hey, he's single, too! My ex, I mean."

Imo fingered her apron. She wasn't quite sure how to say

what she had to. "I . . . I don't want to find a new man, Wanda. It's taken me till now to figure out what I need to be doing instead."

"What then?"

"Taking care of Calvary's shut-ins."

Wanda laughed. "I know you're joking, dear. But let's get serious now. I have just the thing for you right here." She dug around in her purse until she came up with a piece of paper.

Imo pursed her lips. How silly she'd been to think it might be enough to simply tell Wanda she was no longer interested in finding a man. "Come have some apple pie, dear," she said. At least pie would keep Wanda's mouth occupied. Sighing, Imo led her to the kitchen table, pulled out a chair, and grabbed a knife. She settled down into the chair across from Wanda. The pie on the table was cool enough. She sliced a piece and slid it over to Wanda.

"How many of these things did you make?" Wanda surveyed the counter top.

"Six in all." Imo swept some crumbs from the table into her palm and folded them into her napkin.

"Look at you," Wanda said, "making six pies spells L-O-N-E-L-Y. You really need that man."

"Hush, Wanda," said Imo.

"Now, sweetie," Wanda said, "there's lots of other places to look for a man. I said to Martha this morning, I said, 'Martha, I've found the perfect solution for Imo.'" She looked down at the pie slice and fanned her face. She smoothed out the slip of paper. "Right here under part-time employment it says sales clerk needed part time at Serenity Retail Showroom."

"What?" Imo blinked.

"I bet money lots of eligible men hang out at that place," said Wanda, jabbing a pink fingernail at the paper. "I mean, it's got to be a natural draw for your target audience. Plus, it wouldn't be like it was at Kroger. They'd come to you. Like flies to sticky paper."

"That sounds terrible." Imo did not even allow herself to linger on that idea. She gave Wanda what she hoped was a resolute frown.

"Listen, if they're regulars and have some account set up or something, you'll have access to their personal information. Perfect, huh?"

"Hush, Wanda."

"So, you ever had a job before?" Wanda lit up a cigarette.

"Worked at the peach-packing shed every summer of my life, after I turned fourteen, and right on up until I was twenty-three." Imogene waved away the smoke.

"Listen, this job sounds perfect for you."

Imo's toes still pulsed with the memory of the cruel sandals. In her mind's eye, she saw herself off at a job while the garden got full of engorged tomatoes, splitting their skins, needing to be put by.

"Uhm, Wanda?" Imo began, "I hate to tell you this, but I am not going to look for a man."

"You can't just sit here and dry up, sweetie. You've got to grab life by the horns!"

Imo thought of grabbing a bull by the horns. Dangerous business. "I don't think so," she said quickly. Wanda smiled and hopped up to affix the scrap of paper to the refrigerator with a magnet.

"What's that smell?" Wanda's nostrils flared.

Imo smiled modestly. "The pie. It's Mama's old recipe, lots of cinnamon and nutmeg."

"No, I mean, it's a burning smell. Look!" Wanda cried. Imo turned to look behind her and there was smoke pouring out from around the oven door.

Imo set the charred pies out on the back steps and opened up the windows. As the kitchen cleared, she and Wanda stepped outside into blinding sunlight, then walked over to the shed. "Like I said, let my ex come do your oil." Wanda slapped the hood of the Impala. "He's got the cutest buns! Bring him a glass of tea out here and if you can catch him bending over into the hood, you'll think you've died and gone to heaven!"

Imogene felt her neck get hot. "I bet the kitchen's cleared out by now."

Wanda turned around and looked at Imo's face. "Oh, hon', I'm sorry, I shouldn't have said that about dying. Now you're going to hate me . . ."

"Oh no, that's not it. I'm just . . . just . . ." Imo didn't realize how sad she must look until she saw Wanda's face. "Don't you want your pie?"

"I'm on a diet, and I better get on back. I've got a perm coming at three." Wanda patted her tummy and hurried to her car.

Imo went inside to clean up and portion out the collards. She hung up her apron. It was quiet. Jeanette was napping. Lou was probably down at the bottoms. She arranged the food into baskets and set them into the trunk of the Impala, trying not to think of Wanda's ex's cute buns. She walked out past the garden and hollered, "Lou-ti-shie!"

There was no answer and she went back inside and slumped down into a kitchen chair. She was tired, and a little sad about the burned-up pies. She spied the classified ad up on the Fridgidaire. Well, come to think of it, she was a bit lonely, too. But if she listened to Wanda this time, it might be even worse than the Kroger incident.

Another week passed. A week of almost unbearable loneliness that made Imo work harder in the garden. Despite the drought, the tomatoes were tall and stout.

"I'm doing just fine," she insisted when Martha called her. But the truth was that the place just seemed so vastly empty these days.

She tried to concentrate on removing the faded flowers from her crepe myrtles and drying hydrangea blossoms. Then she pinched the chrysanthemums and pulled up poppies to shake the seeds where she wanted some to sprout next year.

Imo pruned the roses that were finished blooming and

fed her azaleas and camellias. There was some joy in this while she was actually doing it, but it didn't last, and she kept wondering what she could do to overcome the loneliness that dogged her. At first she tried ignoring it. After all, it could be just a stage she had to go through.

She went inside and called all the girls in the Garden Club to talk about ordering bulbs for fall planting. When she went to the mantle to get her gardening catalog, she noticed a film of dust on the photographs there. She dashed into the pantry for a dust rag and took a deep breath when she remembered what her dust rags actually were. They were Silas's old threadbare undershirts. Imo's eyes blurred. She swiped the dusty glass of one photograph and found herself peering right into Silas's eyes.

"We had fun fishing, didn't we, Imo?" he seemed to ask her. She sat down, holding the picture of her and Silas at Cooper's Lake. First, she pictured him coming in the back door with a grin stretched from ear to ear. In his left hand was a tackle box and under his right arm, two poles.

It was early at Cooper's Lake, still cool, as they set up folding chairs and baited hooks. They spent the day propped against each other, complacently quiet in the way only two soul mates could be.

That memory was so satisfying that the next afternoon she pulled down another picture of her and Silas at the county fair. Suddenly, she was with Silas again, holding a paper cone of cotton candy and walking the dusty midway beside him.

She savored each moment of these trips down Memory

Lane. They made her feel so happy she was light-headed. She felt young again.

But now she had a new problem. When it was over, the memory, that is, there was this raw ache in her heart, and she felt drained. The memories from the third, fourth, and fifth trips left Imo so sad when they were over that she couldn't get up for several hours.

It was probably the way it was with alcoholics. She could see now how enticing it was to get drunk—a temporary, wonderful high. But you had to pay for it when it was all said and done. You had to endure the hangover. It was a beautiful experience to escape to the past with Silas, but one of these days it was going to put her over the edge.

"So, stop it, Imogene," she told herself. "That life is behind you and this is killing you! You are going to be a basket case if you keep this up."

Previous work experience. Imogene tapped the clipboard with her pen. How could she fit raising Angus, making apple jelly, composting the garden, feeding the chickens, and canning tomatoes in that tiny space?

Standing underneath a long blue banner which read "We Bill Medi-caid/Medicare For You!" the manager of Serenity watched her.

Lining the walls were wheelchairs, respiratory equipment, lift chairs, bath safety rails, and the largest selection of canes and walkers she'd ever seen.

First she thought: *What in the world am I doing?* Her next

thought was that the walker section would remind her too much of Silas's last months.

But then again, she reasoned, she could meet another Silas Lavender in this joint. A man certainly didn't have to be feeble to visit the store.

She toyed with the idea of adding the summer peach-shed-packing job. Where it asked: "How many days did you miss in the last year due to illness?" she proudly wrote none.

On the back of the sheet she was supposed to write down any experiences related to this job. It was the first time, since Silas had been diagnosed with prostate cancer, that she had stopped and summarized the past year. She wrote about buying his walker and about nursing him in his last five months.

Reading over the essay, she gave it a satisfied pat and returned it to the manager.

"If you can wait a minute, I'll look this over before you leave, Mrs. Lavender," he said. She nodded and stepped to the front of the store.

The entire store front was glass with a base of red brick that had two feet of dirt between it and the sidewalk. If she was hired, she was going to speak to him about planting some dianthus out there.

Since Serenity was situated in the heart of downtown Euharlee's only intersection, it was perfect for people watching. She stood there looking out when a young man walked by outside, wearing only red nylon athletic pants. He stopped when he saw her and turned to face her. She smiled and waved with her free hand.

He looked at her with bloodshot eyes. He bent his knees, tipped his pelvis forward, and grabbed his crotch in a vulgar gesture. Pulsing his hand, he rolled his eyes up in mock pleasure and mouthed words she could only imagine.

It was like when she was paralyzed in her dreams. She could not move or turn her head away from his leers. He was obviously delighted with her expression because he took both hands and made vulgar squeezing motions in the air like he was massaging two water balloons.

"Just don't make eye contact. Somebody needs to teach you some street smarts." It was the young lady, Angie, who worked in Serenity after school. "It's like when you were little and your mama told you to ignore kids who were picking on you. What people like that want is a reaction."

Imo could not speak. This was the kind of thing that made a person love plants.

"Welcome aboard," the manager walked over smiling, his hand stretched out. "We do on- the-job training here at Serenity. Can you start tomorrow?"

"I have changed my mind," she said.

That night Imo lay down beside the ever-present shape of loneliness. A memory nudged at her, and she was too tired to fight it.

"The fish are biting," Silas whispered. He slid out from underneath the covers whistling his way to the kitchen.

Silas reappeared with coffee, his feet making soft padding noises on the wooden floor. He placed the cup and saucer on her bedside table. "Grab your pole and grab your hat, leave your worries on the doorstep. Just direct your feet to the fishing hole with me," he sang, dancing and bowing like Fred Astaire. He gathered their poles and tackle boxes, loaded the truck with a quilt and a radio, singing as he went.

The sun spread its tender morning fingers out over the pastures as they made their way to Cooper's Lake. They parked and settled down at the base of an old pine tree in the warm complacency and joy of a companionship where idle chit-chat is not needed.

The whole memory dissolved when a woodpecker attacked the tree just outside her bedroom window. *Come back, Silas.* She squeezed her eyes together tight, begging him to return. She was desperate to crawl right back into this particular memory and stay there. Forever.

She sat up and rubbed her eyes until it dawned on her that she was still alone.

"You can't hug memories," her sub-conscious therapist said, "you've got to go and find that man." She crawled out of bed and slipped off her nightgown. It was dark enough in this corner of the bedroom to conceal the purpley spider veins, but not dark enough to hide the fact that her bosom was no longer firm and high and that she wasn't as tall as she had once been.

"Well, like it or leave it," she said to all the eligible men out there and pulled on a housedress to go make the coffee. The girls were still asleep at this hour, so she carried her coffee outside to the glider, along with yesterday's newspaper.

Under the obituaries, the words "Notice of Public Hearing" caught her eye. She lowered her bifocals to read the fine print.

"Come join us to stand up for your rights!!! In an effort to gauge public concern and support for the farming community of Euharlee, Georgia, there will be a meeting Saturday, July 19th at the VFW building on Rainwater Road. Lack of involvement means you, the farmer and property owner, will lose!

"Proposals to restrict future agricultural activities and limit farm pursuits, including federal/state government programs that intend to reduce odors, noise, chemical use and manure spreading, are threatening our way of life. Recent complaints about these aforementioned items may force demands to halt operations or to give up the land altogether.

"Mark your calendar and plan to attend!"

This sounded like something she ought to go to. She cast her eyes around the farm. A handful of cows, some chickens and one dog, and the garden, which was not for commercial use. It wasn't likely to affect her place, but still, it wasn't fair for whoever these people were, government officials or maybe city people moving out this way, to complain about farming. That made her mad. Farmers were the lifeblood of this great nation.

She went inside to call Martha. "Some ornery old coot from Tea Creek's at the back of it," Martha said.

"Is it true, though? The part about the government coming in?"

"I reckon so, Imogene. You know how that goes."

"You going?"

"I imagine I ought to. Lots of the congregation are farmers," Martha said. "Listen, hon', you sound a whole lot better today."

"I do?"

"You surely do. Come with me to this meeting."

Imo said she guessed she would, hung up and walked through the garden. Without thinking, she plucked a bloom off a tomato vine. Independence day was coming up soon, she thought, twirling the little yellow flower. She sat down on an overturned feed bucket between the rows of tomatoes and closed her eyes.

When she opened her eyes she was staring at a perfect red orb. The first ripe tomato! Hallelujah! At long last the fruits of her labor were here. All her life, for as long as she'd been big enough to garden, Imo had been as tickled with the first ripe tomato as God must have been with Adam.

She touched it. Warm from the fat sun and powdery with a little Euharlee dirt. She twisted it off gently and pressed it against her cheek.

Now this was living! She swiped it clean against her sleeve and chomped down into its flesh. Juice and seeds slid down her chin to her collar. She didn't care. She looked around, there were bushels of them, hanging like giant rubies. She would carry some to her shut-ins. Oh, she was definitely moving forward now!

Loutishie's Notebook

Toward the middle of June, Imo practically lived outside. We replenished the mulch in the garden and re-staked the tomatoes twice. They were so tall at that point that I had a vision of them stirring the clouds like Jack's bean stalk. She fed her roses and she planted more gladioli and chrysanthemums. She started her seeds of cleomes and zinnias and pinched back her petunias and pansies.

It was comforting to have her outside with her sleeves rolled up, since that was where she seemed the happiest. What was even more comforting was that she was turning back into herself. No longer dressing fancy or putting on rouge and eye shadow. And when she had her hair up inside of her straw gardening hat, you couldn't even tell it was two-toned.

One Saturday, I was down at the bottoms, and I heard the bell up at the house ringing. The bell was our emergency signal for everyone to come quickly to the house. Alarmed, I took the shortcut through some barbed wire fences and the side pasture. I found Imo standing in the kitchen, surrounded by boxes and baskets, a list in her hand. Jeanette stumbled into the kitchen, too.

"What's the matter?" I said, breathless.

"Girls, I've found the first ripe tomato in the garden!" She looked from me to Jeanette, her eyes dancing.

"That's why you rang the bell?" Jeanette studied her face.

"Well, that, and it's time to visit my round of shut-ins," she said, handing me something wrapped in tin foil. "You girls come on and help me, hear?"

There were six Better Boys, still warm from the sun, on the kitchen table. Imo's eyes were dancing.

"This will certainly help us get our minds off our own troubles, won't it girls?" she said. "And there's nothing like fresh vegetables to perk those old folks up. A lot of them can't even get out anymore."

"I'm not going," Jeanette said, rolling her eyes.

"I'll go!" I said, glaring at Jeanette.

"Come on and help me tote all this food, Jeanette," Imo said.

"I don't want to go." Jeanette started crying.

As Imo and I rumbled off down the road, she asked me what was wrong with Jeanette. I shrugged. What was happening to Jeanette was far beyond anything I had knowledge of. Seemingly overnight, she had gone from being my friend and sister, who loved to run down to the bottoms with me, and Imo's faithful daughter, who would follow her anywhere, to an easily tearful young woman who kept her nose in trashy magazines.

SEVEN

Rain in the Forecast

*"That's nothing. My Truett always said she knew it
was going to rain when the bees were heading to
their hives. Or, when the swallows were circling
and swooping low. Hoo-wee, that woman was
one great weather forecaster!"*
— HENRY PRITCHETT
ornery old coot and suitor of Imogene Lavender,
discussing his dead wife

*A*ll her life Imo had heard that it was a woman's
prerogative to change her mind. That made her
feel better when she called Wanda to touch up
her roots. Also, she put the photographs of Silas into the
trunk of winter blankets. She traced the outline of his face.
"I'll let you out when I'm a little stronger."

The evening of the farmer's meeting she put on her lipstick, a bit of blush, and a light smear of eye shadow. She
told herself that gussying-up for a cause was not vanity.
Certainly, the good country folk of Euharlee needed to
look sophisticated tonight.

She climbed into Martha's Dodge and placed her hand-bag on the floor at her feet.

"Looks like we might get a sprinkle this evening," Martha said.

"I hope so," Imo said, leaning out the window. The sky was low and threatening, a dusky gray canopy.

"How long's it been? Since we had a drop of rain?" Martha stuck her arm out and waved it around.

"About two weeks now," Imo said.

"If we don't get us some rain soon, it won't be the government or the city folks running the farmers out of business."

"My tomatoes are doing the best ever."

"Is that right?" Martha pressed the accelerator and turned off Paris Street onto the highway.

Ahead in the dusk, they saw the neon lights of the Dairy Queen. Imo spied the Impala parked at the DQ. At least Jeanette had been telling her the truth when she asked if she could drive to the DQ tonight. Maybe Jeanette was eating all her meals at the DQ. That would certainly explain a lot.

Martha steered them right up to the door of the VFW post. "We're early," she announced. "I'm going to open up and get the refreshments ready."

Imo smiled. She helped Martha tote in some boxes.

"Now, I think folks'll come to this no matter what," Martha said, "since their livelihood's at stake, but it's always nice to have a little something for them."

Martha and Imo nibbled on mints as they unfurled a long tablecloth and set out the food.

"Here comes somebody now," Imo watched a man get out of a pickup. The hairs on the back of her neck stood up. If she believed in ghosts, she would have run to him shouting, "Silas!"

Instead, she marveled at the familiar shape of a man who was the spitting image of Silas. He had the same shaped head and the lowering sun was shining through his large ears from behind. Sparse hair was combed in straight furrows over the shiny dome of his head. He had on a cotton plaid work shirt and khaki trousers and sturdy boots. He was holding the familiar green cap of the Feed 'n' Seed.

Imo's heart rate accelerated. Every time she saw a man with one of those caps, she thought about Silas. Of course, she realized that a lot of old men got rather homogenous as they aged. But this was uncanny! One glaring difference she made out as he got closer was that this man had no right hand.

He stuck his head in through the double wooden doors. "Anybody home?" he bellowed.

"You are the early bird," Martha chirped, without looking up from the cheese straws. "Come and get your worm."

He laughed. "Much obliged, but I got to get the overhead projector set up."

Martha looked up at him. Imo could tell she thought it was Silas for a minute, too. "Uh, you must be Henry Pritchett," Martha said. Almost speechless for once.

"Yep. Mighty nice of you ladies to fix all these goodies."

"Our pleasure," managed Martha.

Imo stood there with her mouth open. It wasn't long before folks started dribbling in. There was quite a crowd for a Euharlee Tuesday evening.

"Isn't this something?" Martha nudged Imo's arm as they sat in folding chairs at the back, waiting for the meeting to start.

Everyone's attention was on a clipboard that had a petition fastened on it that was going up and down the rows like a church collection plate. Random jaws worked on tobacco chews and there was a cough here and there.

She knew most of the folks from church or town and they nodded hellos. Finally, Mr. Henry Pritchett came through the side door carrying a yard stick.

"I'd say it was Silas 'cept for that hand," Martha whispered.

Mr. Pritchett's voice was strong and persuasive. "If we don't step forward," he boomed out, "what will happen to our livelihood? I ask you to realize, with me here tonight, that there are proposals to restrict future agricultural activities right here in Euharlee."

Everyone sat in rapt attention, watching his shining face as he hopped around the podium. He leaned over the microphone, waving his stump. "Folks are complaining about foul odors and day-to-day farming activities. Yes, the same people who enjoy a Sunday dinner of fried chicken and snap beans and squash." His voice boomed out and echoed against the brick wall in the rear. "What do they expect? A bed of roses?"

Laughter.

"Friends," he said, "these ill-conceived complaints will

not go unchallenged! We must step forward to work toward a solution together. As local farmers, it is our duty to protect our future!"

He went on about forming committees for research, and for taking the case to local governments and ended with a call for a Farmer's Coalition.

Applause like corn popping.

"Listen to me," he said, goaded on by their reaction, "I've been called an ornery old coot by some, a yokel by others. Nobody's complained about my cornfields, but some say my poultry operation is a blight on the face of the Earth, or should I say, a stink!?"

His country boy image was perfect for the job, and his speech was as smooth as the Etowah. Every face was riveted to his words. "Listen, friends and neighbors, we won't take this meekly." He waved his arms like a revival preacher. "You local farmers have to stand up and fight. Do you hear me?" He cupped his hand around his ear and beckoned with the other hand. "What is at the heart of America? Can't hear you," he coaxed. "Say farming, say it loudly."

Finally, the voices surged up from the audience, starting softly and then crescendoing as people felt the comfort of numbers.

"Yes," Mr. Pritchett went on, "I see people here tonight who care about the future. People here who are willing to fight. We will show those government bureaucrats we won't just sit back while they threaten the survival of agriculture in rural Georgia!"

Imo found herself clapping along with the rest of them.

It seemed like the only thing to do was join the cause. Was it for the cause that she would do this, or was it for this man who was like Silas on the outside? She wasn't certain, but she knew she had to get near him.

Martha grabbed her by the elbow. "C'mon honey, he's winding down, we've got to start dipping punch."

Imo kept her eyes on Henry Pritchett as she blindly ladled the orange sherbet and ginger ale mixture into plastic cups.

"Watch out, Imogene," Martha warned her, "you're making a mess."

"We're in this together!" Mr. Pritchett cried. Everyone clapped, and he announced the next meeting.

"Spittin' image. Don't you think?" Martha whispered.

Imo didn't answer. She listened to him announce the refreshments and thank everyone for coming.

When Imo picked up the phone the next morning she hadn't had her coffee yet and it took her a minute to place who Henry was.

"Mighty purty day out, Mrs. Lavender," he said. She listened to him talk about the weather and then his chickens, until it dawned on her it was Mr. Henry Pritchett. "Just thought we might like to get to know each other a little better." He paused.

She pressed her left hand over her heart, drew in a deep breath, and sat down on a chair at the kitchen table. "We could ride around this Sunday," he said. "Around two o'clock or so?"

She smiled into the phone. "Yes." She bit her lower lip. "I'd like that, Mr. Pritchett."

Imo hung up and sat there awhile. This was certainly a surprise. Her heart swelled with thoughts of love. Look what had happened! She hadn't even had to chase him a bit. Barely even got up the nerve to speak to him at the meeting.

This was meant to be. That's what all this was about. She got up and brewed her coffee extra strong. Let's see, this was Wednesday, and that meant four nights to get through until their date.

Forty-nine years since she'd been on a first date! She closed her eyes. She wondered if she could really do this. She went into the bathroom and washed her face. What should she wear? She looked into the mirror and smoothed on extra facial lotion. Maybe she'd wear her black short sleeve dress and then try a little of the darker lipstick. Maybe some of the emerald green eyeshadow with that?

"Now where in tarnation did I put my sunglasses?" Mr. Henry Pritchett searched the visor and the seat for his clip-ons. It was five o'clock, and the sun was low and bright, bouncing off the hood of his pickup.

At first Imo found it easy to talk to him because he looked so much like Silas. For three hours, they'd been riding and talking. Gradually, though, she'd realized that there were some major differences in the two men, and she wasn't even thinking about the missing hand.

First of all, he mentioned his dead wife far too much.

"Let's get ice cream," he said.

"Fine," she said. She thought of cool butter pecan ice cream sitting on her tongue. Mmmm. A crunchy cone, too. The perfect summer treat.

"Now, Truett had to have cherry vanilla. If they were out of that she would take strawberry. But what she really loved was cherry vanilla."

Imo sighed. He had mentioned Truett sixteen times already today, and it was beginning to tire her.

At first, Imo had been entranced, like having a private view into another woman's world; hearing about how she gardened, how she preferred dark meat to white, and what she did with the grandchildren at Christmas.

But now it was exhausting. You would have thought the man wouldn't be so focused on her after she'd been dead four years. She was wondering how long it would be before she didn't think of Silas so often. But at least she didn't talk about him to Henry non-stop.

Maybe being around me will purge the habit from Henry, she thought. He was nice enough, and he was a pleasant companion.

She turned her attention to the scenery outside. The Queen Anne's lace was at its peak. Every summer she put out two big feed buckets filled with colored water: one with blue and one with red. She let the girls gather armfuls of Queen Anne's lace to dye. She knew Lou would be up for it this fourth of July, but Jeanette would most likely roll her eyes and sigh.

Jeanette didn't appreciate the fact that Imo tried to think of things that they could do together. Just last week, Imo got the sewing machine and several yards of fabric out to teach Jeanette to sew curtains.

The sullen girl came into the kitchen and sat slumped on the phone stool in a bored sort of way. Imo hoped some small part of her realized the importance of domestic knowledge. But by supper time, they'd gotten nowhere.

"What's the matter, sugar foot?" Imo asked.

Jeanette's face was pale. She started to say something, but then she jumped up and ran into the bathroom. Imo excused her from the lesson and sent her to bed.

"Purty out this way, ain't it?" Henry asked.

"It certainly is," she answered, grateful for the new subject. "My hostas are the prettiest they've ever been."

"But it's been a terrible dry spell, eh?"

"Oh, yes, my water bill was double." She could get used to having someone who shared her concerns.

She looked over at Henry. She stared at his hand. It had plump purple veins just below the surface of thin skin with the watery brown spots of old age. She wondered when the time would be that they'd first hold hands.

The Ice Cream Churn was an oasis in the middle of the rural outskirts of Euharlee. It was really more of a filling station and convenience store, combined with a bait and tackle shed, than an ice cream parlor. It had four stools growing out of the floor in front of a small glass case which held eight cardboard cylinders of ice cream.

"Treats on me." Henry squeezed her elbow as she peered up at the menu. "They've got cherry vanilla today. My Truett was partial to the cherry . . ."

"You've already mentioned that." She hoped her voice didn't sound as irritated as she felt. "I'll have two scoops of the butter pecan," she said to the girl behind the plexiglass.

The girl, about Jeanette's age smiled pleasantly and scooped down into a container. "Cup or cone?" she asked Imo.

"Truett always ordered the cup," Henry said. "She was a real tidy girl, didn't want that drippy cone all over her."

"Cone, please," Imo said overly sweetly, through clenched teeth.

Henry ordered himself a plain scoop of vanilla in a cup and they sat on the barstools eating their ice cream and looking out through the convenience store part of the establishment.

"This is good," Imo said. "I was getting right hungry." She took a cold, creamy lick of her ice cream. She still couldn't get over how much this man looked like Silas.

Henry smiled at her. "Wanna see my place?" he asked. "It's only about five miles from here." He looked like such an eager beaver, nodding his head with his eyes so wide open.

Part of Imo thought maybe she'd be better off going back to her place and forgetting this whole thing. Finally she said, "Mmm hmm." She supposed it wouldn't hurt to take a polite look at his place.

Henry drove well enough with only his left hand, but Imo

kept thinking that she wouldn't be able to scoonch over next to him and clasp his right hand if their relationship progressed to that point. Well, she could turn herself into one of those modern dating women and pick him up in her car and drive with her left hand and hold his hand that way.

Like he could read her mind, he nudged his stump against her thigh. "Nice dress, Mrs. Lavender."

"Thank you. You may call me Imo." She slid toward her window and tucked her dress in around her legs.

"I know you'll like my place," he said, sucking at something between his teeth, "prettiest place in my neck of the woods."

She smiled and said she was sure it was. Then he lit into how Truett had transformed it from a scrubby pasture into a gardener's show-case. "We couldn't drive two miles without Truett ordering me to pull over and stop the car. She could spot an old abandoned house site through a three foot thicket. Dug up many a crepe myrtle and flowering dogwood."

"That right," Imo said.

"Yessum. That girl was a real artist with flowers and trees." His voice was husky with emotion.

"Well." Imo said, hoping that her skin wasn't as green as her heart.

"That woman grows azaleas as big as pines. . ."

Imo ground her teeth together so hard it hurt. Grew, past tense. The woman grew.

By the time they were in sight of Henry's house, she was fed up with Truett.

"Looka' yonder," he crowed as they turned down the driveway. "See her cornflowers just a bloomin'!"

Imo peered out at a lush carpet of blue covering the banks where the yard met the highway.

Henry parked beside an old-timey hand-plow sunk into the ground with a mailbox fastened on top. The prettiest purple clematis Imo had ever seen was wrapped around it. Henry pranced over to her door and helped her out.

"Welcome to Tara, my dear," he said in a silly Rhett Butler voice. She let him propel her along the walk to what was actually just an old white farm house with a new tin roof glinting in the sun. There were concrete steps painted green, spilling over with pots of cherry tomatoes and petunias. Azaleas encircled the front of the house and spice pinks and verbenas lined the walk.

Imo couldn't let her jealousy cloud the beauty of this floral paradise. Her chance at love either. Well, maybe just companionship. She had a fleeting vision of this being her place.

Imo knew one thing: She and Truett would have been great friends if they'd had the chance.

She pulled away from Henry to wander around the yard. His mouth fell open, and she imagined him thinking what an independent woman she was.

"Do you like it?" He asked from behind her.

"Oh, yes. I like it." She walked around and out back, surveying a small barn with a trellis over the door laced with Carolina jessamine. There was a thick mat of honeysuckle covering the roof of a well nearby, too.

She couldn't stop. She knew it was rude, but there was something inside propelling her onward. Henry looked like a lost child as she stopped at the edge of a cold frame near to where the back yard proper ended.

"Real pretty, Mr. Pritchett."

"Henry," Henry said. "You get carried away by flowers too, don't you?"

She smiled, and he hooked his arm through hers and sailed her off across the yard. "Wait'll you see this," he said and waltzed her around a little Monet garden of Queen Anne's lace and lavender blue petunias, stopping at a kidney-shaped garden pond. She looked into the eyes of Saint Francis of Assisi who was standing in the center, pouring water out of a cistern.

Imo caught her breath. She counted seven exquisite water lilies skimming the surface of the oasis. Henry was rocking back and forth from his heels to his toes and grinning like a mule eating briers.

"Speechless, huh?" He looked so eager. "Have a seat." He deposited her into a wrought- iron chair where she sat like a princess in someone else's world. There was a little stone footpath leading to what, she guessed, from this far away, was a rose garden.

What caught her eye was the trellis at the start of the path, so covered-over with blooms that it looked solely formed of roses.

She rose up, heart pounding, and made her way over to the arc to enter a land of floral enchantment. Eve couldn't have had it any prettier. She stepped, with a wild picture of herself

as a girl in her grannie's garden in her head. Ensconced between gigantic boxwoods there was a pomegranate tree, its
blooms unfolding like little birds. A scent of honeysuckle and
the peppery smell of roses mingled into an intoxicating fu-
sion. She walked in a trance.

"Want to see my corn now?" Henry shattered the moment.

She didn't tell him she'd rather stay right here and not
move, forever.

They walked a quarter mile to a cattle gate, and he un-
latched the chain and swung the gate open, holding out
one arm like the man on *The Love Boat* show.

"After you, my dear," he said. They walked into a field of
precise geometric patterns carved in the red earth. Alternating
lines of green, brown, and green again. Corn shoots about
knee high.

"How nice."

"Fifty-seven acres of Silver Queen," he said, shielding his
eyes and peering out like a sailor at sea.

"My goodness," Imogene said. She could tell him that
Silas planted Silver Queen, too. But, she didn't feel like sliding his name out right here in another man's field.

"Started growing corn when my harvesting equipment
wasn't nothing but a shucking hook, a team, and a wagon
with a bang board."

"How nice, Henry." There, she did it. Used his first name.
She bent down and touched a tiny stalk.

He seemed to be waiting for her to say something more.

"You must be real proud of this corn," she ventured.

"Uhm, yes I am. It's worth all the sacrifices." He was standing there staring at his stump. It looked like a weenie to Imo, the way it was all puckered up on the end. He cleared his throat and glanced at her.

"How'd you lose your hand, Henry?" she smiled to encourage him.

"Fall of fifty-seven. I was on the corn harvester. Had my work gloves on. Stepped on the clutch and the thing grabbed my glove and pulled it right in. Chewed up my hand."

This news didn't really startle Imo. She'd heard worse. But she still couldn't think of what to say. "I swanee, you sure do manage good without it," she said after a minute.

"Yep."

That was probably the wrong thing to say. Made him think she was uncaring and callous to his pain. He was still staring down at his stump like he wanted her to kiss a boo-boo.

"I'm so, so sorry that happened to you," she added.

He bent down and started plucking up stray blades of grass among the corn shoots.

"I see you've got a lot of work to do. I reckon I better be getting on home," she said, wiping her brow in the sweltering sun.

He stretched back up, arching his eyebrows in surprise. "You can't leave now. I haven't even shown you inside the house yet. All her quilts. Or her vegetable garden."

"Another time," she said. She felt her neck muscles tense up the way they did when she listened to the Democrats on TV.

"Won't take another twenty minutes." He pouted. "We're already this far . . ."

"I have to go home right now. Need to check on my girls."

"Won't take no time at all." He grabbed her elbow like she hadn't uttered a word of protest. The man was obviously used to getting his own way. "Get you something to wet your whistle."

Imo drew herself up stiff as a board. She could play this game, too.

"I reckon I should've carried you to the Red Lobster in Oak Grove. You're mad at me over the Ice Cream Churn." He poked out his lower lip.

"No, that's not it," she said. "I had a fine time getting ice cream. And your place is lovely." She hung her head. This was her chance, and she was probably messing it all up.

"What, then? Is it my hand? You don't want a cripple? An imperfect man? You probably want two hands to hold you tight."

She blushed and shook her head. She should tell him about the fibroids in her uterus. But that was way too intimate, talking about private parts. Even she and Silas never talked about it explicitly, referring to it only as her "female problem."

"I'm worried about my Jeanette," she whispered as she

made what she hoped was a very serious, concerned face. "She's been sick."

"They broke the mold when they made you, woman!" Henry's exuberant shout startled her. "Here you are on a date with one of the most eligible men around, a man who wants to pamper you and escort you around on a tour of his castle and feed you dainties, and you're thinking of your daughter." Henry's face was shining. "Everybody in Euharlee must look at you and say what a good, God-fearing woman you are. Putting others before your own pleasure."

She smiled and said, "Thanks."

"I reckon I'll get you on home, then. We'll walk back by way of Truett's vegetable patch. I'll carry you inside next time."

Imo had half-imagined him clubbing her on the head and dragging her by the hair into the house, so she didn't even protest going by the garden.

The garden was neatly outlined in marigolds. Tomatoes and asparagus stared her in the face. It was strange to be looking at another woman's prize garden when she wasn't around to tell about it. Like looking through her panty drawer. She wondered who kept it up since Truett's death. Did Henry do it as his shrine to Truett?

He grinned. "What do you think?"

"Nice." Imo couldn't keep from smiling. It was her dream of how her garden ought to be. Not an insect or weed in sight. No aluminum pans flapping on baling twine or eggshells covered in coffee grounds peeping out from the soil. Stout green plants lined up and spaced as evenly as soldiers. She felt his eyes on her. *Say the right thing, Imogene. Don't mess this up.* Huge red orbs of tomatoes hung like volleyballs and she could not resist touching one. Warm and firm.

"Big," she said.

"Truett had one once that weighed in at two pounds and five ounces!"

"Great." She tried to sound enthusiastic. After all, the Bible said to rejoice with others over their good fortunes. But she'd never grown one that big. It seemed like he was daring her to top Truett.

"It's been a lovely tour, but I must be getting on home."

They walked back to the pickup in silence. She wished she didn't feel so envious of a dead woman, but the way he kept on was intolerable. She opened her own door and climbed up to tuck her dress in around her thighs.

"All righty," he said, "let's get you home, dear girl. Before I decide I just can't let you go." He touched her cheek and she didn't move away. "You are an angel, Imogene Lavender. A true Christian woman." His forehead wrinkled up in sincerity, and his voice was reverent. "Yep. I knew it the minute I laid eyes on you. You are a rare gem!" cried Henry. He closed his eyes and sighed.

Her body tingled; warmth spread to her fingertips and she floated on air. He was really taking a shine to her. Maybe her refusal to go inside counted as playing hard to get. She had an urge to ask him in to stay for supper. But after thinking it over, she decided it was a little too early to introduce him to the girls. Jeanette might be in one of her moods tonight.

The miles flew by. Henry said how Channel Five News said there was no sign of the drought letting up any time soon. He'd have to buy one of those irrigation outfits for his corn.

Imo said, "You can't really trust what those weathermen say. They're only right half the time. I always look at the clover leaves."

"How's that?" Henry asked.

"You know, if they're curling, it's a sign it's going to rain. Hasn't failed me yet."

"That's nothing. My Truett always said she knew it was going to rain when the bees were heading to their hives. Or swallows circling and swooping low. Hoo-wee, that woman was one great weather forecaster." He shook his head like Truett had been too wonderful to believe.

Suddenly, Imo couldn't wait to get home and jump out of his truck and never hear his voice again. And here she had barely mentioned Saint Silas, and he'd done nothing but extol the virtues of a dead woman. Why, she'd been gardening by her wits and by natural signs all her life, and she wasn't crowing about it. *Try raising foster children, your sister's child, and heading up the Garden Club and the shut-ins care group, and then see how big your tomatoes are, Truett.*

"I can stand inside my kitchen with the curtains closed and tell it's going to rain," Imo snapped.

He grinned. "Is that a fact?"

"It certainly is. I know when my salt gets damp and cakey and my dishes get a film on them."

They drove past the Dairy Queen in silence. Henry invited Imo to his house for dinner the next evening, "I'll cook us up some ham 'n' eggs," he said, then parked at her mailbox and scurried out and around to get her door. She was too fast for him, though, retrieving her handbag from the seat like lightning.

"Tomorrow is just too busy," she said.

"How about Tuesday then?" He asked. He must see her neck getting all flushed. "Take you out to the Red Lobster."

"Tuesday's busy, too." She marched up the walkway and gave him a curt wave when her key was in the door.

❧ ❧ ❧

Loutishie's Notebook

I walked around the whole month of July praying for rain. But even though the Bible says God makes the rain to fall on the just and the unjust, it just wasn't falling on Euharlee.

I daydreamed about rain. About huge fat soaking, sopping clouds pouring down onto Euharlee. Just once we had a sprinkle. It was only enough to get our hopes up and before it even hit the garden, it was dried up by that fat greedy sun. Still, Imo and I kept that garden thriving.

We were having to work hard making sure the garden stayed

alive. We spent a lot of time listening to weather reports on WNRG, lugging water to the garden, and breaking up the crusty soil. We got the job done, but it was exhausting.

One late evening, I heard Imo pulling into the shed. I was at the table having a bowl of corn flakes for supper. When she stepped inside, her eyes flew to the stack of plates and silverware in the center of the table. She swung open the Fridgidaire and looked at the meatloaf, whole and cold under its plastic wrap. "That your supper, Lou?" she asked, looking confused. She'd also left a salad and some rolls, but since it was just me eating I didn't go to the trouble.

"Yes," I said, "want me to heat up some meatloaf for you?"

"No, sugar foot. I filled up at my meeting," she said, walking down the hall.

"Was it a prayer meeting? For rain?" I was hopeful.

"No," she said, opening the door to the bathroom. "A Save-The-Farmer meeting at the VFW. Where is Jeanette?" Imo had her hands on her hips, swiveling her head from side to side like Jeanette might be playing hide and seek.

"I don't know," I said, trying to sound soothing. "Somebody picked her up."

"Who?" Imo's eyes were wide. "I thought she was feeling poorly again."

"I don't know. Somebody in a black car."

Imo's shoulders drooped. "Did she say where they were going?"

"Nope."

Imo's face crumpled. "I just can't manage things anymore, Lou," she said.

I couldn't tell if she meant the drought or Jeanette. "I'll help you haul water up to the garden," I said, plunking my cereal bowl into the sink.

The drought was a lot easier to manage than Jeanette in those days. She was hot and cold. Distant. But one late night, she was feeling talkative. She sat down on the foot of my bed and pulled her knees up inside of her nightgown, right underneath her chin.

"Look at me, Lou. I'm Dolly Parton."

I laughed.

"Who do you like?" she asked me.

"Tara, Monica, Imo, you . . ."

Jeanette rolled her eyes and sighed. "No. I mean, what boys do you have a crush on?"

"Nobody," I said.

"Come on. You can tell me. How about Danny Powell?"

"He's in high school, Jeanette."

"So."

"I don't have a crush on anybody."

She smiled at me like I was this pathetic little kid. "Well, I'm in love," she said, twisting a strand of her hair. "He's much older than me."

"Who is it?" I asked.

"His name's Dipafloda. He works at the Dairy Queen. I'm thinking of marrying him if he can get a divorce."

I must have turned white because she clammed up and hopped off my bed. My mind raced with images of Imo fainting if she knew about Jeanette and this married man. I recalled sev-

eral of Reverend Peddigrew's comments on the sacredness of
the marriage vows. Surely Jeanette hadn't forgotten them.

We kept on going to Calvary on Wednesday nights and on
Sundays. Finally, though, one Sunday Jeanette refused to go
with us and Imo very calmly said just to let her be.

Well, that Sunday Reverend Peddigrew passed out twenty
dollar bills. I was real excited because usually he was asking us
for money. They were all folded up like the little notes we passed
around school when the teacher was writing on the blackboard.
It made me think, at first, that, boy, Jeanette was going to be
sorry when I told her.

But I was sorry when I unfurled it and it was only real on one
side. The other side was a gospel message that read:
"Disappointed? You shouldn't be!" It went on about heavenly
riches being better than gold, and it had the plan of salvation
below that.

"Drop these around town," he was saying, "at the laundromat,
the grocery or the Feed 'n' Seed . . ."

I didn't know why he didn't just say to put them where the
real bad sinners hang out, like the liquor store parking lot or the
7-11 where they sell dirty magazines. I was planning to tuck
mine into Jeanette's purse, next to her green vinyl pouch with
the cigarettes and lighter.

Jeanette had hardened her heart to spiritual riches. And if the
Rapture happened while she was kissing on that married man at
the Dairy Queen, then she wasn't going to inherit eternal life. Or
see Uncle Silas either.

That night, I couldn't settle down, so I went into Imo's room and climbed into bed with her, right into the sunken spot where Uncle Silas used to sleep. I reached out to touch her face and her cheek was soaking wet. She was crying again.

I think that's the scaredest I've ever been in my life, even more than at Uncle Silas's funeral.

EIGHT

Gardening Strategies

"Remember that to make a truly divine tomato sandwich, you need four ingredients: hearty white bread that can handle the onslaught of juice, may-onnaise slathered onto that, and a dead-ripe tomato, sliced thickly with a sprinkling of salt. A word of CAUTION: It is critical that you realize tomatoes have their best flavor when you use them straight from the garden, still warm from the sun. The very instant you pluck them from the vine, they start losing flavor and nutrients."
— HEAVENLY BANQUET COOKBOOK
by the The Women of Calvary Baptist

Imo wandered around in her weedy side yard, musing over adding a garden pond. The place was covered with straggly bindweed and leggy phlox. The flowers there were all old common Southern staples like spider flowers, china pinks, and money plants. Boring. She needed outlandish colors and exotic varieties. Old Truett wasn't the only one who had a green thumb.

She got down on her knees and rooted out the bindweed, meditating on a showplace of boxwood hedges surrounding islands of camellias. She closed her eyes to fix this scene in her mind. Bus tours would come from all over to see her paradise, and reporters would beg for her garden secrets. When she opened her eyes, Lou was standing there, staring at the pile of blooms and roots.

"Imo, what are you doing?"

"Transforming our yard, child. You get breakfast?"

"Yes'm."

"Good. I'm planning to get rid of the phlox after I'm done with the bindweed."

"But you love phlox."

"Well, not anymore. We're going to have a row of double-flowered holly hocks right here. Poppies over yonder."

Lou put her hands on her hips. "Why?"

"Because." Imo tugged at a stubborn root. Her head hurt from turning the Henry dilemma over and over in her mind. Working out here was supposed to get her mind *off* of him. She had decided that Henry was just going to have to make do with the untarnished memory of Truett as his companion. He had made his bed, and now Imo had made up her mind.

There was no reason she couldn't grow her own floral showplace.

Lou was down on her knees petting the phlox. "Think I'll move these over near the well house," she said, looking at Imo shyly.

Dear Lord, she'd snapped at sweet little Loutishie. The only sane one of the whole lot.

She managed a big smile for the girl. "You do that, Lou. What do you think about a little ornamental garden pond over by the weeping willow? With a statue in the center?"

Lou sat down beside her. "Are you serious?"

Imo squeezed the girl's knee. "Perfectly. It'll jazz up our yard. I want something fancy," she said. "Something not so country-fied. A place where we can have garden parties and wear hats and gloves."

"You mean like that stuffy old Barnsley Gardens place we visited last spring?"

"Yes, that's it! We can scatter some pretty stones over there near the side of the barn."

Lou glanced in the direction of the barn. "You're not talking about where Uncle Silas plants the pie pumpkins, are you?"

Imo smiled. "I want to gussie this place up." She took off one glove and grabbed Lou's small hand in her own. "Transform it."

"But I like it how it is."

"Things change. Life's about changing," Imo said.

Lou's nose turned pink and her eyes glistened with unspilled tears. "A *place* can stay how it is, and we need the pie pumpkins for our Thanksgiving."

"Martha will give us as many as we ask for. She's always got them running out her ears."

Lou hugged herself. "I hate fancy gardens!"

"You'll like it once we get going on it."

"I won't."

When Lou stomped off, Imo had to fight the impulse to scrap the whole landscaping endeavor and go running after her small figure. *Think of red tulips against the barn; Imogene, Lou will get over this.* She saw them in her mind's eye and went right on ahead, weeding out the phlox.

The same night, after she had gone to bed, a question nagged at Imogene. She couldn't remember how it felt to fall in love. Was she giddy? Did she hear violins? Was she walking on air with a song in her heart?

Maybe she and Silas had moved so gradually into love over their five months of courting that there was no definite moment of "knowing" they were in love. Maybe, she thought with fear, they'd never really fallen in love. Getting married had just been a practical decision, stemming from the fact that they were from similar enough backgrounds and it was time. And then they just got so used to each other that they loved one another like you do your arm or leg.

So how did you know, then? About love. Maybe there was love at first sight, but she didn't know anyone who'd had that experience. A good number of her friends just tolerated their husbands, fearing more the prospect of being alone than making sure it was true love. But if all her girl friends were able to get their marriages to the place where they put up with some things and rooted others out over time, then maybe that was the way of the masses.

The thing was, Henry passed in the looks department. Probably because he looked like Silas. Oh, and he was competent mentally. And they had enough in common. He was a Baptist. A farmer. Southern. His first spouse was deceased, too.

However, that last one was where his major flaw came in: talking about Saint Truett too much. Now, if Imo could bring herself to mention Silas time for time, maybe it would make that behavior extinct.

Or maybe it would wear off after they spent time together. It was probably just a nervous habit, and she could hang in there through the end of October and see if he improved.

Because if she wanted someone to share the rest of her life with, she couldn't afford to be so picky. She would train herself to dwell on Henry's good points. Look at all the irritating habits of Silas's that she had learned to live with. The man had not known what a laundry basket was for, he salted all her cooking before he even tasted it, and he never once in all their married life put a new roll of toilet paper in the bathroom.

Yes! If she could get Henry to leave Truett in the ground, dead, then he would be good. Because she felt he *was* perfect when she first laid eyes on him. She reckoned it was true about familiarity breeding contempt.

The next moment, the strangest vision of a tomato sandwich swam through her mind. Imo sat back and closed her eyes. She thought of a helpful hint from one of her cookbooks. It said something to the effect that the instant you picked a tomato it started to losing its flavor and nutrients. To get the best sandwich, you should use a tomato fresh from the vine. Too much familiarity with said tomato and it was inevitable that it would not leave as good a taste in your mouth.

Wasn't it like that with men, too? When you first met them, you saw only their good points for the most part. But you had to be practical and consider that of course everyone has their faults. Getting to know a man would bring his imperfections into view. At that point you could will yourself to overlook his faults.

Plus, after ten years together, she and Silas both were totally different people than they had been when they met. Twenty years after that they had metamorphosized yet again. They weren't the same two who had gotten married that sunny June day in Calvary's chapel.

All of these realizations told her something. Loving a man was just making a decision. You picked somebody, plucked him off the vine, and maybe when he became familiar he lost some of his perfectness. He would change over time. But also, over time the two decision-makers literally grew on each other. She could again with Henry!

Imo squeezed herself. "I'll say yes when he calls me," she whispered into the sheets.

Now that she'd made this decision, her spirits were lifted. She began to enjoy the anticipation of another date with Henry. After she tamed his Truett obsession, she would have him out to the house for supper and reveal their intentions to Jeanette and Lou.

The energy this thought gave her helped her summon up the gumption to clean out the refrigerator, a once weekly chore she had not touched since Silas died. She hummed along as she tossed out a moldy hunk of carrot cake wrapped in cellophane and the contents of three unfamiliar containers. She stacked them in the sink to wash later and noticed the names of three ladies from church on rectangles of masking tape.

She'd never properly thanked them for their funeral offerings, and here were their Tupperwares five months later! She began to make up a conversation with them.

"Thank you for your delicious Jell-O salad," she said, and returned a spotless container to Maimee Gordon.

"You're welcome, Imo. You think nothing of it. I know it's been hard without Silas. But you're holding up really good."

"It's hard."

"I can't imagine how you do it," said Dot Jarrett, "what with all your responsibilities."

"Well, you have to keep going. The girls really miss him, too. So I can't just think of myself."

"I bet. It's probably a relief to you that Silas is out of his misery now."

"Yep. He's in a better place. Happier than we are."

"You were such a good wife to him," said the youngest church lady, Donna Pardue, somewhere in her early forties.

"Why, thank you, dear."

Donna said, "He's probably looking down on you, smiling away."

"Wants you to be happy," said Dot.

"You think so?"

"Lord, yes, Imogene. If anybody deserves to be happy, it's you."

There was a pause, and then Imo said: "It's right lonely, though. The girls are busy with their own lives."

"I'm sure it is. I agree with Martha, Imogene, you need a man. It wouldn't mean you care any less for Silas."

Imo held onto a near empty jar of chow-chow she found wedged in the door between some muscadine preserves and a bottle of soy sauce she used when she was in the mood for foreign food. "Silas was the only one who ever touched this stuff," she told one of the ladies.

"I don't see why you'd need to keep it, Imogene."

"Time to move on, for Heaven's sake," Maimee grew stern with her.

Maybe she should keep it around in case a visitor wanted it. Someone who liked it as a side with his black-eyes. Too late. She tossed it into the trash. Won't be needing you either, she said to some sardines on the bottom shelf.

Soon, half the contents of the refrigerator were in the trash, and the memories came back to Imo so thick and so piercing that she worked harder. She scrubbed the shelves, watching Silas fry fatback in a skillet in her mind. There he was, making one of his pancake suppers for them. They were all laughing and sitting eagerly at the table while he made five-inch high stacks of pancakes, setting them in the oven to keep warm. They begged and begged to start putting on the butter and syrup, they'd just eat one each, they promised. But he never let them start till the last one was perfectly browned and they had said grace. And boy, were they good. Everyone talked with syrup running down their chins and wrists.

She finished, hauled the trash out of sight, and sank down onto the sofa.

The news was on TV. Must be noon. Maybe Henry was waiting to give her a call after he finished his lunch. She didn't have to worry that he *would* call today, it was just a matter of when. He was so clearly smitten with her. Why in the world had she turned him down? She couldn't remember. She was probably just tired and not thinking clearly. Being a fresh widow was wearing her out and getting back into the dating scene was not as easy as one might think. So much had changed since Silas had courted her. Plus, she wasn't as free and easy now that the girls depended on her to hold body and soul together.

She carried the cordless phone outside with her to work in her yard. At five she carried it back inside, checking to make sure the phone had a dial tone. It did.

The second day, the phone woke her up just as the sun lightened the sky. Imo was breathless when she picked up the receiver and said her cheeriest "Hello!" It was Rhetta Williams calling about the next Keenagers get-together.

She was through washing up the lunch dishes and was

paying the light bill the next time it rang. She jumped and dropped her checkbook, running to get it.

"Hello?" Imo held her breath and sat down at the kitchen table.

"Hi dear," Martha said, "you doing all right?"

She said, "Yes, fine."

"I imagine you're coming along on the Keenagers trip to the Tennessee Aquarium?"

"Might."

"Might? Might meet somebody . . ."

Imo didn't mention Henry.

"We're going with West End Baptist from Polkville," Martha went on softly. "I hear they got two single men in their group."

Imo laughed, sighed, and rubbed Bingo's head with her toes. "I reckon it can't hurt a thing to go. Even if I don't meet anybody, it'll be nice to get away."

Sometimes, she wondered if she wouldn't just turn into a total recluse if she didn't have Martha. Probably never leave the house unless it caught on fire.

That night she stretched out in bed and waited for the tears. She went over the disappointments of the day . . . how sad it was the way she sprang up every time the phone rang . . . how Henry didn't even call her.

While the rest of Euharlee slept, Imo cried into her pillow.

The next morning, wide-eyed and jumpy from no sleep,

she noted how nice the weather was while scraping leftover grits into Bingo's bowl. She thought she'd get her laundry going and work in the garden. Praise the Lord for cordless phones.

Imo put on her straw hat and gloves, then carried the phone out with her to the garden.

She plucked and dug, sifting through the soil like it was gold. This was just what the doctor ordered. This connected her with the heart of the universe. If she could only bottle this feeling she had right now and carry it around with her and dip into it when she was feeling down, life would be a lot easier.

Wouldn't it be fun when Henry saw her garden? This thought satisfied Imo in some deep-seated way as she worked, concentrating blindly on her patch of Euharlee.

At four, Imo's throat was parched. She went inside for tea and turned on the TV. A Tide commercial was on when Lou huffed through the den. Poor child. She still hadn't gotten over the pumpkin patch incident.

Chuck Woolery came on announcing *The New Dating Game*. Maybe this could be like school for Imo, showing her the fine points of flirting. She got a glass of iced tea and sat down on the sofa.

Chuck had his arm hooked through a ditzy blonde girl's arm. Her skirt was so tiny that no matter how much she wiggled and tucked it in when she got up on the stool it didn't leave one thing to the imagination. Chuck introduced her as an elementary school teacher from Sacramento. Didn't look like any elementary teacher Imo had ever known.

"So, Sandy from Sacramento," he bubbled, "there are three eligible bachelors who just can't wait to meet you!"

Then came the part where they gave the ages and occupations of three men. Less than half Imo's age and silly as teenagers, they were grinning eagerly and punching each other in the arm.

"Okay, Sandy!" Chuck said, "Let's get down to business!"

"Bachelor Number One," she breathed. "Eating ice cream in bed is one of my guilty pleasures. Can you tell me one of yours?"

Number One wrinkled up his nose, raised his eyebrows and grinned wickedly at Bachelor Number Two. "Eating ice cream off of you in bed, Sandy!"

Cat-calls, whistles and hoots erupted from the other bachelors and the studio audience. Sandy loved it, too.

Imo stiffened. Such filthy minds. And imagine, a grade school teacher. Surely a parent or even a child home sick from school could be watching this.

"Bachelor Number Two," Sandy giggled, "same question."

Bachelor Number Two pursed his lips and scratched his head in mock seriousness. "Sitting on the bed, watching you and Bachelor Number One eat ice cream off each other."

A really big explosion on that one. Imo wasn't going to wait around to see what Bachelor Number Three might say. Surely they didn't really allow this kind of smut on TV. She turned the channel to a cooking show.

She had only a moment to watch them making egg rolls

before the phone rang. It was in her pocket and she almost jumped out of her skin when it went off.

"Hello?" She held her breath.

"Hi, Imogene."

"Oh, hi, Martha."

Martha chattered on about her granddaughter's piano recital while Imo paid half a mind. "Well, I know you're real proud of Tiffany," she said.

"The real thing I was calling about, dear, is to see if you'll go to another one of those save-the-farmer meeting with me tonight. That Henry man's been away stirring folks up in the surrounding counties. Now he's back in Euharlee."

"Really?" Imo's heart pounded.

"Yessum. Going like some mad man. Meetings twice a day most days. Going right up to farmer's doors, riding out in fields. Printing flyers. . . "

"Oh . . ." A light came on in Imo's brain.

"Yes, and tonight he's back here. We really ought to go support him."

Imo felt a floodgate of relief open throughout her body. "I'll go, Martha."

She was so excited, her hands were shaking. She went to stand in front of her closet. Oh, she was silly for even doubting that Henry was still in the picture. The man was just so busy caring about other people. That was all. She searched through the closet for the right dress to wear.

The hours careened by, and Martha drove up, honking the horn. Imo grabbed her handbag and made her way out, locking Lou and Jeanette safely inside. It was the first time in a month of Sundays that all three of them were there together in the evening, and a part of her was reluctant to leave.

But a bigger part of her was concentrating on what she was going to say to Henry. She hadn't felt this jittery and slightly nauseous since she used to stand and recite poems in front of her eighth grade classroom.

She sat down inside the VFW hall, energized by snippets of a dozen conversations going on around her. She looked at a sea of serious faces stretched out toward the front of the room and realized she was now a member of a group of enraged citizens, defending their constitutional right to go on farming. And she, Imogene Lavender, was the girlfriend of their dynamic leader.

The meeting was adjourned, and a flock of folks clustered around Henry up at the front where he stood talking and shaking a handful of papers. Time to make her move.

Imo touched up her lipstick and remained in her folding chair, mentally planning her invitation. Saturday night for fried chicken and biscuits. She sat there five minutes working on the side dishes and waiting. The little flock of women up there that just wouldn't hush were certainly irritating. She wished she could sweep them aside like checkers on a game board. She was tired of being patient.

By the time the rest of the crowd had thinned out, Imo had become the tiniest bit frantic. Martha was still talking away to old Mr. Smith across the room, but she signaled to Imo, by tapping her watch, that she was almost ready to call it a night.

Imo sucked in her breath. It was now or never. She looked at Henry, and his smile dried up her hesitancy.

He was the one for her, and tonight was her move! Imo felt daring, now that she knew what she wanted, and all she had to do was trot right up there and claim it!

She stepped into the center aisle and made a bee-line for the podium. Henry gesticulated, fascinating the hopeful old biddies. He dipped his head in her direction to acknowledge her, without missing a beat. She took this as her special cue and went around behind him, to say *we're an item here, I'm staking my claim, so don't get your hopes up, ladies.* She set her handbag down next to his feet.

Finally, she could feel whole again. Martha would get off her back about it and there would be a man around the house to balance things out and fill it up with masculine smells.

She studied Henry's face. Of course, that part of him would take no getting used to. Should be easier on the girls that he looked so much like Silas.

Henry laid his wad of papers down on the podium and clutched his shirt over his heart. He was illustrating his love for something he was talking about. Imo leaned forward so she could hear better.

"After the drought of 1948, I had a bee-u-ti-ful crop of corn," Henry said. "When it matured, nearly every stalk was bent plum over with the ear to the ground." Spittle was glistening on the corners of his mouth.

The silly old biddies hung on every word he said.

"Yep, I started picking the corn early September and

didn't finish till the end of January. Just me and my shucking hook, a team and a wagon with a bang board. That was it!" He glowed.

He thought he was the only one who'd ever harvested a big corn crop. Imo had already heard this one out at his place. She had never pictured herself as intolerant, but she was certainly tempted to stuff a sock in his mouth. Just wait until they were Mr. and Mrs. She knew a lot more now at sixty-four than she did at sixteen when she'd married Silas. There were things that were in her power.

She hooked her arm through Henry's, used to his stump now. "Well, good night, ladies!" she interrupted him. "Our hero needs his beauty sleep. Ha ha."

Their faces fell and she couldn't keep a big grin off her face. She felt Henry stiffen and grab onto the podium with his hand. *Come on, Imo, all you have to do is gently pull him toward the door and whisper your invitation into his ear.* Fried chicken, biscuits, collards, tomatoes, and his all-time favorite, corn. Corn fried in a skillet with a bit of bacon grease.

"But I haven't gotten to Truett's prize tomato story yet." He pouted like a three year old.

"I'm sure they don't want to hear about that. They've probably all got their own tomato stories."

Henry did not bat an eye. She unhooked her arm and marched toward the side door alone, looking over her shoulder. *Come on, big boy, you know you want me.*

"Truett," Henry said and closed his eyes like he was praying. "That lady grows the hugest tomatoes! She crossed a

Better Boy with a Beefsteak and came up with a two-pound-five-ouncer. I near about called the folks at the Guinness Book, gosh a mighty. Good Lord in heaven, He broke the mold when he made Truett!"

That was the line he had used on *her!* She fumed. Silly old fool women were hanging on every word.

"Did I tell you about her flowers?" He touched the middle woman's hand. "Not only does she amaze me with her veggies, dear girls, she's like one of them French painters, the way she works magic with her flower patch."

Those women were putty in his hands. Imo hurried on out to Martha's Dodge, her face hot as the blazes. Suddenly, she saw herself as one of many in a humongous herd of desperate single women cuckolded by Henry's charisma. What an idiot she'd been. She settled herself into the passenger seat. Well, she was smarter now, at least. Maybe it had been too much to ask that the first one would be the one.

"What is it?" Martha asked, backing out of the gravel lot. "What's wrong?"

"Nothing." Boy, was she glad she hadn't told a soul of her fixation on Henry.

Martha pulled up to Imo's mailbox. All the lights were on in the den and Imo could make out Lou and Bingo's silhouettes in front of the TV.

"Listen, hon'," Martha had a very serious look on her face. "Are you sure you're all right?"

"I'm just bone-tired, Martha. Going right on in to bed."

❧ ❧ ❧

Loutishie's Notebook

August turned out to be the longest month of my life. Imo was ripping up stuff in the yard, and Jeanette was wilder than ever. One morning, I got out of bed and trudged to the kitchen. Jeanette was gone, and a note on the table said Imo was at a Garden Club meeting. The house was a mausoleum.

I sank onto the sofa, scattering a stack of Jeanette's magazines. The headlines read: "100 Ways to Please Your Man in Bed," "Beauty Secrets From the Stars," "True Love or Steamy Sex?," "I Slept With My Boss." and "Husband #2?"

That last headline caught my eye. Gossip travels fast in a small town. One day Imo was a grieving widow, and the next thing I heard she was out chasing men. At first, I laughed right into Angie Holland's face when she told me a friend of her mama's, who lives next door to Viola Sneed, who goes to the Kuntry Kut 'n' Kurl every Friday for a wash, set and style, said that Mrs. Sneed said that Imo was on a man-hunt. Maybe even dating somebody.

"You're crazy," I said to Angie. I wanted to punch her in the face.

"Lou," she stared right back at me, honest as a morning glory, "I'm just telling you what I heard."

"Well," I said, my nose tingling the way it does before I start to cry, "she still loves Uncle Silas."

I kept thinking about it though, and the more I thought about it, it would explain several things. Her beauty makeover and silly giggling moods and her carrying the phone into the washroom to talk.

But then I convinced myself it was just a mean rumor. The woman was simply crazy from grief. Because, look, she was still so grief stricken that she wasn't taking proper notice of what old Jeanette was reading these days. If she had seen it, and there it was, right under her nose, she would have been horrified. She would have burned it up. She would have plucked Jeanette back from the brink of hell before the Rapture surprised us.

It only took me ten minutes to walk that mile to the Dairy Queen. It certainly looked like the place for summer socializing in Euharlee. There were lots of kids walking around the parking lot and hanging out by the pay phone. Some were lounging on the hoods of cars.

Inside was cool. Cardboard signs twirled above orange stools. A pimply-faced teenaged boy stood behind the counter arranging plastic spoons in a bucket.

"What do you want?" He asked.

"I'm looking for somebody," I said. "Jeanette?"

"Try the office."

Down a short greasy hallway I heard a sound I hadn't heard in quite a while. Jeanette's giggle. The door was ajar, but the lights were off. I stood there and listened.

"Dee," Jeanette's voice was teary, "you've got to!"

A man said. "No can do."

"Oh my God, you have to, Dee." Jeanette stomped on the floor.

I pushed the door open and stood there.

"What are you doing here?" Jeanette was scrambling around, pulling her shirt over her head, and grabbing her pocketbook.

I leaned against the door frame and crossed my arms.

Jeanette came out. She had a swollen red face and under-eye bags she would die over if she knew. "What's wrong?"

"Imo," I said as coolly as I could.

"What?" Jeanette panicked a little. "She okay, Lou?"

I said, "She's worried about you."

"Is not. She don't even care where I am."

"You were kissing that man," I said.

"Duh, Sherlock." Jeanette lit up a cigarette. "Mind your own beeswax."

"Imo's not going to like this one little bit."

"She's not my boss. But if you say one word to her about this, I'll never speak to you again as long as I live." Jeanette walked as fast along the dusty road as she could in her heeled sandals.

"Wait up," I called to her stiff back, but I could feel her anger, and I knew talk was useless.

When we got to the house and went inside, I noticed Jeanette was crying. "What's the matter?" I asked her.

She rubbed her nose on the back of her hand. "Nothing. Got something in my eye."

Jeanette didn't fool me any.

"You ever ask her," she said through sniffles, "why she don't give all these old hats away?"

I shook my head, looked up at Uncle Silas's prized collection of bill caps hanging in three lines right above the washer and dryer.

There was one from each county fair since 1975, three from the
Citizens Bank, two John Deere, one Caterpillar, one Copenhagen,
and a bunch of others. I guess I'd never thought about them as
anything but a permanent fixture, like a light or a windowsill.

By early evening, Jeanette was going to be my best friend if I
promised not to mention Dipafloda to Imo. Starved for human
companionship, I said I wouldn't if she'd come out to the garden. She sighed and straggled out there behind me. Barefooted.
Her pearlescent pink toenails shocking in the twilight dirt.

All through July, Imo and I had worked hard out there. Our
reward for this was that the garden was so laden with harvest
that it was overwhelming. That pulsing place inside me that was
terribly painful at times would quiet down when I was hauling
water, hoeing, or weeding. I felt this connection with Uncle Silas
out there, and I believed that Jeanette would feel it too.

However, Jeanette wasn't exactly thrilled to be out there. She
slumped down between two rows of limas and stared. But, I told
myself, given time out in the garden, the scales would fall off her
eyes, and I would be rewarded with a new Jeanette.

I worked along, filling the plastic laundry basket I'd wedged
into my Radio Flyer wagon with enough squash and green beans
to feed Africa. The corn and okra were just beginning to make,
and there were so many tomatoes that I got this panicky feeling
just looking at them.

When it was time to haul my wagon load up to the house,
Jeanette wasn't between the limas. I called out her name, and
she didn't answer so I decided she had gone on in.

I wheeled along the short side of the garden, when out of the corner of one eye I noticed her, squatting with her knees beside her ears.

Jeanette licked her fingers. Her eyes met mine.

The hairs on the back of my neck raised up. She had dirt smeared all over her cheeks and chin. "What are you doing?" I squeaked.

She smiled. Her teeth were muddy.

"You're eating dirt! Are you okay?"

"I reckon." She sounded sane.

"Let me help you back inside and clean you up."

"Okay, but don't tell mama . . ."

I left the wagon, grabbed her bony wrist and pulled her to the house. "You've been starving yourself," I snapped. "Just look at you. Eating dirt!"

I sat her down at the table and poured her some milk.

Jeanette's hands shook around her cup. She kept on starting the same sentence. "Lou, there's something I want to . . ." and then stopping halfway through it. I kept wiping her chin with a wet dishrag. Then she put her head down in her hands and cried. It was awful. I couldn't imagine what had come over her for her to be eating dirt.

Remembering how Imo always rubbed circles on my back when I was upset, I did the same for Jeanette. "There, there, now, Jeannie. Every little thing's going to be all right," I murmured.

"Lou," Jeanette's shoulders were going up and down while she got her breath, "I . . ."

I patted harder to help her get the words out.

"I'm pregnant," she spat out, mouth gaping and eyes shining, white streaks where tears ran through dirt.

"You're too skinny to be pregnant! You're not pregnant!" I put my arms around her. I could feel her ribs through her shirt. "I'll make you some oatmeal."

I fixed a big bowl and brought it to the table with a box of brown sugar and a stick of butter. "Look, here's you some dirt." I laughed and sprinkled brown sugar on top, then floated a pat of butter on that until it made a yellow puddle. "Better eat it or I'll tell," I teased.

Jeanette stared vacantly. I spooned up a big blob and pressed it against her lips. "I'll tell," I sang out till she opened her mouth.

A long pause. "He was everything to me." Her lip quivered, and she took a deep breath.

I searched for words. I waited for her to tell me more, but she didn't. I said, "Well, looks like you'll have to get married. You should hurry up before your stomach pooches out."

She started bawling."Don't cry anymore, Jeannie," I said. "Eat this stuff so you won't eat dirt. That's probably bad for the baby."

"I'm so stupid," she said finally. "He can't leave his wife. He loves me, but he can't leave his wife!" She shut her eyes. Her blouse was sticking to her bony chest. "You can't breathe a word of this to Mama."

"Shhh," I whispered, "I won't tell." I reached out and hugged her, thinking of the seed she was carrying around inside her.

NINE

Putting-By

"Hey, Imogene, reckon what it is that comes out of the garden that starts with the letter M ?"
— SILAS LAVENDER
scratching his head and musing on the contents of metal cans—cooked and sealed and chugging along the conveyor belt of a community canning plant, Euharlee, Georgia, 1954

Well, it was probably good that old Henry didn't work out. Imo should not ever have dismissed his multitude of faults. She would have gone batty trying to fix the man.

Once again, she found herself heading to the garden to collect her thoughts. She pulled a folding chair from the well-house and set it up at the end of the tomatoes. She sat down to enjoy the view of tomatoes literally dripping off the vines. The peppery smell sent her back to the summer kitchens of her childhood.

Every August, her mama had pulled out the covered wash-boiler. Clicking and clacking, jars of tomatoes boiled along on the stove-top. No one used wash-boilers anymore, except as decorative planters or to add to their antique collections. Imo owned a pressure canner she bought from the farm supply store. Stainless steel and with its own pressure gauge and safety valve. A real modern advancement.

Poor Mama. Who said they were the good old days? That woman spent weeks on her feet, putting by the garden. Harvesting, washing, peeling, cutting, stripping off skins, blanching, scalding, and canning. Saving the things they didn't have to use at the moment, against the time that they would need them.

This was, Imo decided, her answer. She should teach Jeanette and Lou to can! Plus, canning tomatoes was the most methodical and labor-intensive thing that Imo could imagine to do. It would give her time. Enough time to instruct the girls and enough time to think about and plan her next move.

She rounded up some Mason jars and set them in the sink. "Hello, girls," she said to Jeanette and Lou, who were in the kitchen eating breakfast.

"Hey," Lou said. She looked tired. Jeanette said nothing.

"There's a fine mess of tomatoes ready for canning!" Imo said to Jeanette's swollen face.

Jeanette stared at her like she'd sprouted horns.

"We've got our day cut out for us!" Imo said after a minute. She smiled her most encouraging smile.

Imo fastened on her wide straw hat as she eyed the vines. "Goodness," she said. "We may have to can for quite a long time! Run get your buckets." She waved a hand toward the barn.

This was a trip down memory lane. Lou and Jeanette out in the garden with her. She studied them down at the end of the row she was on, and she felt like singing. Maybe this would coax them back into feeling like a family.

"What a fine mess of tomatoes!" she said to Jeanette's pale back. She had on a halter top that let Imo see her spine as she bent over.

"This enough yet?" Jeanette groaned and set down her half-filled bucket.

"No, child. Let's make hay while the sun shines."

"It's too hot out here," Jeanette wailed. "Why don't we just go buy them at the store?"

Imogene shook her head. What was it with the younger generation? "You just cannot compare a home grown tomato with what they sell at the grocery," she said, indignant.

They worked until they filled up six five-gallon buckets and the pockets of Imo's apron. And still there were more.

"Girls," she said to them as they made their way back to the house, "I had an idea while we were picking."

Jeanette gave her a quick, venomous look. "What?" she licked the sweat from her upper lip.

"How about we take a trip to the beach once we get the garden all put by?" Imo looked from Jeanette to Lou.

Loutishie's eyes were wide. "Yes!" she shrieked. Jeanette loped along without a word.

The girls watched while Imo filled the pressure cooker

with water deep enough to cover the Mason jars. She set it on the big back burner. Doing this made Imo feel like the generations were connecting. She clung to the hope that all their communication blocks would dissolve in the heat of the kitchen.

"Now let me tell you something real important," Imo said, grabbing the whistling kettle from the front burner. "Pour you some boiling water over your lids and bands and just let them drain in the sink. That way you won't have to stop later and tend to them." She hoped all this domestic knowledge was sinking in. There were things these girls had to know. Household knowledge would help them get a man and keep him.

"Now," Imo said and looked right into Jeanette's eyes. She could read nothing. "Your job will be to peel the tomatoes. Do you remember that from two summers ago?"

Jeanette shook her head. She was slumped forward on the kitchen stool, heels hooked on the lower rung. "Hot in here," she muttered.

Imo fought a hint of irritation. She hurried over and got the floor fan, plugged it in and aimed it at Jeanette's legs. She decided the stomach aches and the napping were caused by Jeanette's grief. People experienced a loss in different ways. Hard work would be good for the girl.

"Get out that wire basket, Jeannette," Imo instructed, "and we'll dip them in boiling water a minute or so until their skins crack. Then you'll be able to peel them lickety split."

The lid on the big pot of water bumped and burped. "It's ready!" said Imo, turning to Jeanette.

The girl didn't move. "Get busy," Imo urged, "or we'll never make it to the beach." She had imagined this going much smoother. "Look, Lou can quarter them once you've got them peeled, Jeanette, and I'll fill the jars." Imo stood up tall and straight and breathed in like this was the most satisfying thing a person could do. "Many hands make light work," she announced, her voice high and light.

She watched the thermometer. The clicking and clacking of the jars soothed her. "I know what," Imo said, "I'll tell you girls a funny story while we're waiting. It's a true story." She rinsed the sink and hung the dishrag across the faucet.

"About thirty years ago, the county started a canning plant where you carried your garden produce and they'd put it in cans for you. It was run by the Ag teachers. They'd put your things in metal cans and cook them and seal them up."

"Bet that was nice," Jeanette muttered.

"Yes, it was." Imo laughed. "Silas and I carried our garden in, and we were so excited. We came back to fetch our cans when they told us to, and while we were standing there waiting for ours—see, we'd labeled the can lids with our name and the first letter of what was in there—these cans came by on the conveyer belt. . ." Imo started laughing and couldn't stop enough to finish.

"What's the funny part?" Lou studied her face.

The laughing subsided into fits of a snort, and Imo wiped tears out of her eyes. She added salt to the quart jars and pushed the tomatoes down so that the juice covered them.

Finally she got her breath. "Hand me that spatula, Lou. Got to get rid of this air." She pressed the shiny tomatoes down until she no longer saw any bubbles. "Wipe those jar necks," she pointed the spatula in Jeanette's direction. "Then screw the tops on loosely."

"So what happened?" Lou tapped her foot.

"Well, Silas and I looked at these cans of somebody's coming along and they had big M's written on them above the person's name, and for the life of us we couldn't figure out anything that came from the garden that would start with M." She started laughing again. She clenched her teeth to get a hold of herself. "So, Silas, he asked the old country boy standing there waiting beside us if they were his, and he said 'yes', and Silas asked, 'well, what in the world does M stand for?', and that old bumpkin just looked real hard at us and bellered out, ' 'maters, you fool! 'Maters!" Imo really let go now, and her sides were shaking so hard she had to set down the spatula and hold onto the counter.

Lou chortled a bit, and after a minute Jeanette said, "So, they still have these canning plants?"

"Nope. Didn't last long."

"Imo," Lou said, "it's time to put them in the canner."

She brought herself to the present. "Yessum, you are right." She lifted up a hot jar of ruby red tomatoes and sank it into the bottom of the canner. "Beautiful," she sighed.

"Can I go yet?" Jeanette slouched like she had no spine.

"Go?" Imo said, her voice rising, "We're not near done here. We can visit for the forty-five minutes till these quarts are sealed. You girls are lucky."

When the girls didn't respond, she said, "They don't teach this stuff in the schools anymore."

There was a smirk on Jeanette's face. "I'm thinking about dropping out of school," she hissed.

A chill ran up Imo's spine and clutched at a muscle in her neck. "Oh, sugar foot. Don't *say* that! You've got to plan for the future," she said, her voice cracking. This wasn't turning out to be the warm fuzzy experience she'd planned. It was time to talk. "You cannot drop out of school until you are eighteen. Look up here at me, young lady," Imo said. Jeanette slowly lifted her eyes again. "Do you understand me?"

Jeanette nodded ever so slightly.

"What has gotten into you?" Imo asked, cradling hot tongs.

Lou stood deathly still at the sink.

"Drugs?" Imo asked in a whisper.

"No." Jeanette shook her head.

"You still have an upset stomach?"

"Nope."

"Good," Imo breathed out. She supposed that if it wasn't being sick or drugs, it was something that would just work itself out given time. Drugs were one of those mysteries she knew she wouldn't be able to handle.

"Now, about our little beach trip. We can ride to Atlanta on Saturday and buy swimming suits." Jeanette wasn't arguing. She'd probably realized what fun they could have together. Look at how close they'd gotten while canning!

By late afternoon the counter top was laden with warm

quarts of tomatoes. Imo sat in the den and planned their beach trip. She thought it would be good to leave in three Fridays—a week before school began. By that time, surely the tomatoes would be finished.

Loutishie's Notebook

The end of August was so miserably hot that Imo made a gallon of tea every morning, and by supper time it was gone. She ran in and out of the house, harvesting the vegetables and then freezing or canning them.

She was energized by garden abundance, as if a freezer and pantry full of food was the answer to life's questions. That's about all she did. She'd stopped going to those help-the-farmer meetings. At least Imo's tearful nights were over. She talked about our Florida trip every chance she got, and she seemed happier.

My aunt was so busy putting by the garden that I was 100 percent positive she wasn't on a man-hunt, and I figured that the ugly gossip would just dry up.

Watching Jeanette begin to bloom, I had a vision of the impending storm. I was so scared sometimes I could barely swallow. To me, Imo's happiness at that point was like a delicate, glistening bubble teetering on the edge of its life and about to burst into smithereens.

One afternoon, Jeanette said she felt the baby move, and she called it Peanut and started crying and rubbing her stomach.

"Don't cry," I begged, sitting at the bottom of the sofa, rubbing her feet.

"You haven't said a thing to Mama about me, have you?" Jeanette sniffled.

"Nope, Jeannie, I promised. But she's going to find out sooner or later," I said. "You can't hide being pregnant."

"I can hide me. Go away somewhere. Give the baby away."

I didn't know what to say back. That was what happened to her and look how it messed her up. Up till she was twelve or so, she nursed the insides of her upper arms at night so bad she had continual bruises on them.

"I'm sleepy." Jeanette settled down onto the sofa with a cigarette. Her face was pale. Everybody knew each cigarette took one minute off your life, and so I knew it couldn't be good for the baby.

I spent the next two days trying to get her to eat something healthy. I offered her fresh blackberries and a lot of vegetables. I decided to walk to the clinic and pick up some of the pamphlets on having babies that the school nurse showed us in health class.

I set out on foot toward town with Bingo. The clinic was literally in the heart of downtown Euharlee, below and to the left of City Hall. "Seven miles is nothing," I said to Bingo as we passed the Dairy Queen. He was panting and walking so slowly I figured we'd never make it. I turned around and stuck out my thumb at a blue Ford pickup coming toward us.

It kicked up a cloud of dust that settled all over Bingo and made him sneeze when it stopped. It was Mr. Royce Sosebee, a man I knew from riding out to his farm with Uncle Silas.

"Hi, Mr. Sosebee."

"Get in." He scraped a tangle of paper, styrofoam cups and candy bar wrappers off the seat.

"Mighty nice of you to stop," I said.

My main memory of Mr. Sosebee was his huge arrowhead collection and the way he would use his tongue to suction off his upper denture plate and thrust the teeth out at me and laugh. That was when I didn't know about false teeth, and I'd spend hours trying to poke mine out.

Mr. Sosebee was one quarter Indian, but he could pass for a whole one with his dark eyes, big humped nose and wrinkly brown skin. He had on overalls with no shirt, and a greasy gray braid hung down his back. "Where you going?" He puffed out a long stream of smoke.

"Downtown," I said.

"Don't you know better than to hitch-hike? There's bad folks, even in Euharlee."

Glancing over, I caught his anxious stare. "I was going to walk, but Bingo got worn out."

"Where to?"

"Post office," I said.

"Y'all need anything over at your place? I mean, ever since Mr. Silas died, I've been meaning to come round and offer to help. But I've been sick myself . . . "

"We're managing," I said. I knew he had no wife to bake stuff or write a fancy card with flowers on it.

"It's no excuse. Your uncle was a good man. Helped me out many a time," he said, stopping in front of the flat gray post office. "Need a ride home, gal?"

It broke my heart, the way he called me gal, the same as

Uncle Silas did. Something else in his voice made me decide to tell him what I was really doing downtown. Before he could lean across the seat to jiggle my door open, I could feel the words rising up out of my throat.

"So, you haven't told your aunt?" Mr. Sosebee gave me a swift, searching look.

"Nope, I promised not to. Jeannie says she's going to run away when we're in Florida. Change her name." My heart beat hard against Bingo.

"I see." He drummed his fingers on the steering wheel and stared straight ahead. Then he closed his eyes and started this strange humming. I kept glancing at his profile, his big nose like the side of a mountain, while he sat like a wax figure, humming away for five minutes or so.

I was about to quietly slip out of there, run to the health depart- ment, and get myself home somehow when he opened his eyes.

"The Great Spirit gives wisdom," he said in a hoarse whisper. "Yes, you must tell your aunt."

His words felt like alcohol poured into a cut. "I can't. I promised."

"Go on, get your stuff. I'll wait." His voice moved through the sunlight streaming into the pickup's cab and reached my brain. I didn't give myself a chance to think it over. I hit the sidewalk.

I ran between the Dixie Chick and Dub's Gas to the back of the flat brick clinic. There were stacks of pamphlets on a long table just inside the door. One had a profile of a rounded girl with an upside down baby in her stomach. It was called "The first nine months of life." I snatched it. Mission accomplished.

"Alrighty, gal, let's get you home," Mr. Sosebee said when I got back to his pickup. Mr. Sosebee cleared his throat. "I made a decision while you were in there. I'm going to offer my services to your aunt."

"Fine," I said. "But please don't tell her about Jeanette."

When we reached the house, Imo's car was gone, and Jeanette was asleep on the sofa. She jumped when I shut the door.

"Mr. Sosebee's here," I announced. "He gave me a ride home."

"How do?" he said.

Jeanette wiped the drool from her cheek onto her shoulder and sat up.

"He's going to help Imo," I said.

Mr. Sosebee leaned against the counter which separated the kitchen from the den. He must've seen Jeanette's ashes in a coffee cup on the counter because, the next thing I knew, he had a cigarette hanging on his bottom lip.

"Care for one?" He asked. My mouth flew open, but Jeanette was up and over there in a flash.

He reached in his pocket and I could not believe it when he pulled out a pack of Marlboros, shook one out and handed it to Jeanette. He even lit it for her. He aimed the pack toward me and raised his eyebrows. I shook my head so hard I heard my brain rattle.

Before I could utter a word, Jeanette was puffing away and smiling at Mr. Sosebee. She didn't like hardly any adults, so I bit my tongue. There would be time when he was gone to give her the pamphlet I felt in my pocket.

Imo invited Mr. Sosebee to stay for supper when she got

home. All during supper I was nauseous, praying that he wouldn't betray me. All he talked about was cows and the up-coming fall.

Jeanette was fairly civil and even ate a little bit of her meat loaf and butter beans.

During dessert he said, "I hear you all are going to the beach," and looked hard at me.

A bit of pie stuck in my throat when Jeanette said, "I've got something to tell y'all."

"What is it, Jeannie?" innocent Imo asked. She was glowing because Mr. Sosebee said he'd never in all his life tasted such fine cooking.

Jeanette bit her bottom lip and smiled.

I heard myself swallow. All right, here it goes, the end is here. I stared down into my lap. I couldn't stand to watch Imo get hurt.

"I went and bought myself a swimsuit for Florida," Jeanette said.

I took a deep breath and then I laughed so hard I spit out some tea.

Imo said, "You did? I thought we were all going to ride to Atlanta together and get suits." She looked disappointed.

Of course a five-months pregnant girl wouldn't want to parade around Rich's swimsuit department for her mama to see. Plus, Imo's idea of a swimsuit for us looked more like a toddler's romper, rather than the new French-cut maillots Jeanette admired in the advertising circulars that came with the Sunday paper.

"Listen, girls," Mr. Sosebee said to me and Jeanette, "we need to let Imo in on a little secret, don't we?"

We were walking along the dirt road that led to the bottoms while Imo cleaned up the supper dishes. He stopped and looked right at Jeanette.

She bristled. "What?"

"She's a tough woman. Stronger than you think."

"I don't know what you're talking about." Jeanette turned and inspected my face.

I didn't dare look at her, just kept walking along slowly.

"You have a big mouth, Loutishie. I can't believe you did this!" Jeanette's voice trembled behind me. "I had a plan and now you've gone and told. Mama doesn't have to know—I trusted you!"

"But you don't have any money, Jeannie. And I was scared."

"I can take care of myself, thank you very much."

"What about Peanut, then?" I walked over and patted her belly which was poking out just the slightest bit now. In fact, if you didn't look real hard, you still wouldn't know she was expecting. "Don't you know Imo will go crazy if you run away?"

"Listen, squirt. Why don't you mind your own business."

Mr. Sosebee began to sing real low, under his breath, while we were arguing. It was in some foreign tongue that was mostly vowels, with his eyes closed and his adam's apple bobbing up and down.

"This guy crazy?" Jeanette asked.

I shook my head, but I wasn't so sure. I was just relieved she was still talking to me.

We heard footsteps then and spun around, shocked to see Imo practically jogging through the cattle gate, toward us. I'd never seen her prance like that, with her face lit up. I was embarrassed for her. She stopped short when she saw Mr. Sosebee.

"Goodness," she giggled, "what's he doing?"

"Talking to the Great Spirit, I guess," I said.

"Well." She patted her hair and tucked her blouse into her slacks.

We all stood there in the gathering dusk with Mr. Sosebee's voice a sonorous background for the crickets and the nightbirds which were beginning to call.

Imo looked happy. Jeanette bit her nails, and my insides were a mess.

Mr. Sosebee got quiet, opened his eyes and took a deep breath. We turned to look at him, and he raised both palms solemnly toward us like he was surrendering in a Wild West shoot out.

"This is a time for strength and celebration," his voice was deep and gentle.

"Mr. Sosebee," Imo chirped, "what are we celebrating?"

He cleared his throat and looked pointedly at Jeanette. She laughed hoarsely, but she didn't utter a word.

"Alrighty!" Imo said in a thin voice, looking back and forth at them. She touched her throat. A whippoorwill called out from the thicket of trees behind Mr. Sosebee.

"Shall we continue?" She smiled and picked up her right foot like she was about to march forward in some parade.

"Say it then!" Jeanette yanked Mr. Sosebee's arm. "Say it and get it over with!"

"Jeanette is going to bear a child," he said gently.

Imo covered her mouth. She shook her head and looked at Jeanette. "Is this true?"

"It's true," said Jeanette, gazing down at the grass.

T E N

Annual Panic

"Too bad? I've got bypass surgery next month and do you think I have anyone who cares? Anyone out in the waiting room, rubbing their hands together nervously while the doctors are cutting me open?"
— MR. ROYCE SOSEBEE
lifelong bachelor, discussing his upcoming heart surgery

A panic seized Imo. The annual angst that the garden's abundance always brought was magnified a thousand times. She stood in the middle of the garden with an engorged tomato in each fist. The tomatoes had split their skins, and their bulging sides reminded her of pregnant women.

Always it overwhelmed her, but *this*, this plethora of produce, she could handle. She could can, freeze, blanch, pickle, and dry till the cows came home. She would give up sleep happily, shoot, give up eating, to get it all put by.

But Jeanette she could not fix.

She blamed herself for Jeanette's predicament. With every prayer, every kind word of encouragement, every instruction in righteous living, every tear, every bounteous table she set, and with all her generous love, she had succored the child. Imo had believed that if she set forth her personal example of virtue and the strength of hope, if she loved her enough and was patient, if she carried her to Calvary enough, then the child would walk the straight and narrow path.

Mr. Sosebee regarded her from across the squash vines with a pitying smile. He was waiting for her to speak.

"It certainly has been a dry summer," Imo managed. Her face burned. Mr. Sosebee really should just go on home and let her deal with this alone. When she had hightailed it back up here to the garden to think, he'd followed right along, clueless to the signals her folded arms and annoyed sighing were giving out. She hummed a hymn to herself and even bent down to pluck up a few weeds to discourage him. She couldn't think very well with Mr. Sosebee looming there.

"Yep, dry alright." He puffed on a cigarette. "Look, I been meaning to get over here and offer my help and I knew when I gave Lou a lift this morning that was a sign. I know it's hard, you alone and all. Now, what needs doing?"

Imo tried to concentrate on what he was saying as he picked up an overripe tomato that had fallen off the vine. She felt drained—like all the life had just been washed out of her.

"I want to help out," he said after a moment when she still hadn't replied.

"That's nice." She watched Bingo lift his leg onto Mr. Sosebee's truck tire.

"Put me to work. What's the first thing?" he insisted.

She wiped the dust from a cucumber on her sleeve and stuffed it into her pocket. Did he mean with the farm or what? He leaned in close to her. She shrugged. It was a strange world she was living in, up and down like a roller coaster.

Mr. Sosebee touched her shoulder, and she jumped. "I know you're worried about Jeanette," he said gently. "She didn't want you to know. Lou said she was planning to run away when y'all were down in Florida."

Imo imagined herself and Lou walking along an empty expanse of white sand calling out *Jeanette! Oh, Jeanette!* "I don't imagine we'll be taking a Florida trip now," she said. "I'm going on in the house, Mr. Sosebee." She handed him the cucumber.

"You don't want my help then." He sighed.

You have no troubles, she thought, staring at his brown teeth and growing more annoyed with his presence as dusk sank over the garden.

"Must be easy for you. No family and all," she snapped.

In the uneasy silence that followed, Mr. Sosebee pressed his right hand, with the cigarette, over his left breast. "It's the opposite, actually," he said in a faltering voice.

She looked out over the horizon, her jaw thrust out.

He said, "You don't believe me."

"No." She felt mean and childish.

"Imogene, come closer." He crooked a finger and beckoned to her.

She was startled to hear him use her name so intimately. She moved within half a foot of him.

"Listen. Listen to my heart. Hear that?" His eyebrows raised up.

She did hear a clicking noise.

"That's my heart. Valve. Been through one surgery. I'm like that gator in Peter Pan."

"That's too bad," she said. *Better than a broken heart. At least medical science can fix yours.*

"Too bad? I've got bypass surgery next month and do you think I have anyone who cares? Anyone out in the waiting room, rubbing their hands together nervously while the doctors are cutting me open?"

"I had no idea." She pressed her fingertips against her own heart. She felt her chest ache in sympathy. Poor Mr. Sosebee. She bit her lip.

"Look, I shouldn't have dumped my burden on you. You've got enough to deal with already. Just tell me how I can help."

"Well now, I don't know." Imo blushed.

There was a long moment of silence. They stood in the dark heat of the garden until there was the sound of a door slamming and the lights in the kitchen came on.

"There is one thing you can do," Imo said.

"What?"

"Jeanette likes you, I can tell, Mr. Sosebee. She doesn't take to many people, and she won't listen to me anymore. It was Silas that had a way with her. Talk to her. I believe she wants to drop out of school. Talk to her about staying in, and find out about the baby."

"I'll try." He thought a minute. "But I don't rightly know what to say."

"I don't mean the actual *birth*. What I mean is: talk to her, find out who the father is. Maybe they can get married real quick. I've got the Florida money to pay for a wedding." This all occurred to her while she was saying it, and really, it made perfect sense. Even though Jeanette said she thought it was five months or so along, she wasn't showing too bad yet. There could be a quiet little wedding.

He smiled. "I'll do what I can."

She walked toward the house. One thing was for sure, there was no way out of this one. But here was help that had walked right up to her and volunteered when she needed it. Plus, maybe it would take his mind off his heart.

Mr. Sosebee was right on her heels as she sank down onto the warm glider. The August moon shone down on them and made long shadows at their feet. Imo was lost in thoughts about the wedding when he touched her arm. She jumped.

"A penny for your thoughts," he said gently.

"Uhmmm . . ."

"You don't want to tell me." He shook his head. "You barely know me."

"No, it's not that." She hoped her tone was warm. She just needed a moment of quiet to plan, and this man was worse than a fly buzzing in her ear.

She was thinking of her wedding dress. Would it fit on Jeanette? She could take out the seam at the waist and put in a few darts for the tummy. Then she was thinking she'd carry the girls to Reverend Peddigrew's revival Friday week.

Perhaps *this* was God's way of showing them where they needed to be, instead of headed for the beach. But how would she keep Martha's nose out of this? She closed her eyes. "Sweet Jesus . . ."

"What's that?"

"Nothing," she said. He wouldn't understand. She wanted him to go.

He took her hand, squeezed it gently.

"How shall I say this?" He leaned forward and murmured so low she had to get right up to his lips to hear. "You look . . . well, I don't remember you ever looking so pretty." He shook his head. "Heck. I shouldn't have said that."

"It's okay." She was used to people commenting on her new look. Usually she just laughed and told them she was a walking advertisement for Wanda's Kut 'n' Kurl. The truth was that although she still fussed with her bobbed haircut, concealed the gray, and put on the modern lip color, most days she didn't put on the full face. Around the farm, she was back in her cotton house dresses.

"Thank you," she said, casting a sideways glance at him, aware of his ticking heart. It was almost a comforting sound. Steady. She wondered how it sounded if you put your ear right up on his bare chest. It was, Imo decided, a really sincere man who would reveal his personal agonies.

"What I was thinking was I'd carry the girls to church with me next week. Jeanette's not really showing yet . . ."

"No, she's not."

"I mean, I love Martha to death, but you've got to understand that she's got the biggest mouth. . . . There's no need to tell her about anything."

"Of course not." He withdrew his hand to light a cigarette.

"We could sit on the back pew . . . "

"Sure." He blew his smoke away from her. "I know something that'd be good for you."

"What?"

"Bingo. Come with me Friday night."

"I'm not much for games, Mr. Sosebee. And you saw that garden. Just plum running over with things to tend to." What she needed now was plain hard work. It was also time to step up her instruction on virtuous living while there was still a chance for Lou.

"Call me Royce," he said, eyes shining. "Come with me Friday night."

"Can't," Imo said.

He tucked a wisp of her hair behind her ear. "Look, you deserve to get out. Do something for yourself. And if you're not having the time of your life, say the word, and I'll bring you right home."

She felt a burning hot place where his fingers had brushed her cheek. "Maybe. Well, okay," she said. She couldn't remember the last time she'd played a game.

Imo loaded up the trunk with an old laundry basket and two feed buckets full of squash, tomatoes, and cucumbers to give out after the revival meeting. She tossed in a clump of plastic grocery bags for parceling the vegetables out. Food for the body after food for the soul, she reasoned.

She ought to have invited Royce to come to Calvary with them, but she would wait and see how the Bingo episode went.

It still seemed unreal that Jeanette was having a baby. Maybe Imo was stuck in a dream and would wake up and laugh her head off. Sometimes, lately, she actually confused dreams with reality. She would have a fleeting thought, and she'd have to stop and think, did that really happen or was that part of last night's dream?

But no. This was real. She still hadn't talked it over, or even mentioned it again to Jeanette. And when Imo said she wanted them all to go to tonight's revival, she expected a sneer and a "no way" from Jeanette, but she said "fine."

So Imo set the problem of planning the wedding on what she called the back burner of her mind to simmer a while. She'd at least wait until Royce had his talk with Jeanette.

Tonight they would pile into the Impala and go put themselves under the cleansing and scrutinizing eye of Reverend Peddigrew. For once she was glad about how sullen and disrespectful Jeanette was to her elders. She sure wouldn't be chatting with old big-mouth Martha.

Jeanette looked pale and washed-out when Imo saw her in the rear view mirror. Hadn't even managed to do her lips or eyes as far as Imo could tell. Poor thing was gaunt and hollow-eyed.

"How about some ice cream after the meeting?" Imo ventured as they passed the Dairy Queen.

Lou said, "Yes!"

"Jeannie? I said we're going to get ice cream after Calvary," Imo said.

"No! I mean, no thank you." Jeanette shook her head. Her chin quivered.

Imo was trying. Lord, how she was trying to do and say the right things. She'd always thought pregnant women *craved* ice cream.

They passed a huge corn field. The sun was setting back behind it, bathing it in an unearthly golden light. Maybe heaven would look like that. It would be nice to be dead right now, she thought. Wouldn't have to deal with all this.

But at Imo's last check-up the doctor said everything was as stout and strong as it had been when she was forty. Her only hope for escape was the Rapture of the Saints, which was one hot topic with Reverend Peddigrew. That was the whole reason for tonight's meeting. It sure would be wonderful if the Lord came and fetched her. She would fling herself into Silas's arms and forget all this.

She pulled into the parking lot as a hymn drifted out from the church. "Love lifted me, love lifted me. When nothing else could help, love lifted me." The chorus of voices bathed her in hope. They slid into the back pew after the singing was over.

Reverend Peddigrew led a long prayer, and Imo let herself look around. It was such a sweltering evening that the other ladies on the back pew forsook any semblance of modesty and sat with their feet flat on the floor and their knees apart, fanning up under hem lines with offering envelopes.

Her girls were wearing shorts, and it tugged at her heart to see Jeanette's spindly, vulnerable legs and Lou's, all skinned and stained like a child's.

She heard the Reverend praying for the congregation to have strength during trials and testing. That was it! God was testing her with this newest calamity in her life. She would prove herself worthy. She closed her eyes for the last of the prayer.

Reverend Peddigrew said that plummeting morality was the first proof that the Rapture was imminent; young people today were flinging aside their parents' values. She glanced at Jeanette, slouching and staring vacantly toward the pulpit. On the other side of her, Loutishie was ram-rod straight, leaning forward to absorb every word.

Imo leaned back. She listened. The next topic was Israel's rebirth in 1948. Reverend Peddigrew said Israel was God's "time-clock." She never thought much about foreign places, and the idea of God needing a clock tickled her. The way the Reverend was carrying on about all these fulfilled prophecies and his "ten compelling proofs that Jesus was coming soon" was enough to make the congregation expect Him to float into their midst at any second.

But Imo had sat through enough sermons on the Second Coming to temper her own expectation and agitation about it. He may not be back for 100 years. You had to get on with this life and tend to your troubles. Jeanette could use some shaking up, though.

When he was close to proof number nine and winding

down, Martha turned around to mash a spider on the pew back behind her and spied Imo. She waved a *let's talk after the message*. Suddenly Imo was intent on getting the three of them out of there pronto.

Of course, she should let Martha know of this latest travail, let the church undergird her with prayers and Godly counsel, but she just couldn't endure any more pity at this moment of her life.

"Girls," she whispered, bending over their laps, "get your things together. We need to hustle on out of here."

"Why?" Lou whispered back, not taking her eyes off the Reverend.

"I don't feel well," Imo said.

The crickets sure were making a racket in the privet, and Imo winced under the full moon which hung over Calvary like the eye of God. They were all belted in by the time the rest of the congregation spilled out onto the front steps. Martha flapped her hands and scurried out toward the Impala. Imo yanked the car into reverse, then forward so fast she flung gravel as she scratched off.

"Cool," Jeanette murmured.

Imo made it five miles before she remembered the trunk full of vegetables. She pressed the accelerator to keep herself from turning around. Anyway, all those folks at Calvary had gardens of their own. She swerved into the parking lot of the Dairy Queen.

"I thought you was sick!" Jeanette shrieked, then fussed and flopped her head back hard against the seat. "I ain't going in."

"You don't have to. I've got something I need to carry inside."

"What?!" Jeanette stiffened.

"You two stay here. I'll bring you a Dilly Bar, Lou. What do you want, Jeanette?"

Jeanette burst into tears.

Imo turned and patted her knee. "Alrighty. Sit tight and I'll be back in a jiffy." She wrangled the baskets and buckets from the trunk, balanced them on her hips like the African women they showed on Channel 8, and carried them into the dining area. She wrote, "Free. Help yourself," on a napkin and wedged it underneath a tomato, then went to the counter for three Dilly Bars.

Loutishie's Notebook

At the beginning of August, I was back in school, and the garden was slowly moving toward a dormant state. It was funny, Imo said she was relieved and sad at the same time. Of course, there was still the corn and sweet potatoes to harvest, and she was talking about planting her onion sets for winter.

I wish I could say that Imo told everyone in Euharlee the great news about a new baby coming, that Jeanette was feeling great and went on back to high school to get her diploma, and that Mr. Sosebee and Imo were just buddies.

But what happened, though, was Mr. Sosebee was hanging around way too much and being way too cozy. That man showed up everywhere. We'd come in from the garden and there he'd be, sitting on the sofa next to Jeanette and puffing away on a cigarette. Bingo would dart up to him and stand there until Mr. Sosebee leaned down and rubbed his ribs to get his back leg going. I wished he didn't like Mr. Sosebee so much. I wished Jeanette didn't either.

Maybe he would die soon, I told myself. During his open heart surgery he kept talking about it. Bad thoughts were like wild horses in my mind. They bucked and pranced around and no matter how hard I tried, I couldn't get a bridle on them. I kept telling myself that Jesus could come and blow the trumpet any second and there I'd be, caught with the sin of wishing Mr. Sosebee would drop dead.

It was bad that he encouraged Jeanette's filthy habit, but what was worse was that he sat so close to Imo in the glider and held her hand. It would be hard to describe how I felt whenever I saw Imo and him laughing together the way she used to do with Uncle Silas. What I did was to block their intimate moments out of my mind. I told myself she was trying to convert Mr. Sosebee from faith in The Great Spirit to faith in God.

Still, a part of me had to know the truth about Mr. Sosebee's intentions. Then I could stop lying in bed at night and wondering. One night, things had reached such a boiling point in my mind that I decided to confront him. It was dark by the time he climbed into his pickup where I'd been waiting quietly for him to say goodnight to Imo.

"Hi," I said from the passenger side.

He was startled and banged his head on the cab. "Dern it, Lou!" he said, all breathless after he saw it was me.

"I need to talk to you," I said. I was so nervous I could hardly breathe.

"What?" He eased into his seat, rubbing his head and whistling softly.

"Uhm . . . why are you doing so much work around here?"

"Listen, gal," he said and opened up his door so Bingo could jump in his lap. "Your uncle helped me out more times than I can shake a stick at. Plus, I'm crazy about your aunt. Crazy about all of you. She's crazy about me."

Around me, everything blurred. My chest tightened. "I'm not crazy about you!" I yelled.

The world was yanked right out from under me. I must've opened the truck's door and run across the front yard, up the steps, across the porch, and into the den, where I flung myself onto the sofa. But I only remember Imo standing over me and saying, "What's wrong, child? You look like you've seen a ghost!"

I looked up at her in the half-light of one lamp at the other end of the den. You should feel terrible, I thought, running around on Uncle Silas like this. But I didn't say a word. She bent over me and put the back of her hand on my forehead. "Let's get you to bed," she said.

I turned my head away and showed her my displeasure by giving her no goodnight hug. I didn't want to go to bed. I wouldn't be able to sleep anyway, I reasoned. I went outside. I contemplated running away to sunny Florida by myself. Then they'd all be sorry. Instead, I climbed into the back seat of the Impala along with Bingo. I quietly eased the door closed and lay down.

The sun was almost over the pecan tree when Jeanette found

me the next morning. Her hair was damp, and her purse was slung over her shoulder. She opened the driver's door and stood there for a moment like she saw a snake.

She let out a long breath and pointed at me. "You scared the shit out of me, you little twerp!"

I sat up, rubbing the life back into my aching arms and legs.

"God, it stinks in here!" She ran around flinging all the doors open.

I sat there and swiped the white crust of drool off of my cheek. "Don't take the name of the Lord in vain," I mumbled.

"Shut up, Lou."

She was really ornery today. This was too early for her to be up and dressed.

"Imo know you're out here?" I asked, figuring maybe she was running away.

"Yeah." She looked miserable.

"Where're you going?" I asked.

"To the baby doctor in Cartersville. I promised Mr. Mabry."

I fluffed up Bingo's neck while he did a slow stretch. I couldn't walk just yet, and when he yawned in my face it was ghastly. "Can I go?"

"Hurry, run get ready."

I ran in the house, got myself cleaned up, and tucked my fake $20 bill into my pocket..

We rode toward Cartersville with the windows down to root out the dog smell. Leaves were turning brown and yellow, and the sky was losing it's summer pastel shade.

It was a few minutes after nine when we pulled up at the doctor's office. A few acorns bounced down on the car hood and Jeanette drew a deep breath. "You wait out here. I'll leave the keys and you can listen to the radio."

I sat there and wondered if Imo even thought of Uncle Silas anymore. There was something crazy about a woman her age running around like that. I was still hoping Mr. Sosebee would die. I sure hated to think of how my heavenly account was looking in the thinking department, so I wrapped the fake $20 bill around Jeanette's lighter in the pocket of her cigarette pouch.

"Hey kid, time to go." Jeanette had a big white bottle of vitamins in her hand, and she was popping gum.

When we pulled out of the parking lot a flurry of leaves left the hood and skittered up the windshield. Jeanette dug around in her purse and came up with the green pouch. She opened the ball clasp expertly with two fingers and slid out the pack of Marlboros.

Well, here goes, I thought.

She placed a cigarette on her lower lip and worked her lighter up from the side pouch. She felt the paper and looked down at it, puzzled.

We wobbled all over King Avenue as she unfurled the bill, rubbed it between her fingers, flipped it over and read it. She spit her chewing gum into it and wadded it up into a little ball and tossed it over her shoulder into the back seat.

Her laughter bounced off the dashboard.

E L E V E N

Picking a Winner

*"Store-bought tomatoes (those commercially grown)
have to be harvested when they are still hard and
green. That way they can hold up to the rough
treatment of picking and shipping. Then they treat
them with ethylene gas to make them turn red.
That's why they don't taste like a thing."*
— THE SOUTHERN GARDENING BOOK

"Pick you out a winner, darling," one of the cheer-
ful-faced ladies of the Women's Auxiliary told
Imo as she followed Royce into AMVETS Post 5
for Monday Night Bingo. He peeled off a ten dollar bill
from his wad of money and bought them each a book of
games, just as he had done the other times.

There were seventy-five or so of the churched and the
unchurched gathered in the cavernous smoke-filled hall.
Imo discovered she knew a good number of them.

Imo decided it was a fine time to do something so unpro-
ductive as playing games since it was a relatively in-between
time in the garden—the tomatoes and cucumbers were pe-

tering out, and she had a while before she sowed her turnips and beets. Even the Garden Club members were slacking off. At the September meeting, all they'd done was talk and arrange an assortment of lillies, dahlias, and delphiniums according to a book Myrtice had called *Artistic Flowers*.

What a strange few weeks this had been! Imo was exhausted and dizzy and wobbled around on her feet the same way she did after a roller coaster ride.

It was still hard for her to confront the fact that she'd failed with Jeanette. When she let herself think about it, her heart fluttered so badly she had to press on it with her hand.

Royce sure seemed to think she was fascinating though. He often praised her cooking and her beauty. So far, they'd been to bingo three times (if you counted this one) and to the fish house twice.

There were three weeks to go until Royce's bypass surgery, and he was not supposed to be smoking. Imo thought that just walking into this place was equivalent to smoking a whole pack all at once.

The smoky room took shape all around her as she settled into a folding chair and watched Maude Simmons getting ready to call the game. Maude was an immense woman with bright orange lips who sat between the light-up Bingo-King scoreboard and a microphone. She tended a box full of fluorescent lights and bubbling Ping-Pong balls.

Royce spread out his cards and laid a gray arrowhead above them. At least his good luck charm was not as tacky as a lot of these people's. There were a good number of unicorns, Teddy bears in ungodly colors, and some real raunchy figurines.

"I win, I carry you to the movies," he said.

Imo's heart swelled. One day soon she would call Martha up and tell her about him. She wouldn't mention Jeanette though. There was no need to, she would just say "fine" when Martha asked her usual, "how are the girls?"

"This game's the seventy-five-dollar one." He patted her knee. "Block of nine anywhere on the board will make you the . . ."

"Royce, what did Jeanette say?" She interrupted him.

"Uh, when?" He was distracted as the first Ping-Pong ball was selected and displayed on the closed-circuit TV which hung on the wall to their right.

"When you talked to her after supper." She cleared her throat. It was like having a conversation with a brick wall.

"After supper. Yes. She . . . She said . . ." He paused to flick the cap off of his bingo- marker.

"Go on."

"She said . . . hey you got it too, Imo! That it's a boy."

"What?"

"The doctor took a picture inside, and it's a boy."

"No, I know that. Did she say who the father is?" Imo asked, holding her breath.

"Mmm-hmm," he said.

"Well?"

Royce stared at the TV screen.

"Who?" Imo's voice was high, and she held one hand over her heart.

"Who," he echoed, eyes fastened on the most recent number.

"Who is it?!" Imo shouted over the talk and laughter in the room.

He waved a hand in her direction. "Just a minute."

"Who?" Imo begged, tugging Royce's shirt sleeve. He was oblivious to her, and so she raised herself up and got between him and the TV.

He blinked.

"Who is the father of Jeanette's baby?" Imo asked, twisting the fabric of his sleeve tighter.

"He's married. Gone now," said Royce.

Imo closed her eyes and sank back down in her chair. She wasn't breathing well. Married? Gone? She hadn't allowed herself to think those words. But what had she expected? Maybe it was too much to ask that the baby's father stay in the picture. She had no idea of what she should do now. She vowed to keep her cool, think things through, and make a new plan.

The shout of "B-6!" brought Imo back from her thoughts. Royce happily stamped three of his cards and one of hers. He fumbled in his shirt pocket for his cigarettes, shook one out, and stuck it between his lips without lighting it.

Imo resigned herself to finishing the game before she could talk to him and make any sense out of it.

She swigged her Pepsi and listened halfheartedly as another number was called out.

The tension was thick after the next five minutes. She watched Royce gnaw on his unlit cigarette.

At the table behind them, she heard the excited murmurs of someone close to winning. *Please Lord, let this game be over*, she prayed.

Royce kept his marker poised above his cards. He was breathless, lacking just one square on two different cards which would make him a winner. He was practically eating the cigarette.

Suddenly, one of the women directly behind them yelled out "bingo!" and jumped up waving a lucky card.

Royce quickly swept away their cards. "Dadgummit!" He chuckled.

"Can we talk about Jeanette now?" she said, forcing control into her voice.

"Go ahead." He moved so close to her she heard his ticking heart.

"I just wondered if she has considered her future. What'd she say she was planning to do? Stay in school? Find a husband?" For a moment Imo felt like she might cry.

"She said she's dropping out."

"Of school?" Imo felt numb.

Two ladies in pink smocks were walking around the tables, picking up discarded game cards and selling new ones for fifty cents apiece. Royce waved a fifty dollar bill at one of them and said, "Two books, Pearl."

Pearl handed over two more and placed a couple of twenty dollar bills in change at his elbow. "Good luck," she sang out, making her way to the next table.

Royce stiffened. His nostrils flared. He gritted his teeth.

Imo saw him bite his cigarette in half. "What's wrong?" she asked.

"Pearl!" He bellered.

Pearl hustled back with wide eyes. "Yes, Mr. Sosebee?"

"These bills bear the image of Andrew Jackson!"

"Sorr-ee sweetie," Pearl sang out. She replaced them with four tens and patted his shoulder. "I plum forgot."

Imo grabbed Pearl's arm, pulled her down, and whispered, "What's wrong with Andrew Jackson?"

"He hasn't given you one of his Indian preachin' tirades, sugar?" Pearl looked at Imo like she had turned purple. "He's the president who ordered the removal of the Cherokee Indians. Made them leave here and march to Oklahoma. Trail of Tears, I believe it was called."

"Oh," Imo said.

There was a lot about this man she didn't know. He was probably putting his best foot forward with her. Maybe he had that type-A personality, and it was wrecking his heart. She looked hard at him. He was fiery. A fiery Injun with his ponytail in a sloppy braid tonight. His spunk could come in handy, though. She checked her handbag to make sure she carried no twenties.

They started a new game. Bingo etiquette required that everyone keep quiet during the game since a good number of folks were playing eight cards at a time and needed their concentration. This one was called Big Picture Frame and the prize was $100. Imo wasn't concentrating the way she needed to. She was exhausted. All these late nights with

Royce were exhilarating, but they were tuckering her out, too.

The skinny man at the table directly to their right was close to bingo. His hands twitched above his cards while he waited on the next number.

Maude Simmons read out another Ping-Pong ball. "O-60." The tension in the room was palpable.

Royce sighed. "You're not covering your numbers, Imo." He made a few quick stamps on her cards.

"Sorry."

"All you need is O-64 and you got it."

It was the first time in all these games Imo had even been close to winning. She decided it was improper to pray for luck while gambling, even though it was legalized. But if she won, she sure would have Royce's full attention.

Maude called out O-64! Yes! Imo was breathless. "Bingo!" Her arm flew up with her card.

The skinny man glared at her and the women behind her sighed.

As if a spell had been broken, Royce blinked and turned to her. "That's a good bingo you got there, Imo."

"Thanks. Ready to go?" She saw no point in staying any longer.

"You serious?"

"Perfectly. Got a chess pie waiting at the house." She squeezed his knee.

Someone said, "Time to play blackout!"

Oh Lord, Imo sighed. Even though blackout was the last game of the evening, it took forever for someone to fill up their entire card.

Royce stroked his arrowhead a minute and turned halfway in his chair. He pulled out a fresh cigarette and lit the first one of the night. He met her eyes, looked up at the Bingo King scoreboard, then back at her.

Okay. She sensed that this was a test. Her or bingo.

He studied her and inhaled, narrowing his eyes.

She smiled to beat the band. She'd walk home if he chose bingo, tired or not. She could deal with some things, but she wouldn't put up with coming in second to a *game*. She raised her eyebrows at him.

He closed his eyes and started singing vowels. It wasn't too long before he stopped, though, shook like a dog does when it gets wet, stood up, and said, "After you."

Imo's heart fluttered. She hadn't been so sure about his priorities for a minute there.

"Good win," he said to her and stuck another cigarette between his lips as they pulled out on to Hardigree Drive.

He bounced the cold cigarette up and down with his teeth and felt around the dash for his lighter.

Hardigree Drive led straight into downtown. The radio played Solid Country Gold, and she hummed along with the words as they drove through the darkness.

They passed the Welcome to Downtown Euharlee sign, the courthouse, and the tiny library. The truck rumbled and shuddered as Royce pulled into a parking place in front of Mozelle's Supply Co., a deserted dry goods store. Moonlight made the town square romantic.

"Nice evening," Royce said.

She felt her pulse racing as he reached for her hand. She wished she could think of something witty to say, but the truth was that she couldn't get her mind off of Jeanette at the moment. "Yes, it is." She felt a little thrill as he inched closer. He held her hand.

"I want us to be more than bingo partners," Royce whispered.

She closed her eyes. She smiled in the dark. Why not? Why not him to grow old with? "Yes." If smoking was his only vice, and she was almost certain he wasn't a drinker, then she would overlook it. The man was clearly besotted with her. Anyway, everybody had their weaknesses. She decided to call the Indian thing just a charming eccentricity. Something she and Martha could laugh about.

"Well, I'm sorry there'll be no wedding for Jeanette," Royce said. He was puffing on a cigarette like there was no tomorrow.

"If I could just get her to stay in school, I'd be almost . . ." She wouldn't say happy, that would be a lie, but at least Jeanette would have a shot at a future.

"Maybe I can convince her," he said tenderly and touched Imo's cheek.

"It'll all be okay," she said with a teary laugh, then covered her face and began to cry.

He put his arms around her. "There, there now," he whispered into her ear, "I'll take care of you."

She cried, listening to his heart tick, and letting the tears run rivers through her face powder. It sure was nicer than crying into her pillow. But it was more than just having this pillar of strength to lean on. She strained up so that her forehead touched his lips, and it sent a volt of heat through her limbs.

There was chemistry between them!

He felt it too because he dipped down, and their lips touched. Zing! She ignored the taste of the cigarettes.

A Z-28 circled the square. It stopped and headlights encased them in a golden glow. There was a honk, a boy's voice hollered out "Get a room!" followed by laughter.

"Oh!" she jerked away.

Royce blinked. "Let's finish this at your place."

That night she went to sleep instantly, spiraling down into the vortex of a dream where she was an Indian squaw wearing two long braids, and moccasins made of deer hide. She was snapping ears of corn off of stalks twice as high as she was. She stroked the tassels on the corn, which were the sweaty scalps of feverish infants. "Poor things," she crooned and lined them up on the packed red clay. She picked up two to comfort. Peering into their tiny sad faces, she saw it was Jeanette and Loutishie.

Imo wished she had thought to bring her mending, a little

something to keep her busy while she sat around the hospital. She'd already thumbed through all the dog-eared issues
of *Woman's Day* and *Better Homes and Gardens,* and she
avoided *Field and Stream* and *Cosmopolitan,* the only other
magazines there. It made her mad that people tore recipes
out of waiting-room magazines without thinking that someone else might want to read the words on the back of them
or that someone else might want a chef's secret recipe for
chicken divan.

Imo was sitting in the surgical waiting room with Lou
while Royce had his heart procedure done. Martha said she
was coming by to sit with them.

Martha's first question when Imo revealed that she had a
boyfriend was "Where does he go to church?"

"The woods," Imo said. "He worships The Great Spirit
in the woods."

Martha looked hard at Imo. "Well, God must be using you
to convert him, then. A believing wife can sanctify a worldly
man. Use your Baptist faith and win him to Jesus."

Imo knew this would preoccupy Martha for hours and
keep her on the phone for days. She waited a week before she
mentioned his surgery. "Listen Martha," she said, "would you
just come and sit with me Wednesday week during Royce's
surgery?"

"What?!" Martha shouted so loud Imo had to pull the receiver away from her ear.

"Just a standard little procedure, hon'."

"Well, what is it?"

"It's not cancer. It's his heart."

"That's not a standard procedure, Imogene. I don't think you're thinking straight."

"I'm fine . . ."

A long silence, then Martha said, "I'm serious. Heart surgery is serious."

"Just put it on the prayer chain, Martha." Imo hung up.

Before they wheeled Royce into pre-op she held his hand. He became such a little boy, hiding his lucky arrowhead underneath his back when the nurse asked him to remove glasses and any jewelry. He pressed his head into her thighs. Imo indulged him by talking about how they would go to bingo as soon as he was able.

"You don't know how much you being here means to me," Royce said.

"Don't you think a thing about it," said Imo. "You are practically family."

This really *was* an intimate thing to do. He could die in there. It meant they were serious when they walked through the valley of the shadow of death together.

Imo glanced at Lou, who was watching a TV up in one corner of the waiting room.

Imo had been avoiding the fact that Royce could die in there. Lots of folks didn't make it out of the operating room. She wished she could will away the thoughts that were battering her now. Of course, she'd known when she'd picked him that this valley was on the horizon. Known there was a possibility that he might not make it. Yet, she'd gone right on ahead.

She squashed that thought quickly and told herself that

she would nurse him through his post-op period. This heart problem wasn't like cancer, which had such an ominous sound. This operation was just some cutting and moving around and stitching, like making a quilt or mending, and it would not ruin her wonderful romance. It was just something to get through that would bring them closer.

Several other clumps of people were there, too, but it was so early, they had not yet exchanged pleasantries. Everyone just sipped their coffee and looked up anxiously each time a doctor appeared in the doorway.

Out of the corner of her eye, she saw Jenny Jones come on the TV. Jenny delivered her monologue seriously while they all sat there staring vacantly. A parade of blonde-haired, well-endowed ladies, wearing pink-frosted lipstick, sashayed out onto the stage while the TV audience clapped furiously. The topic was girls who put themselves through college by dancing topless.

Seductive music played while cameras panned in on undulating hips and thighs, with the privates covered by tiny triangles of gold lamé.

Imo took a gulp of her lukewarm coffee and trained her eyes on some plastic geraniums next to her. Her neck grew hot. She could only imagine what they'd show next. She squared her shoulders. "Lou," she hissed, crooking a finger to call her over.

The girl trudged over with a pained expression.

"Flip that TV to something decent, sugar foot."

"People are *watching it*, Imo. Please. Just leave it on."

That's how it had been with Lou lately. Teenager-hood, maybe. Or else Jeanette was rubbing off on her. She'd even said to Imo's face she didn't care for Mr. Sosebee.

"Run turn it to another channel. Now." Imo hated to get stern with her.

"P-l-eee-a-s-e," Lou groaned.

"Run on. I can't get up that high to change it," Imo said, forcing control into her voice as she studied the faces in the waiting room. They were transfixed on the screen.

Every eye in the room blinked when Lou got up on a chair and flipped the TV to *Little House on the Prairie*.

"Well, at least they're dressed a little nicer," Imo said to the stunned man on her left.

Finally a grim-faced doctor stood in the doorway with his surgical mask down around his neck. His eyes panned the waiting room. Watching him, she gripped the sofa's arm, and her breath stuck in her throat.

She'd better prepare herself. Please God! She prayed. But didn't the Lord give *and* take away?

"Sosebee?" she asked.

He looked at her blankly and shook his head.

She wilted back down into her seat and glanced at her watch. She was tired and her stomach growled. Where was Martha?

Finally. Martha's voice, breathless and concerned, floated into the waiting room before she did. "Oh, Imo, I'm sorry I'm running so late. How is everything? Have you talked with the doctor?"

"No word yet,"she sighed through a tired smile.

"You look weary, dear." Martha touched her arm, and she jumped.

"Hungry."

"Here." Martha fished a Wintergreen Lifesaver from the bottom of her handbag.

"Hello, dear!" Martha said to Lou.

"Hello, Mrs. Peddigrew."

Martha bent down to pat Lou's knee. "And where is Jeanette?" she asked.

"Oh, she's busy today. You know young people," Imo said, her voice rising. "Let's go get us a bite. I am about to cave in."

They took the elevator down to the main floor.

"You reckon they'll know to come down here if there's any news?" Martha asked.

Imo nodded. "I told Lou to come fetch us." She selected a golden crusted biscuit with a slab of country ham flopping out the sides and scooped up some scrambled eggs from a steaming silver warming tray. "Real nice of you to come, Martha."

"Well. I thought it might take your mind off of Royce if we planned the Garden Club's Christmas party while we're waiting."

"Oh yes, the party."

"This is your year, Imo, you know, to be the hostess."

"Oh-h-h-h-h." Imo let that soak in.

"Now, I've got the amaryllis ordered. Went on and got twenty-four of them."

Cleaning up the house for the Christmas party and getting things baked and decorated was a lot to handle by itself. But you add in the annual planting of the amaryllis and the fact that the second Tuesday in December was also Jeanette's due date, and you could almost have yourself a stroke.

"That's just great, Martha." The noise in the crowded dining room closed in on her. She opened a cool little tub of apple jelly and spread some on her biscuit.

"I'll do my cheese straws," Martha went on, "and if you'll do your sausage balls and Myrtice brings her coconut cake . . . you've got a punch bowl, don't you, dear?"

Imo nodded. How long did heart surgery take anyway?

Martha reached across the table and patted her wrist. "You're mighty quiet today."

Oh, this was all so hard. Having to balance friends and family with a boyfriend and his surgery, and then a Christmas party with a baby. Would she ever have a relaxed moment again? One where her insides weren't all twisted up?

With every minute that passed, life got more complicated. Even Loutishie was being secretive and difficult. Once a sweet, communicative, and respectful child, she was turning into a stranger. Maybe she was smoking dope.

Surely not. Surely God wouldn't add another complication to Imo's life. She already felt like Job, except her body wasn't covered with painful boils and the cows appeared to be healthy.

It was two cups of coffee later when Dr. Ellis found her. "Mrs. Lavender?" he said "Everything went as well as can be expected. He is recovering nicely."

"Thank you," Imo said and cried a little. She felt like dancing.

"You okay?" Martha asked as she left.

"Yes." Imo smiled.

She went down to the gift shop to buy a stuffed cow that held a plastic sign saying "You mooooove me." That ought to brighten up Royce's room. She took it home to wrap it up, get a bath, and fix her face and hair.

Royce would make everything better. She'd nurse him back to health in no time and then a man around the house would do the trick.

Loutishie's Notebook

In the weeks that followed her trip to the doctor, Jeanette seemed to mellow a little. She took her vitamins faithfully and kept the volume of 96 Rock turned down low.

It wasn't too long after that I found myself at the hospital, in the surgical waiting room while they cut Mr. Sosebee open. I remember looking at Imo's face, and at the same time I was hoping he'd die, I was praying he wouldn't. When the doctor came to the door, I held my breath until I heard he was okay, and then I hugged Imo.

Only a week or so later, we were heading to the doctor again. This time it was to a baby specialist in Atlanta for Jeanette to get some tests done. By late morning, Imo began to pack a lunch to take with us.

"Don't forget the good knife," she said to me as I put the

bologna into a Tupperware container and wedged a cantaloupe into the corner of a pasteboard box. Imo put the mayonnaise, and a tomato into a small cooler and filled up an empty milk jug with tea.

"Alrighty." She swiped her hands together to show things were ship-shape. "You get the loaf-bread, Lou?"

"Yes ma'am," I said and followed her into the den.

Imo's breath was short as she helped Jeanette out of her chair. "Run lock the front door, Lou, and get my handbag."

As I went to lock the door, I heard a big "Oomph!." I flew back to the den and saw Imo, spraddle-legged on the floor.

"Ouch!" she squawked, "Like to broke my hip." She winced and rubbed her thigh.

"You okay?" I bent over her.

"I reckon," she said and pulled herself up and hobbled to the door. "We'd better get a move on." She sucked in a sharp breath.

It made me ache to see her so helpless. She was getting old. The hair dye could hide the gray, but you just could not ignore the fact that she was not as spry as she used to be. I wondered if I should let her lean on me to get out to the car or act like nothing had happened.

Imo was silent as we headed to Atlanta. I sat in the back and watched her face in the rearview. Her jaw was clenched. Maybe she was in pain from her fall. I wondered what in the world she was thinking.

"You haven't mentioned Jeanette's condition to anyone, have you, Lou?" Imo's eyes met mine in the rearview mirror. I jumped at the serious sound in her voice. "Only Mr. Mabry," I said.

It was past two when we left the doctor's, and I was starved. It was our plan to stop at a little country church outside of Oraville that had three cement picnic tables out back beside the cemetery. Imo said that since it was Baptist, we were affiliate members, and they wouldn't mind as long as we left the place tidy.

Before we even got the big box out of the trunk, it was discovered that we'd left the tiny cooler with the mayonnaise and tomato back at the house.

"Doggit!" Imo said, which was the closest she ever came to cussing. "What good's a bologna sandwich without mayo and a tomato?" She had this look on her face like the world was coming to an end. "Get back in, girls."

"We're going home?"

"We," she said, her voice slow and controlled, "are going back up the road a piece to that big fancy grocery."

Imo unfolded three ones and handed them over the back of the seat to me. "Jeanette and I don't need to go in, you run in and get us a tomato and a jar of mayonnaise. Now, don't get one of the little bitty jars, you'll pay a good bit more per ounce."

"Yes ma'am," I said and ran across the parking lot of Publix, my sandals making a slap-slap on the hot pavement.

A blast of cool air hit me as the second set of glass doors slid open. I walked beyond a dozen check-out lanes and stood there. You could get lost in here. I felt so country in my Keds and cutoffs. There were women wearing what looked like skirt versions of men's business suits, complete with hose and heeled pumps.

By the time I found the produce section, I figured Imo and Jeanette were impatient and sweating out there in the parking lot, so I grabbed a cellophane-wrapped green plastic basket full of four hard tomatoes. The price sticker said **$2.89.** If I bought them, I wouldn't have enough money left for the mayo. I picked up a single lemon shaped tomato with what looked like an outie belly button on one end. Nope. I put it back. No telling what that would taste like.

Finally, I found a bin of loose tomatoes. They were fairly red and I plucked up the biggest, prettiest one. Hard as a baseball, but I slipped it into a plastic bag and headed for the aisle marked condiments. I found a jar of mayonnaise for $1.89 and ran up to the checkout.

What happened next really confounded me. When I got to the cashier and she rung it up, I was twelve cents short. A man behind me paid the difference.

"You just return the favor to someone else," he said and winked at me.

To look at the tiny bag, you would not have dreamed it could be that expensive. I reached in and fondled the rock-like sphere that was the tomato.

Imo had the engine running, blasting icy air onto Jeanette. I climbed in, and she held out her hand for the change, and I shook my head.

She turned and looked hard at me, and I got ready for one of her childhood stories about an entire box of Kellogg's Cornflakes costing a nickel. "Let me see that receipt, Lou."

"My stars." Imo stared down at it and then shook her head. "$1.30 for one tomato!"

Imo ran the store-bought tomato underneath a spigot near the church's cemetery. She said no telling how many sets of nasty hands had handled it. Folks at those packing plants picked their noses and no telling what all else.

I had our sandwiches ready and laid open to receive the slices which turned out to be a pallid pink.

"Bless this food to our bodies and our lives to your service," Imo prayed before she opened the bag of chips and sprinkled some onto our plates.

We didn't say a thing as we sat there silently chewing our food like cows and staring up at the blue sky laced with feathery clouds.

I chewed the second bite of my sandwich slowly, waiting for the spicy zing of the tomato to hit my tastebuds. Finally I used my tongue to wedge the bit out from between the bread and bologna and rubbed my tongue over the flannel-textured morsel. Disgusting. Flavorless. I slid the rest of the slice out onto my paper plate. Imo always said that if you don't care for something, **quietly** place it on the side of your plate and don't say a word about it.

I managed to eat half of my sandwich before Imo laid hers down. All of a sudden, her face looked like somebody had punched her in the gut. She said, "doesn't even **taste** like a tomato!"

She dipped her head over towards Jeanette. "What do you think, Jeannie?"

"I think it sucks," Jeanette said.

Trying to say something to keep the mood from getting too gloomy, I smiled and said, "The lettuce sure is good." I was wondering if I hadn't just picked up a bad tomato and all this was my fault.

Imo smiled, but it was a pitiful smile, like **what's the world coming to?**

Jeanette was tired, so Imo and I went for a walk in the cemetery. We wandered around in a daze, squinting against the sun, not even reading the tombstones or musing about the folks buried there.

"Didn't even taste like a tomato." Imo sighed.

"I'm sorry," I said, trying to show in my expression that I shared her indignation.

"There's a lesson in this, Lou." She closed her eyes and dabbed her sweaty forehead with a wadded up napkin. I thought maybe she was praying for wisdom to impart to me. It was the longest time after that when she said, "There's only two things money can't buy."

I figured she would say salvation and probably a good conscience, or maybe a good night's sleep. I walked over to the stone lamb on a baby's headstone and traced it with my finger. I studied her out of the corner of my eye.

"Truelove," Said Imo, her voice quavering, "and homegrown tomatoes."

"Really?" I said.

Imo looked at me and nodded. "Heard a song about it on the radio last week."

Something in her face, a vulnerability or weakness I'd never seen, scared me. I agreed with the part about the tomatoes after today's purchase, but I'd never been in love before. I wanted to believe that love was a natural, pure wonder, too, that you couldn't just will it to happen or wander into a supermarket and buy it.

"I don't know anymore, Lou." Imo had tears in her eyes. She leaned back against a monument, crossed her arms and hung her head.

I hated it when I had to play the adult. I went over, wrapped my arms around her, and pressed my face into her bosom.

"Well now," she said, snorting and laughing through tears, "silly old me, crying over a song."

I knew it wasn't the song or the tasteless tomato she was crying about.

Late that night, in bed, I panicked. I ran barefooted out into the steaming garden and pulled a tomato off the vine. It was as warm as the soil. I hunkered down with Bingo and sank my teeth into its spicy sweet flesh, letting the seeds slide freely down my chin.

TWELVE

Earthy Desires

"I've got it, girls! If I can get hold of some of that Viagra, I'll add it to my fertilizer. That way I won't have to stake up my tomatoes!"

— FLORENCE BYRD
Garden Club member, musing about gardening possibilities
while at the annual Christmas party

*I*mo felt it first in all of her joints. Knuckles, elbows, hips, knees, and ankles ached like you wouldn't believe. Then it settled into her stomach and head.

Sometime after the roosters quieted down she realized she was not getting out of bed, and she snuggled down into the sheets to brace herself for another wave of nausea. The thought of coffee made her feel green and woozy.

If she had to be sick, she reckoned it was a fine time with Thanksgiving done and the garden hibernating and Lou out of school for the Thanksgiving holidays. Plus, she had already pulled up most of the spent plants from the garden and drained the gas from the roto-tiller.

Most importantly, Jeanette was feeling stronger, and Royce

was through his surgery. She had nursed him faithfully. Sat by his bedside for days after he returned home; spooning soup into his mouth, reading books on Indians to him, and playing checkers until her eyes crossed.

He told her he'd have been helpless without her there. Speaking of helpless, she was now having a bout with chills. She shook involuntarily and considered the electric blanket folded up in her closet. No, she always needed a cool spot to slide her toes into.

At noon, she managed to dial Martha.

"Hi, hon'," Martha said. "Lovely day, isn't it? Been out planting my peas."

"I wouldn't know, Martha. I'm sick as a dog."

"Uh oh. Let's hope it isn't that old fashion flu. What are your symptoms?"

"Chills right now. Upset stomach. Achy."

Martha said, "Sounds like flu."

Imo's teeth chattered into the phone.

"Did you say chills?" Martha asked.

"Y-e-e-e-s-s-s."

"Listen, get one of the girls to fix you a hot water bottle. Unless you can get Royce to come warm you up," ha ha ha, laughed Martha.

Imo was shocked at Martha's racy talk. But it would be nice when he got there, just to have him near her. Imo said, "I imagine he'll drop by to see about me, run pick up some Jell-O and soup, sit beside my bed."

"Listen, I'll bring you by some soup."

Imo smiled, but that hurt, too. "Royce will take care of things, Martha. Thanks, though."

"Bye now."

"Bye."

When Lou looked in, Imo sent her to the hall closet for the hot water bottle. The child came back and said it was all dried out and cracked open. Useless. Lying there she could appreciate the good health she'd been blessed with all her days. Hot, then cold, she swam in and out of consciousness.

"You okay?" Lou asked sometime in the twilight of late evening.

"Still f-f-freezing," Imo managed. Her limbs were ice. "Royce call?"

"Yes."

"Well, what did he say?"

"I told him you were sick."

"And?"

"And he said he'd call back later. He was going somewhere."

Imo stared at the ceiling. "Lou?" she called feebly.

"Yessum?"

"There is something you could do for me," Imogene said. "Heat me a brick up. In the oven. Then when it's good and hot, wrap it in a dishrag."

"What?" Lou stepped closer and peered at her.

"When I was little, and it was so cold in the winter," Imo said, pulling the quilt up over her chin, "we'd heat a brick on the hearth in the evenings and then carry it into bed with us. Warms up the sheets."

Lou stared at her.

"Just run get a brick out of the potato house and put it in the oven at 400 degrees."

Lou raised one eyebrow. "O-kay."

Imo smiled and drifted into sleep listening to the background noise of Jeanette's TV. A grandma. She'd be a grandma soon! She had to face the music. But not now. She had all she could deal with at the moment with this flu. *But Royce'll be a comfort when he gets here . . .*

Imo jumped when Lou slid a warm brick between the sheets. "Royce?" Imo surfaced slowly from sleep. She had dreamed he was there, with ginger ale and crackers. For an instant she imagined the brick was him.

"No. It's me," Lou said. "Martha came by with chicken soup."

Four days had passed, if she was correct on her days and nights. She cringed at the high volume of Jeanette's TV show. Her legs still ached, but now she was hot. The fever sent her brain places she wished it wouldn't. Terrible images of herself falling off a cliff.

"Lou?" she called out feebly when she heard a knock at the door.

Lou seemed so small as she stood in the doorway. Pale and small.

"Mr. Sosebee here?"

"No. It's Martha again. She wants to know how you're feeling."

"Tell her I'd rather have a broken leg. Thank her for the soup."

"Yes ma'am."

Suddenly her brain changed tracks. It went to the one where Jeanette lay, swollen with child. "Don't let Martha in the house!" she yelled to Lou. "Don't want her exposed to this!" She was breathless. "Tell her I'll call her about the Garden Club Christmas party."

"Okay," said Lou.

Imo relaxed when she heard Martha's car shift from reverse to forward and go crunching away on the gravel.

She wondered what had become of Royce. Maybe she'd call him. Then she wondered if she could tolerate the smoke from his cigarettes with the way she felt now. Oh well, if they meant him, she would have to. She dialed his number and put the phone up to her hot ear.

"Royce?"

"Hello, Imo."

"How are you?" she peeped.

"Doing okay. Listen, I'm on my way to bingo. Running late as it is, can I call you when I get back?"

"Yes, goodbye," she said, and hung up. She lay there picturing him at the bingo game with his lucky arrowhead, smoking away.

To her surprise, he was still smoking like a chimney, gob-
bling up high fat foods, and avoiding his three mile a day
walk. Three things the doctor said would extend his life.

He was set in his ways. If *she'd* gone through heart surgery
twice, she would follow the doctor's orders to a T. Silas had
done all he could once he went to the doctor and got his di-
agnosis. But at that point, no amount of carrot juice or
chemo could give him back his vitality.

She guessed it was unfair of her to compare Royce with
Silas. He surely didn't measure up. The Lord knew she was
trying to go forward and not to look back, but her heart had
a mind of its own, and lying in bed was hard work, and really, she had no choice but to dwell on her life. On Silas.

Back in the back of her memory, it was *Silas*, holding her
now while she was so sick. She sipped some warm ginger
ale. This relationship she had with Royce made her stop
and think about how wonderful Silas was.

Relationship. The word rolled over her with the tingle of
a mild electric shock. She had never imagined the com-
plexities of merging two people who'd lived separate lives for
so long. The smoking and the bingo, she had decided she
could tolerate, but this really disappointed her. Not showing
hide nor hair in her hour of need. She could forgive him for
not coming around at the height of her fever, with his weak
heart and all. But a whole week was inexcusable! And after
she'd nursed him so tenderly following his surgery.

She sighed. No flowers, no candy, no pretty card, or bal-
loon. Imo heard the organ chords that announced the five

o'clock news drift across the hallway. She lay there in disbelief. A still small voice told her this flu was actually a good thing to test the mettle of Royce's commitment—before she hitched herself permanently to him and they hit a real valley together.

Think real hard, Imo. Yep, it was a *brick* that kept you company and gave you some relief.

The bathroom and the baseboards were the places Imo planned to tackle first. Four days to clean, polish and bake until the Garden Club Christmas party.

Pale December light scattered in through the open blinds. She liked the thought of giving the place a thorough cleaning because being in bed for a week had really left a film of dust and cobwebs everywhere. Lou had done a lot for a fourteen-year-old child, but you could not expect her to think of details like scrubbing the toilet. Poor child had had enough just keeping them all fed and tended to.

She pulled up her rubber gloves with a tidy, satisfying *snap!* and poured a quarter cup of bleach into her bucket.

Imo scrubbed away and sang "The Old Rugged Cross," a hymn that always comforted her. She couldn't think of one thing better for helping her wounded spirit. "I'll cling to the old rugged cross, till my trophies at last I lay down," she puffed out in rhythm to her labor. "Yes, I'll cling to the old rugged cross, and exchange them someday for a crown, A-mennnn," she drew out the ending.

"A brick heated up in the oven!" She shook her head. Well,

Royce was a book she had closed. *Move on, Imo, and don't look back.* Maybe she'd start a home-business selling bricks with names like Joe or Bill that had batteries inside to heat them up. She smiled for the first time in over a week. Chasing men had brought her nothing but trouble and heartache. She didn't know why she'd convinced herself that was the thing to do. They weren't worth it.

Except Silas, of course. But that was another story. She'd never be able to replace him. She would just forget the man-hunt and get along much better with her life.

Imo sprinkled Comet into the sink and scoured away. She paused to stare out the bathroom window at the crepe myrtles which had finally turned. December was a little late for that, but Euharlee was always unseasonably warm. Christmas day usually meant iced tea and potato chips, instead of hot cocoa and chestnuts roasting over an open fire. Christmas without Silas wouldn't be easy, she thought. She would find a way to get it behind her.

Martha appeared while Imo was sucking up dust balls with the Hoover. She startled Imo.

"Howdy, howdy," Martha said. "I came to help."

"Oh, how nice," Imo oozed sweetly while thinking fast. "All I've got left to do is the fun part. Baking and decorating. Why don't you just go right on back home and cut me some of your smilax for decorating."

"I'll polish the serving pieces." Martha removed her sweater and rolled up her sleeves.

Imo untied her apron. "No, no. Let me walk you outside and show you how pretty my nandinas are."

Here she had cleaned for two days straight. Aired every corner. Not a dust mote left. And even though that stubborn, proud part of her knew she couldn't hide the sullied part of her life forever, she'd be durned if she'd let Jeanette's condition ruin the Christmas party.

Just then, from the girls' bedroom, came a loud moan, and Jeanette hollering, "Will somebody in this friggin' house please come help me?"

Imo froze. "Just a jiffy," she sang down the hallway, "let me see Martha to the door first."

"Hon', you go tend to her. I'll wait."

Imo sighed and raced down the hall. In the semi-darkness of the bedroom she could make out that Jeanette was up on all fours, with her forehead resting on her pillow.

"What's the matter?" she hissed.

"Back hurts like shit." Jeanette started to cry.

"Hush now." Imo rubbed her back. Maybe this was it, she thought, sitting on the edge of the bed. Jeanette hollered again and Imo turned on the lamp. "I'll call the doctor when Martha's gone," she whispered.

Jeanette's nostrils flared with excitement. She squeezed her eyes shut and let out a big breath. "Better now," she said.

"Is this the first pain you've had like that?"

"No." Jeanette shook her head, flopping onto her side and stuffing a pillow underneath her belly.

Martha came into the room, wearing her tending-to-the-sick face. She bent over them with her wide eyes aimed right at Jeanette's swollen belly. "My goodness gracious!"

she gasped, pulling away and blinking."I had no idea!" Martha lifted her chin.

Imo gave Martha her saddest *I'm sorry* smile and sighed from the depths of her soul. "I don't know what's wrong with me, Martha. I should have told my best friend."

Martha closed her eyes. For a minute Imo thought she'd lost her.

"Well, this sure explains a lot of your behavior, hon'. Listen, I never thought you grieved enough for Silas. Remember I used to say to you to just cry it out?" She asked. "Keeping all those emotions over him bottled up inside of you messed with your mind. As the young folks say."

Imo played along. "You surely were right, Martha. You always are. I should have listened to the minister's wife, of all people. I should've cried."

Late in the day, Martha and Imo made cheese straws together while Jeanette slept peacefully. It really hadn't been as bad as she expected. She felt much lighter and festive, too. She put on a Perry Como Christmas album from 1968 and they grated and baked while he crooned melodies.

"Sometimes I can't figure God out, Imo," Martha stirred away.

Imo didn't like the serious tone of Martha's voice. Also, she thought, the Reverend's wife shouldn't talk like that.

"I mean, what do you think He's doing when He lets Vera conceive Loutishie out of wedlock, and her not even wanting a child. And now, Jeanette." Martha shook her head slowly back and forth at the mystery of it all.

"I don't believe we should question His ways."

"Well, I'm not finished. You and that Silas, pining away for fruit from your own loins, and *married*, God-fearing folks, and couldn't even have one." Martha scrubbed the grater in hot soapy water.

One thing about Martha was that she was honest, but sometimes her candor was hard to take.

"There's things I don't understand myself, Martha. But now, I raised Vera, and then Lou. And then I got Jeanette. Didn't even have to go through nine months of being pregnant or the pain of childbirth, either. And look-a-here, now I'm getting another one—that makes four! I've had three already, and I'm getting number four!" She hadn't held a baby in ages.

First Imo laughed about it all, and then she cried. In her heart, she knew her friend was searching for answers to some of life's mysteries, too.

They finished the cheese straws and moved onto pecan fudge. "Reckon we ought to do some date-nut balls?" Martha asked.

"Maybe so. Whatever's left, you and me can divide up and have for our families," Imo said. "If there's still too much, we can carry it out to the old folks' home."

"That's the spirit of Christmas, hon'." Martha gazed out the window while Imo got the pecans out of the freezer.

"I'm wondering something, Imogene." Martha didn't make eye contact.

A silence fell.

"What?" Imo whacked at the dates on the cutting board.

"Who's the father?" Martha asked. "You know?"

"Of course I do." Her eyes filled with tears.

"Why, honey." Martha moved over and patted Imo's shoulder. "You don't have to tell me if you don't want to. I didn't mean to meddle."

Lord God. She was losing it again. Maybe she was still weak from the flu and her break-up with Royce which she still hadn't mentioned to Martha.

Imo swiped her wet chin on her shoulder. "It was one of those foreigners from over at the Sioux Village trailer park."

"Those dark folks?" Martha's jaw hung open.

"Yes."

"He going to marry her?" Martha asked, her voice falling to a whisper.

"No," Imo said.

"What are you going to do?"

"*All is calm, all is bright,*" Perry crooned.

Imo stiffened. "Well, I reckon I'll throw a Christmas party and help raise a baby," Imo said, her voice rising. She knew that wasn't fair to Martha when she was only concerned. But there were just too many things beyond her control.

On the day of the party Imo carried the Christmas table cloths outside. She gave them a snap and draped them over the line to air. She checked the frozen punch ring in the deep freeze. The strawberries and orange wedges suspended in lime Kool-Aid would certainly look festive floating in the punch bowl. She cut some greenery from her holly bushes and settled it around the base of a pink poinsettia. What a pretty sight the living room was! Maybe she'd get through this after all.

Lou was gone to her buddies' house and, so she fed Jeanette an early supper and washed that up. Now, if she'd only drift off to sleep during the party, things would be perfect. But that's not how things were going in her life. Probably Jeanette would have the baby, right in the middle of the festivities.

Bingo got up on his hind legs and pressed a greasy snout on her freshly Windexed window. She went out, grabbed his collar, and dragged him to the barn. She locked him in, trying her best to ignore his whimpers. He was the type of dog to shove his snout in all the girl's crotches, and so she felt justified, even when he looked accusingly at her with almost human eyes. Then a hen strutted right up onto the porch and settled herself in a lawn chair.

"Misery loves company," Imo said, scooping her up and depositing her in the barn with Bingo.

She walked down the hallway to look in on Jeanette. Martha said a baby might mellow the girl, but Imo wasn't even allowing herself to hope.

Outside, the sky was darkening with gray clouds. Maybe there would be a storm during the party. She paused, close to tears. The whole week, up to today, had been so sunny and clear it looked like a painting.

She tried to focus on the blinking golden lights draped around the fir tree. A huge boom of thunder shook the farm house, and the lights flickered. A new fear seized her. How could she have a party without being able to heat the Swedish meatballs and turn the tree lights on? What about coffee? They couldn't have a party or sweets without coffee.

Well, maybe the storm would be over by five.

At four the rain was coming down in sheets and the sky was as dark as Egypt. She rearranged the greenery and simmered some cloves and allspice on the stove. She put on her black pumps, hose and her nice red dress with the reindeer pin fastened at her shoulder. It had to stop by five. There just wasn't enough rain in heaven to keep on like this.

She ran the punch bowl and glass cups under the faucet in the bathtub to knock the dust off and settled herself in a chair to wait for Martha who was coming over thirty minutes early.

Martha came in, breathless, as she untied the plastic straps of her rain bonnet. "The bottom dropped out on us, but we won't let it dampen our holiday spirits, will we? You just sit and relax and let me take over."

Imo watched Martha set a dripping bag down. She hung oranges covered with cloves from the little plastic cup hooks all around the top of the punchbowl. "Now that's real pretty. Straight out of *Southern Living!*" Martha stepped back to admire her work. A minute later Martha hung mistletoe on the doorway from the hall into the den and on the piece of molding which separated the kitchen from the den.

It sure was a comfort to have her bustling around, preheating the oven and pouring herself a cup of coffee like she owned the place. "Alrighty, Imo, time to warm up the sausage balls." She pulled on a reindeer hot-mitt.

This first Christmas without Silas was harder than Imo expected. Each card she opened may as well have contained a photo of him. "Our thoughts are with you . . . . As you sit cozily by the fire with your loved ones . . . .Wishing you and your family the best . . ." and some were even still addressed to Silas and Imogene Lavender. From folks and organizations long out of touch.

Martha rolled up her sleeves and pulled on an apron to mix the punch while Imo set out the cold food and the cake knife.

"I'm going to take down that angel," Imo blurted out with a teary laugh. She grabbed a kitchen chair and dragged it over beside the tree. It was a silver angel Silas had given her their first Christmas together. She thought she could handle it when she put it up there, just treat it like the inanimate object that it was. She said to herself that it should only serve as a reminder of the happy life they had together. Now all she knew was that she had to get it out of sight.

"You do that, hon'. Move that big gold star to the top," Martha ordered.

She did.

"Myrtice! You come on in here and dry yourself off and get a cup of coffee," Martha stood at the door and yelled.

As the girls arrived in the downpour, they spread out raincoats, umbrella's, and even a plastic trash bag over the sofa and the chair backs in the den. Slowly they all got coffee and dried their hair, patting perms and powder and rearranging ear bobs.

Then came the usual holiday chatter about family that was coming over for the dinners and parties and plays. When they asked Imo how she was making out this season and squeezed her wrists, she said, "I'm fine."

"I know its hard, dear," Winnie said. "I cried the whole month of December the year Ed passed away."

"Uh huh," agreed Brenda, "I stayed in bed Christmas through New Years after Tex was gone. Every little thing, especially the advertisements for those little electric shavers that have on reindeer antlers, made me cry."

Brenda turned to face Winnie, and they went on. They could discuss all this so easily, Imo thought, as she listened to bits and pieces of their chatter.

The sides of the frozen punch ring were fuzzy with lime sherbet. Imo ladled the froth into cups as the girls formed two lines alongside the dining table.

"Everything is just scrump-dilly-ishus!" Brenda said enthusiastically, balancing a plate on her knees. The girls all nodded, and Imo turned over the album.

"Oh listen," said Winnie, "I just love White Christmas."

"Me too," Viola said.

"Looks like we'll be singing Wet Christmas," Brenda laughed. A clap of thunder shook the house. "Goodness, I'm glad it's not cold enough to freeze yet."

There was another huge boom, and the electricity went off. Jeanette cried out.

"Oh no," Imo sighed.

The room went pitch black. No one moved.

"I'll go hunt up the flashlight and some candles," Imo said. She felt her way in the darkness to the kitchen. The potholder drawer had three long candles in the back and a book of matches. She turned on the flashlight, lit all three candles, settled them into pools of hot wax on saucers. She carried them one by one into the center of the living room. They sure made the girls look younger.

Next Imo flew down the hall with the flashlight. She slid into Jeanette's room and patted her hip. "Power's out," she said softly.

"I know."

"Probably be back on shortly. You okay?"

"Bored."

"Here's the flashlight. Maybe you can read a spell."

"Don't worry," Jeanette yelled as Imo went out into the hallway, "I'll stay out of sight of all your Christian friends."

That girl had no modesty. Not that it mattered. Imo was sure they all knew about her predicament by now. They just weren't mentioning it around her.

When she got back to the girls, they were ready to play the mystery gift game. Every year, they each brought unmarked gifts of five dollars or less and piled them under the tree. Then they drew numbers out of a hat. Number one chose a gift and opened it. Number two could take number one's gift or pick another one, and so on until the last person had her pick of all the opened gifts or the last mystery gift on the floor.

Martha took over. Everyone squinted through candle-light at Winnie, who was number one. She unwrapped an artificial African violet. The kind they sold at the Dollar Store for a couple of bucks.

Everyone had a good laugh. It was no secret that real African violets were cheap enough and one of the easiest things to keep alive.

Number two opened a rubber finger with a chord hanging out of the end. The tag said it was an electric nose picker. "Guess I'm stuck!" Viola laughed. "No one will try to take this!"

"Alrighty. Number three?" Martha asked.

Glennis Cobb reached into the pile of presents and picked one wrapped in red foil with a wide green velvet bow. "Purtiest one," she said, and unwrapped it slowly and carefully, smoothing out the paper and ribbon in her lap. She removed the lid and rustled down into the tissue paper and pulled out what appeared to be an oversized bottle of prescription pills. She leaned forward into the candle light. "Niagara?" she questioned. "That what it says? We honeymooned at Niagara Fall. What kind of a pill is this?"

Brenda was laughing behind her hand. "Says Viagra. With a V. Found it at one of those Spencer's stores in Atlanta."

Glennis raised up her glasses to read the fine print on the label. Her neck turned pink.

"What is it?" Imo asked.

Brenda said, "It's a wonder drug, darlin'. You haven't heard of it? That's not the real thing though. It's sugar pills. The real thing you have to get from a doctor."

"Well, what is it for?"

"Rejuvenates the sex drive in old men."

"Oh, honey," said Winnie, "I have heard of that." She dropped her voice to a whisper. "I consider an impotent husband a blessing."

"Amen," said Martha, "we older women deserve a break!"

"My Elmer is seventy-seven. Despite his heart, he still wants a roll in the hay several times a week," said Brenda. "I think he needs to take up fishing." Heh heh heh. She gazed off into space.

Viola nodded. "Yessum. I was relieved when Jack hit sixty-seven, and his sex drive finally began to diminish."

Imo glanced around the room furtively. Surely some of the girls enjoyed intercourse. They were all acting like it was just something they endured. She cleared her throat.

"Well, *I* like it," peeped Maimee, the meekest, most unassuming of them all.

"What the hey," said Myrtice, "me, too."

"I like it, too." Imo sat up straight. "Liked it,"she corrected herself.

"Well, not me, hon'. I'm not interested in anything that will pep him up in the sex department." Martha ate a piece of fudge. "A man must've invented it."

Much laughter.

Only three out of fifteen, Imo mused. Of course, not everyone had cast their vote. She took off her right earbob and squeezed it in her palm, remembering Silas and the way he felt in her arms. The earthy smell of his armpits and the salty taste of his neck.

Sometimes she'd see a couple kissing on TV or run across a passionate scene in a novel, and she'd give herself permission to have what she called a bedroom memory. Just for a fleeting moment.

"Your turn, Imo. You're number seven, right?"

She jumped. "Yes. Yes. I believe I am." She concentrated on moving toward the dwindling heap of gifts on the floor in front of her. Finally she chose a gift wrapped in childish Santa Claus paper and returned to her seat with everybody's eyes on her.

Her plan was just to hang onto whatever gift she selected or let any number claim it if they wanted it. She didn't care a fig about the game going on. She had thoughts in her head now that needed tending to.

"How funny," she said when she got it open. It was a little gardening kit that said *You Can Grow The World's Largest Tomato!* The plastic wrapped box contained a pre-fertilized soil pellet with seeds already in it. You just added water to expand the pellet inside of a fake terra-cotta pot to get it started, then you had a little trowel to transplant it and a book on making it grow large.

There were murmurs of interest in the little kit, and Imo reckoned it wouldn't stay hers long. If it did, she'd give it to Lou.

She was right. Viola was number eight and she said she wanted the tomato kit, so Imo unwrapped a little Hershey Kiss encased in a glass dome with a tiny silver hammer. The base of the globe said to break it open in case of an emergency.

"I've got it!" Viola screeched, and they all stopped what they were doing and turned to her. "If I can get hold of some of that Viagra, I can add it to the fertilizer and I won't have to stake up my tomato plant!"

This time there was an explosion of laughter which turned into breathless snorts, and the girls bent over double, holding their sides and shaking. Even Imo laughed.

They kept re-telling the Viagra-tomato joke throughout the rest of the gift game and then collapsing with laughter. In the end Imo wound up with a miniature singing Christmas tree named Everett Green that ran on two AA batteries and that she was sure cost more than five dollars. She planned to give it to Jeanette for the baby.

Later, as the party wound down, and the power came back on, they brewed more coffee and finished up the sausage balls and coconut cake.

It was a cool, clear night when she stepped out on the porch to see her guests off. The yard was full of twigs. Martha stayed awhile to help clean the kitchen and when her Dodge rounded the corner, Imo put on her gardening shoes and walked outside to release Bingo and the hen. She gave Bingo leftover pound cake.

The television was on in Jeanette's room when Imo got back inside. She unplugged the tree lights and crept into her own room and unfastened her festive holiday pin and pulled off her dress. She looked at her shape in the full-length mirror. By lamplight, it wasn't bad. Every woman got a little bit stout after the change.

Her hands trembled when she slipped into her gown.

She crawled into the cold sheets and patted the contours of her body. What was it again that made her think she was through with men? With a relationship that included snuggles and cuddles and flesh against flesh?

Loutishie's Notebook

Getting rid of Mr. Sosebee didn't solve all of our problems. More than anything else on earth, I wanted Imo to be happy, and she was not. She huffed around outside in the garden; working ashes into the dirt around her peonies, and spraying lime sulfur.

Our house was more depressing than ever. Jeanette shuffled around in her fuzzy pink slippers and her maternity gown that made her look like a tent. She was a swollen, weepy mess.

Every chance I got, I ran outside. Into the sunny fifty-degree weather of mid-December. Ran by the sumac and pyracantha, which were laden with berries, down to the bottoms. Fool that I was, I thought my world had already collapsed when Uncle Silas died.

It was Christmas break from school, and it was no break at all. It had never occurred to me that I would ever long to be back in the classroom. My object in life, before Uncle Silas's passing, was to endure school and then race home afterwards, where I could really live. Spending my time outdoors, with Bingo on my heels. That was my definition of the good life.

I could just keep running, I thought to myself that awful December. Live in the woods. Get my food from wherever I could find it. Leave that crazy, sad household behind.

Bingo ran up beside me. "Arrrooo," his throat quivered as he howled. I stopped running.

"I know it, boy," I said, hunkering down beside him. "I miss Uncle Silas, too."

THIRTEEN

Old-Fashioned Gardening

*"Seedless? Nosirreebobtail. Dern foreigners grow
them new-fangled melons that ain't got no seeds.
I like mine the old-fashioned way.
With bees doing the pollinatin'"*
— FENTON MABRY
a farmer selling produce in the Wal-Mart parking lot,
explaining about his melons

*I*mo didn't know what woke her until she sat up and heard it again. Jeanette wailed out into the dark.

It was Christmas Eve.

"Owwwwww," followed by cussing worse than a sailor's, wafted across the hall from Jeanette's room.

Imo's heart moved into her throat.

Stay calm. You're ready. You knew this was coming. In fact, the baby's ten days late. There's time to get to the hospital, though, if she just started her pains.

Imo slid into her shoes and checked her overnight bags, packed and waiting in the corner since the end of October.

She shook Lou's shoulder. "We're going to the hospital. I'll call when the baby's here."

Lou looked at her through the gray fog of the nightlight. "What?"

"You didn't hear Jeannie?"

"Thought it was a dream," Lou murmured.

Jeanette was on all fours in the den, rocking and cussing. Her forehead was braced against the brick hearth with her lips drawn back and her eyes closed.

"Come on, Jeannie. Let's go."

"Cain't," she spat out, rocking forward and moaning.

A surge of adrenalin turned Imo into a quick thinking, take-charge woman. She slid her hands into Jeanette's armpits and dragged her to the car.

"Son of a bitch," Jeanette muttered.

Imo fumbled with the keys in the dark shed. Finally, the cold engine turned over, she scratched out, and flew toward Paris Street.

She craned her ear over the back seat where Jeanette lay wrapped in a quilt.

"How far apart are the pains?"

"Sheee-utt . . . ," Jeanette hissed.

"Jeannie? Don't you push. Five more minutes. Give me five more minutes . . ."

"I cain't. Lord God A'mighty!"

The moon gave a luminous wash to the landscape as Imo accelerated up to seventy-five, then eighty. The Impala shuddered. When she was two lights from the hospital she broke out in song. "Rock of ages, cleft for me, let me hide myself in thee," she sang to block out the foul language that was coming from the back seat.

Imo sped into the hospital lot, parked, and ran in through the emergency room. She grabbed an orderly who wheeled a stretcher out and hastened Jeanette up to the maternity floor. The girl's common streak was really showing now. Imo prayed there would be nobody she knew at the hospital as she followed the stretcher.

An artificial Christmas tree sat in one corner of the maternity waiting room. A few nurses with Santa hats on were walking up and down the hallway.

Imo had a sudden panic. What would they name the baby? Royce had told her that the doctor said it was a boy. It was amazing they could do that these days and Imo wondered how God felt about it. But still, they could be wrong. They could name the baby Noelle if it was a girl. If it did turn out to be a boy, maybe Nicholas.

No, Joseph. A biblical name would be better. Except, Imo always thought the Mexican people were being sacrilegious when they had so many boys called Jesus over there, even though they didn't pronounce it like the Baptists.

The doctor called her name. He was smiling. "Mrs. Lavender, you've got a grandson. Five pounds and three ounces."

"He's okay?"

"He's fine. Small enough that the mother didn't need

many stitches. But apparently healthy, they're running tests. Got a nice set of lungs."

"And Jeannie?"

"She's got a nice set of lungs, too." The doctor laughed. "She's fine." He laughed more and shook his head.

Imo followed him down to the silver swinging doors of delivery. She didn't know what she expected to see, but the sight of Jeanette in a madonna and child pose made her catch her breath. There was a dark little newborn, swaddled in a hospital blanket, laid against her bosom. Jeanette was smiling.

"Hello." Imo bent down to search the tiny brown face. She touched a tiny hand.

"Ain't he gorgeous?" Jeanette's eyes glistened.

Imo stroked his cheek. "What's his name?"

Jeanette laughed. "Peanut."

"What kind of a name is that?"

"Relax, Mama. I'm kidding. I don't know. Ricky or Dusty or Duane or something."

Imo forced a smile. "Oh." With Jeanette, you couldn't state any opinion or offer your own suggestion. She worked in reverse like Brer Rabbit and the briar patch. Imo went out in the hall to find a private phone.

Lou picked up on the first ring. "Hello?" She was breathless.

"It's a boy. Everyone's fine. We'll be home tomorrow."

"Merry Christmas, Imo."

"Why, it surely is. Merry Christmas to you, too. Now

there's some cornbread dressing in the big freezer and a can of cranberry sauce in the cabinet. You call Martha if you need a thing." Imo hung up and hurried back to Jeanette's room.

"I'll hold him and let you get some sleep." Imo scooped the infant up. When she put her hand on his cheek, he looked up and met her eyes, like he was memorizing her face.

Jeanette's eyes were on them. "I brung him a pacifier," she said, and crept over to the shelf in front of the window where her overnight bag sat. Rummaging around in the bag, she knocked it to the floor. A small gold picture frame skittered across the linoleum and landed next to Imo's feet.

"I'll get it dear." Imo cradled the baby with one hand and bent over. She figured it was one of the rock stars Jeanette thought so much of.

It startled her to see Silas looking at her. An old black and white picture taken of him at boot camp, he had the typical army buzz cut and the face of a boy.

Imo's chest rose and fell as she stared at Silas.

Jeanette poked the pacifier at the baby's tiny brown lips. "Silas," she said. "I'm naming him Silas."

Silas sat up on his five month birthday. On his six month birthday he was already scooting himself along and getting into everything. Jeanette and Imo ran along behind him, clearing the floor and buffering his falls.

Every day left them both exhausted. Imo did get a little

bit of a garden in, and she'd managed to water, weed, and mulch enough to get by, but she'd had to depend on Lou for a good amount of the elbow grease.

She wished she could duplicate herself; one to help with Silas, since Jeanette was still so unsure of herself, and one to garden side by side with Lou. There were still some things she craved, and her hands in the dirt was one.

Another thing she was craving was the sweet taste of an old fashioned Crimson Sweet watermelon. She could just about kick herself for not planting any this year.

Today she would go out in search of one. There were plenty of roadside stands with pyramids of melons for sale.

She waited to leave until Silas was down for his afternoon nap, but the interior of the Impala was scorching, and she had to roll down the windows for a spell before she could get in. She walked out to check the garden while she waited. Her three rows of sweet corn weren't quite filled out enough yet, and the tomatoes were still hard and green. She gathered a handful of banana peppers and walked to the side yard.

She paused beside a patch of volunteer black-eyed Susans that were in full splendor. She'd been so pre-occupied with the baby that her fancy city flowers were taken over by fescue.

She paused to think of Henry then, and that led up to Royce. Two that she had scratched off, and here she was, drying up, every day a little closer to the ground, with nothing but memories to keep her company at night.

She straightened the towel she kept on the vinyl seat of the Impala. Cruising the back roads of Euharlee she passed an El Camino full of cantaloupes and some of the long light-green watermelons.

She was looking for the round, dark green ones, so she headed out toward Cartersville. There were occasional road side stands which advertised sorghum syrup, squash, peaches, and tomatoes. The third one she passed had two of the Crimson Sweets on a bed of hay.

She couldn't just take the first ones she came to, could she? The thrill was in the hunt, searching the highways and byways for that perfect melon.

Heat made mirages on the paved roads which ran between lush carpets of kudzu. She rolled down her window and waves of Deep-South heat engulfed her. She snaked her arm past the side of her seat and got the back seat's window down, too.

It cleared her head to have natural air, the way God intended. Imo didn't care about her coiffure anymore. Let the wind whip it where it would. She did good these days, with a baby at her feet, to get on her lipstick.

Imo considered heading to Wal-Mart for formula since she was already out this far. She smiled at an image of little Silas's fuzzy dark hair above his impish face. He got so excited when he saw his bottle coming.

She turned into the Wal-Mart lot. Out of the corner of her eye, she spotted an old '54 Chevy truck at the edge of the lot. That was one vehicle she knew because that was the first one she and big Silas had owned.

There were watermelons in the back of it, and an old

gentleman in overalls sitting in an aluminum folding chair beside it. She'd stop quickly and see if they happened to be Crimson Sweets.

She got her handbag and stepped out into blinding hot sunlight. Shielding her eyes with her hand, she marched up the slight incline of the lot.

Walking around to spy on the type of melons, she said "how do" to the man.

He stood up and tipped his hat. He was ancient. A hearing aid wire traveled from his leathery ear down into his collar. He reminded Imo of those apple dolls you see up in the North Georgia mountains.

"These Crimson Sweets?" she asked.

He inclined his ear to her. "What'd you say?"

"I said, are these Crimson Sweets?"

"Yes ma'am," he said.

How quaint and charming, he called her ma'am! He had a twinkle in his eye, and the knees of his overalls were stained with the familiar red of Georgia clay. She wanted to talk with him some more.

"These good?" she asked.

He was spry enough. He walked over to her, nothing more than a sack of bones stuck inside the roomy overalls. He thumped one of the melons and gestured to her to pick it up and see how heavy it was.

Next he fingered the stem, which was dying back, and then flipped one over to show off its pale buttery-yellow underside.

"If that don't prove it," he smiled, "this oughter do it." He pulled out a pocket knife and sliced one open.

He gave Imo a chunk.

"Thank you," she said, and chomped down into the sweet red flesh. "Delicious. And the heart, no less. The heart is my favorite part, because it doesn't have seeds."

"But spitting seeds is half the fun of eatin' a watermelon," he cackled.

"I'll take three of these," Imo said. Then, "What'd you use for your fertilizer?" to keep him going.

"Well, there you go." He smiled.

"I said, what did you use for fertilizer?" she yelled so hard into his ear that he jumped.

"A little lime. That and some cow manure," he said.

Now this was a man after her own heart, Imo thought to herself. "I don't care much for those yellow-meat watermelons," she confided to him.

"Me neither."

"Or those seedless ones," she went on.

"Seedless?" He shook his head sadly. "Dern foreigners grow them thangs. Them new-fangled melons what ain't got no seeds. I like mine the old fashioned way. With bees doing the pollinatin'."

She liked this man's style. There was no ring on his left hand.

"Imogene Lavender," she patted her chest.

"Fenton. Fenton Mabry."

"Very nice to make your acquaintance, Mr. Mabry." She glanced around for a conversation piece, anything that would keep the conversation going. No, she wouldn't mention the fact that he and Silas had the same truck. There was a bumper sticker on the back that said "My Other Car's a Mule."

"Is that true?" She pointed at it.

"Name's Ruby Jane," he said proudly. "My granddaughter put that on there."

"I see," Imo said, "you have a granddaughter." There was a possibility his wife was deceased, though. "And your wife, Fenton, does she help out with your watermelons?"

"Josephine passed away in '71."

"Oh, I'm so sorry to hear that." She wasn't really, though.

Instinct told her she could leave off the feminine wiles with Fenton Mabry, and focus on gardening and farming talk.

"You know," Imo said, "my tomatoes have been a bit scrawny this year. Now last year was a banner year, but I can't figure out what's going on this year."

He glanced at her. "Eh?"

"That's right. Same thing with my butter beans. Reckon it's been the dry spring we had."

"Dry spring," he repeated, swiping his forehead on his sleeve.

Imo looked at the Wal-Mart, searching for something else to say. There was a line of drink machines and stacks of styrofoam coolers.

"Let me bring you a cold drink," she gushed. "You hold onto my melons, and I'll be back in just a jiffy."

Imo walked on air. Didn't even feel the heat wafting up

from the asphalt. She felt a little thrill as she bought two ice cold Pepsi's.

"I had a mule when I was little," she said to Fenton as they stood at the tailgate. "Daddy hoed the crops by hand and plowed with our mule. Mostly burley tobacco."

Fenton chuckled.

"He raised a few watermelons, too. And beef cattle. Herefords. I've still got a small herd. Prettiest cattle on earth."

"You don't say."

She ran a finger around the top of her Pepsi can. Was she coming on too strong? Too blousy? She checked her watch. Little Silas would be getting up any minute. It was now or never. What would it hurt?

Imogene put on her sweetest Southern hospitality voice. "Fenton," she oozed, "I'd like to invite you to supper."

"I'd be real tickled to come," he said, and leaned over so close she thought he was going to kiss her right there in the Wal-Mart lot.

Loutishie's Notebook

Imo about rocked the rockers off her chair singing to little Silas. I was glad because he took her mind off things.

Nobody said a word about what day it was on the third Saturday in February. I didn't know what I was supposed to do on the first anniversary of Uncle Silas's death. I guessed it was whatever the opposite of a party was.

What I did was, I got a roll of toilet paper out of the towel closet, and begged Jeanette to drive me up to his grave. It was noon when we pulled up to the cemetery. I walked up the hill alone.

"Hey," I said and knelt at the foot of his grave. "It's me. I miss you." I swallowed a lump in my throat. It was harder than praying. "Imo's fine. Jeanette had her baby, you know. Named after you."

I hunched over and tears ran down to the tip of my nose and fell into the soil right about where I figured Uncle Silas's heart would be.

In April, Imo did plant lima beans, cucumbers, tomatoes and bush beans. In July, this ratty old pickup truck with the fenders and the hood shaking came down our road. It shuddered to a stop, and an old man got out.

"How do, miss?" He tipped his hat at me.

"Loutishie," Imo said, "I want you to meet Mr. Fenton Mabry." He stayed for supper.

"Fenton, would you say grace?" Imo asked.

"Our most gracious heavenly fa-tha," he began. It was a loud prayer, asking for rain and that the President of the United States of America would have wisdom to lead us and that all the hungry stomachs in the world would be filled along with having their hearts turned toward Jesus. He was either Pentecostal Holiness or snake-handling Baptist because he asked for the power and glory of God to descend on mankind.

Finally, his voice raised up high like he was about to wind down. I saw Jeanette pushing back her cuticles with the butter knife.

"And Fa-tha," he intoned, "we ask that you keep us ever needful of other people's minds. Amen."

Jeanette giggled first. Then I started and couldn't stop myself. Imo lifted her head and pierced us with a look. "Girls!"

"It's quite alright, Mrs. Lavender," he said. "I believe I did get the end of that thing backward." Then he laughed harder at himself than the two of us put together, slapping the table and slinging spit everywhere.

"Girls," Imo said, "can you tell Mr. Mabry how tasty his watermelons were."

"Great," I said.

"Well, there you go." He helped himself to a biscuit and passed them over to me.

Just then little Silas cried out, and Jeanette ran to get him. Imo laughed. "**That's** the reason I didn't get my melons in."

"Well, there you go," he said.

When Jeanette came carrying little Silas in, Mr. Mabry said, "A baby! I declare!" like he hadn't heard him yowling earlier.

"Back when I was a baby," he said, "Mama put all us young'uns out on a quilt at the edge of the field while she helped Daddy work."

"You serious?" Jeanette said.

"Well, there you go," he said again.

"Tell us about your place, Mr. Mabry," Imo said in the sweetest voice.

"Face?" He touched his cheek. "I got this big old scar when Ruby Jane threw her head up whilst I was unhitchin' her from the plow."

"I see," Imo said, while Jeanette about fell out of her chair laughing. Little Silas slapped his tray.

"Ain't he a handful?" Jeanette said to Mr. Mabry when she could speak again.

"Well, there you go," he answered.

"Girls," Imo whispered, "I don't believe Mr. Mabry hears well. Let's talk loud."

"What kind of farm you got?" Jeanette yelled.

Mr. Mabry smacked his hand on the table. "I didn't even have this thang on!" he said and twiddled a knob on his hearing aid. "Now we go. What harm? Didn't do much harm. Got a few stitches."

Jeanette was out of breath from laughing. "What I said was, tell us about your **farm.**"

"Don't have no farm," Mr. Mabry chuckled. "Don't even own a row to hoe anymore." He forked some okra.

"Where on earth do you grow your melons, then, Mr. Mabry?" Imo asked.

"Same place I grow my sweet potatoes, green beans, corn, peas, okra, and tomatoes."

He let those words hang in the air for a minute while he poured sorghum syrup into a hole in his biscuit that he made with his finger. He smiled. "You wouldn't know it to look at me, ladies. But I'm a millionaire on paper."

"Then why do you sell melons at the Wal-Mart?" Jeanette asked loudly.

He jumped a little. "I'm only a millionaire on paper, little lady. Saved my land from the IRS by donating it to the National Park

Service. I cut me a deal with them to let me and Ruby Jane keep on plowing till we die.

When my brother Benton passed away, four years ago, I got his half of the place. Old feller from the IRS come by and said the farm was not active cuz less than half of it was being farmed on." Fenton paused for a long swig of iced tea. "Meant I didn't qualify for a tax break." He shook his head. "You know, my daddy got that land in 1910 for $75 an acre, and they said it was worth $40,000 an acre now. Yessir, woulda' had to sell the place to them de-velopers to pay the Internal Revenuers."

FOURTEEN

Beefsteak

*"My word! In his eighties? You do realize that
you've got to be married for a minimum of ten years
to collect social security on a husband, don't you?"*
— MAIMEE HARRIS
Garden Club member, expressing concern
when Imogene confides that she's serious about Fenton

This had been a delicious two weeks. Fenton seemed as eager to spend time with Imo as she was to have him out to the house. Five times they'd shared gardening stories, supper, and walks along the Etowah.

He was perfect. In fact, there was nothing he said or did that was contrary. She didn't have to play bingo or inhale his smoke, didn't have to overlook a single thing. She didn't have to fuss with her hair and makeup.

It was like how she was with Silas. Comfortable even in the silences.

Imo stopped to smile at the memory of Fenton bringing another of his Crimson Sweets out to the house on his last

visit. She was planning a special cutting of it this very afternoon. You had to have the right setting to tell the girls
things. You couldn't just spring something this exciting on
them without preparation.

She would lay all her cards out on the table. Share the
joy of new love.

At two o'clock Imo carried the cold melon outside, to the
overgrown yard and spread a quilt on the ground.

She sliced it on a cookie sheet, and each section reminded
her of a big smile.

She and Lou shared a wedge, while Jeanette mashed up
some of the sweet pulp for little Silas. Life was good now.
Imo sat up straight, squared her shoulders, and began the
little speech she'd been rehearsing.

"It's been well over a year since your father passed away,
girls," she said. "You know he'll always be with us and no
one can ever take his place. Not in my heart or yours."

Now they were looking at her with mouths hanging open.

"Listen. I know I haven't known Mr. Mabry for very long,
but . . ."

Lou looked like she'd been stung by a bee, and Jeanette
puffed on a cigarette.

"So," Imo picked up little Silas and said the rest of her
speech into his tiny face, "I want you all to realize my intentions here. I enjoy being with Mr. Mabry. He makes me
feel alive. I believe we may turn out to be more than just
friends. I just wanted you girls to be aware . . ."

Lou's face crumpled. "No!" she shouted, jumping up and heading toward the bottoms.

"Give it time, Lou," she called after her.

Well, that was done. Time to call Martha.

She described Fenton in great detail. "So, what do you think?"

"I think that's fine, hon'. I don't know about the love at first sight thing. But, I reckon you're ready for a relationship, now that you've grieved sufficiently."

Imo closed her eyes. Lord God in heaven, she'd done her grieving. Cried her widowed heart out.

"What does he look like?" Martha asked.

"I'd say rugged. Been out in the sun a lot," Imo said.

"How old is he?"

Imogene squirmed. "It's not the miles, it's the maintenance." She'd practiced that line.

"I reckon," Martha said. "He a Baptist?"

"I'm not certain." Imogene realized she didn't know a lot of details about Fenton. Not his faith, about his childhood, his dead wife; nothing except that he gardened and owned a mule called Ruby Jane. "I'll find all that out and call you."

Martha drew in a quick breath. "Well, you just better be careful this day and age. He might turn out to be an axe-murderer. If I were you, I'd ask Sheriff Bentley to check him out. Run one of those computer things on him. Go to the courthouse and see if Carletta knows something!"

Imo held the squawking phone away from her ear. "Bye-bye, dear," she said when Martha finished. While she folded laundry, she considered things. Was she being foolish and hasty about Fenton?

Whenever Imo had gardening concerns, it was Maimee Harris that she called. A virtual fount of practical wisdom, she'd never failed Imo.

She dialed her. "Maimee?"

"Oh, hello dear."

"Uhmm, hi! Lovely weather, isn't it?" Imo said.

"Yes, yes, lovely. I've been out in my garden."

"That's nice." Imo closed her eyes to think better. "I've fallen in love," she blurted out.

Silence.

"Dear?" Mamie's voice registered concern. "What did you say?"

"I've met a man, Maimee. Someone special."

"Goodness!"

"I think he's the one." Imo smiled.

"Well, who?"

"His name is Fenton Mabry," Imo said.

"That's nice. I don't believe I know the Mabry name."

Imo's pulse raced. "He . . . He's a widower . . . likes to farm . . . grows the sweetest melons you ever ate."

"Farms. That's good." Maimee chuckled. "How old is he?"

What was with these women's fixation on age? Imo decided to be blunt with Maimee. "He's *eighty*-three."

A long silence, then Maimee said, "Imogene, did you say *eighty*-three?"

"Yes."

"My word! You do realize you've got to be married a minimum of ten years to collect social security on a husband, don't you?"

Imo sank down into a kitchen chair. She studied her hands. Why had she assumed everyone would be thrilled about this? "No, Maimee, I had no idea," she said and hung up.

Later she decided that Martha and Maimee were both thinking way too much. In this case, love was not a thinking thing. Imo knew enough just by looking into Fenton's eyes

What could she do to bring Lou around? Martha and Maimee would realize in time, but wouldn't it be nice if she had Lou's blessing at the start? She told herself she'd give more thought to that once she'd made the tea for supper.

She emptied a cup of sugar into a pitcher and plopped a tea bag into a boiler to simmer.

"Have you seen Silas's passy?" Jeanette scurried through the kitchen. "It ain't nowhere."

Imo shook her head. "Run out and ask Lou. She was playing with him last time I saw it."

"Nah," Jeanette said. "She's in a bad mood since you told her you love Mr. Mabry."

Imo clicked off the burner and used a wooden spoon to anchor the teabag to the bottom of the pot while she poured the scalding brew into the pitcher. "What on Earth can I do?" She dropped the wooden spoon into the sink. "It's been over a year." Imo said slowly, taking care not to sound shrill.

"She thinks . . ." Jeanette patted little Silas's hand. "That you oughtn't to get involved romantically. Did you know she keeps Daddy's old boots under her bed?"

"Lou will come to understand," Imo said, hearing desperation in her own voice. Lou had been happier in the last few months, almost back to her old self. She worked her little fingers to the bone out in the garden, humming happily beside Bingo, and Imo had finally stopped worrying over her.

The late afternoon sky was lovely when she went outside with shears to gather an armload of bachelor's buttons. She looked up, startled, as a shadow fell over her. Lou stood there with her arms crossed and her bottom lip poked out.

"Hey," Imo said.

"I wanted to know if you want to go with me up to Uncle Silas's grave?" She asked. "We could take those flowers you're picking."

Imo sat back on her haunches. "It's almost five. Mr. Mabry's coming at six, so I don't have the time today, sugar foot." She held out a hand to pat Lou's arm, but Lou stepped back like Imo was a leper.

Fenton arrived with a big bucket of purple hull peas. "Pay you five dollars to shell these," he said to Lou.

She accepted, and then he sat out on the porch and helped her shell them. "What time does the train run by?" Imo heard him ask Lou about the track on the other side of the Etowah.

"At 7:15," Lou answered in a low voice, staring down into her lap.

Fenton raised an eyebrow and aimed a shell into the bucket they had stationed between them. "Listen, let's us run down there and put a penny on the tracks."

Imo listened to their feet clomp across the porch and down the steps. She sat out on the porch and waited until Fenton and Lou came running up. Lou placed a smooth copper football into Imo's palm. "Feel that!" she instructed. "Still warm."

"Long train," breathed Fenton. He sat down on the steps and wiped his brow. "I remember thinking," he said, "when I was just a teenager, how I could hop onto one of those boxcars and take me a ride if I wanted."

"Why didn't you?" Lou looked over at him and smiled like the same thought had crossed her mind.

"Well, for one thing, my daddy depended on me." Fenton rubbed his chin. "And for another, there was a purty lil' ole gal I had my eye on."

Uh oh, Imo thought, another Henry. Good thing I found out now. She sat ramrod straight and stared out at the barn. She had little Silas to hug on now, anyway.

"What happened?" Lou asked.

"She married my best friend." Fenton laughed and tickled little Silas's dimpled knees. "Showed me a thang or two about unanswered prayers. Yep, there was something even better waiting for me."

"Ruby Jane?" Jeanette asked.

He about fell out of his chair laughing at that one. "No, sugar. Thing was, after she run off on me, I joined the rodeo. Some of my best memories."

Imo relaxed.

"But didn't you get married later?" Lou asked.

Fenton told them all about his life. He threw in his wife, brother, sisters, and children, and talked about them like they knew them as well as he did. He mentioned their foibles and eccentricities, too, like that was as important for them to know as the good.

When Fenton was gone, Imo stepped out on the porch to see a fat August moon hanging right over the barn. Her heart felt full as well. Everything was better now. Just like a miracle, at supper Jeanette announced she would go back and finish high school. She would get her diploma and build a life for herself and little Silas. Imo saw herself with Fenton, sharing Crimson Sweets in the summer and warm nuzzling in the winter and . . .

And Lou would come around. Hadn't Imo seen Lou and Fenton, laughing and talking together like best friends?

Loutishie's Notebook

It was a few weeks after Imo dropped the bomb on us, and Mr. Mabry came for supper again, bringing a big mess of sweet corn. I was out in the side yard with Bingo, who was digging himself a cool hole to lay down in. Mr. Mabry spotted us and came around the corner of the house.

"Purty day, ain't it?" He asked me.

"I reckon," I said.

"Hear you grow some of the finest tomatoes in these parts. Mind if I take a little tour of your garden?"

I jumped up. "Sure!" I felt ten feet tall as I led him to the tomatoes.

He took off his hat, held it over his chest, and blew out a long stream of air. He held a tomato in his palm. "These are bea-u-ti-ful."

We walked over to the squash. "Hear you're starting high school the end of this month," he said.

"Yessir."

"I went to school up to the seventh grade." He plopped down in the dirt. "Had us a one-room schoolhouse. All the grades together."

"Why didn't you finish high school?"

"I was out in the fields helping daddy. The farm was my schooling. Book-learning was for the city kids."

"I'm a little scared of high school," I said.

He nodded. "New stuff is hard. I know. Never did take to them fancy new tractors. Stick to Ruby Jane."

I laughed.

"But you, young lady. You keep it up. Schoolin', I mean. Your aunt is so proud of your good marks. Said you was something else with gardening and critters. Regular Dr. Doolittle. I imagine you could be one of them vets or something."

That was the clincher. The moment I fell in love with Mr. Mabry. Not romantic love, but a deep and fierce respect, and a joy of being in his presence.

The next time he came out to the house, he found me in the garden. "Hi, Lou," he said. "I have a favor to ask."

I nodded.

"Your aunt," he said, "she's a mighty fine person . . . and she told me all about your Uncle Silas. What a fine person he was. A great man."

"Yep. He was."

"How much he adored all his girls."

"Uh huh." I couldn't imagine what he was leading up to.

"And I don't want folks saying his widow is anything but a virtuous woman. Don't want to give 'em no reason to talk."

"Huh?"

"Is it asking too much for you to be our chaperone? When we're together?"

I was speechless. I didn't utter a word until I saw Imo heading our way with some coffee grounds and cantaloupe rinds for the compost heap.

"Yes. Sure," I uttered quickly. "I'll do it."

Imo asked him to come look at her gladiolus with her, and I ran in the house to tell Jeanette. "Hey," I said to her. "Something really weird just happened. Something Mr. Mabry said."

"What?" she asked and I told her about the chaperone stuff.

"You're kidding!" Jeanette laughed like a hyena. "Old as he is? He can't even get it up anymore!"

I acted like I knew exactly what she meant by that. "No, I'm not kidding. He doesn't want anyone to question Imo's virtue or her to get a bad reputation."

When they got inside the house, I wandered in and sat down with a book. Mr. Mabry was very polite. He hung his hat on the back of a chair and waited till Imo sat down. He sat down clear across the room from her. Not once did he lay a hand on Imo. I thought it was more like having a grandfather than a man after Imo.

I knew we were all laughing more when Mr. Mabry was around. Though I had to hang out inside the house every time Mr. Mabry was there, it wasn't as dull as I thought it would be. We played a lot of Scrabble and looked at TV and talked. We ate a lot, too. It was a wonder he was so skinny, the way he ate. Mr. Mabry and Imo were no big secret. Martha knew and that meant all of Euharlee knew.

"What do you think's going on with Imo and Mr. Mabry?" I asked Jeanette one evening.

"I dunno." She shrugged and picked little Silas up. I followed her down the hall and outside, to the well-house to get his stroller.

"You think they're more than friends?"

"I said I don't know. Now why don't you go find something to do?" She buckled little Silas in and set his bottle between his knees.

"Well, I think they're getting serious," I said to her back as she rounded the house. "I overheard part of a conversation with Martha."

"May be," she said.

It made me feel nauseous to hear her agreeing like that. "But maybe not. Maybe they're just staying being friends. Haven't you ever been just friends with a boy?"

She laughed. Bingo joined us, licking little Silas's face.

"I doubt they'll get married," I said. "Do you?"

Jeanette let out a long sigh. "I swannee, Lou. I don't know. Anyway, he's a real old man, and I told you, he can't get it up anymore."

Jeanette laughed so hard I decided not to ask her what that meant. I was really confused at that point. What was not to like about Mr. Mabry? There was no reason for us not to accept him as our friend and welcome him into the bosom of our family. But there was a problem if Imo thought I'd let her marry him.

FIFTEEN

To Everything There is a Season

*"December's real nice for a wedding. You could
have it at night, with candles and some of them
poinsettias they sell at the Wal-Mart."*
— CARLETTA HUGHES
courthouse clerk, advising Imogene and Fenton on setting a date

September was still unbearably hot. What got Imo
through the day while the girls were at school was
the constant attention little Silas required. Fenton's
date-nights were still Tuesday and Saturday and things were
progressing much slower than Imo planned.

The problem was he hadn't so much as kissed her yet.
Lou always seemed to be right there in the middle of things
when Imo wanted to test the waters.

What she needed to do was get rid of the girl for an
evening, like tonight, and get Fenton alone. Let nature take
its course.

"Lou-ti-shie!" She stood on the porch and called out
across the yard.

Bingo scampered up from the bottoms, with Lou not far
behind him.

"I've done all my homework," Lou said, panting. There was a question in her eyes.

"I know you did. I wanted to ask you something."

"What?"

Imo smiled warmly. "Listen. What are your plans for tonight?"

"What do you mean?" Lou stood there with her hands tucked into her armpits.

"I realized you haven't been over to Tara's house in so long, and I thought you might want me to run you over there."

Lou looked hard at her. "Isn't Mr. Mabry coming over tonight?"

Imogene nodded. "What's Tara been up to these days?" she asked.

"I don't know. She's got a boyfriend now," Lou said in that serious way she had.

"Well, how about a movie?"

"No thanks." Lou turned to go back down the dirt road.

"Lou?" Imo sounded so feeble to herself. Once that child had her mind made up, it was impossible to get through to her.

"What?" she called over her shoulder.

"You be careful down there at that river."

She should have said, *I need some time to be alone with Mr. Mabry. So I can see how he feels about me.* But the child's face had stopped her cold.

Imo walked back into the house just as Jeanette seated

herself at the table to do her homework. Little Silas lay sleeping against her shoulder.

At least miracles were still occurring. It wasn't long ago that Imo feared for Jeanette's future. She pictured all of life's ups and downs, probably designed so that not too many things were up or down at one time. Just enough downs not to let you feel like it was all going your way, and just enough ups so you didn't wish you were dead.

However, there were some ups a person could control or at least *try* to control. She sat at the kitchen table and with a trembling hand, she wrote a note:

Do you love me as more than a friend? Yes or no? She put a box beside each possible response. P.S. Don't mention this to Lou, I will tell her about it if you say yes.

She hooked an ink pen onto the folded paper. Infantile? Yes, but she was running out of patience. Plus, after she thought about it, she figured he would think it was romantic. That is, *if* he had those kinds of feelings for her.

Well, she'd soon see.

After supper, Fenton sat in the recliner reading the paper. Imo slipped the folded note into his lap. He jumped a bit and fingered the note. Then he brought it up near his face and read it.

Imo swallowed as he placed a hand on his heart, clicked the point of the pen out, and smoothed the note on his thigh.

Imo's heart threatened to push its way out of her throat as he slid the note into her palm. She was afraid to look, but she did.

He checked the yes box!

Imo raised her eyebrows to ask. He nodded. Lou looked over at them.

Should they kiss? Shake hands? Something to seal it. She blew a discreet kiss.

Fenton came for her in his pickup Friday at noon. It was washed clean of the mud splatters. The dome of his head was softly shining, too. Imo climbed in, wearing the red hibiscus dress for the second time in her life.

"You look lovely," he said.

The truck whooshed by the fading crepe myrtles on the square in downtown Euharlee and pulled up in front of the county health department.

Fenton said, "Reckon they'll believe we're both over eighteen?"

She blushed. "I've got my birth certificate to prove it."

"Yep," he said and patted his breast pocket. He slid out of the truck and hitched up his suit pants. She wasn't used to him in anything but overalls, and he looked so dapper.

The clerk inside the health department gave them two clipboards with forms to fill out, along with a pamphlet on AIDS. Imo looked hard at her.

"Oh. That's required by law, ma'am, doesn't mean a thing."

Next they went by the courthouse. "You two set a date yet?" asked Carletta Hughes, the license clerk. She looked at Fenton. He didn't say a thing.

"December's real nice for a wedding," said Carletta. "You

could have it at night, with candles and some of them poinsettias they sell at the Wal-mart."

"Does sound pretty," Imo said. She turned to see what Fenton's reaction was, and he nodded. He was precious! Letting her make all these decisions.

At four they swung into the Dairy Queen lot for soft serve cones. Imo waited in a sticky booth.

When Fenton returned with two steaming cones, she accepted one and clacked it against his. "A toast," she said, "to happiness."

Loutishie's Notebook

It was the middle of September, a late afternoon, when Imo asked me did I want to go looking for blackberry stragglers.

"Maybe we'll get enough for one last pie." She squeezed my shoulder.

"Fine." I whistled for Bingo.

She strode toward the woods at the far end of the side pasture, her Keds leaving little half moons in the dirt.

"Here we are." Imo stopped near a thicket. "Keep an eye out for snakes!"

She waded in. "Lou?" Imo said when our shoulders brushed. "What do you think of me and Mr. Mabry?" Her brown eyes were eager.

I shrugged and thought of him. How much fun it was having

him around. But, when I imagined it, it was the way it had been. Me and Imo and him as a happy threesome of buddies.

"We're getting married," Imo blurted out.

I froze.

"What do you think?"

"Why can't you just stay friends!" A thorn jabbed me and my eyes teared.

"Oh, Lou." Imo pulled me close while I sucked the bloody place on my knuckle.

"You said," I snuffled, "nobody could replace Uncle Silas . . ."

"He won't be replacing him," she said, and smoothed my hair back behind my ears. "Fenton and I love each other." Imo looked out through the trees.

"How do you know? You thought you loved Mr. Sosebee."

"Well." Imo said. "It's like those cardinal bushes over there."

I looked in the direction she was nodding, at bird-shaped blooms perched on the bush's branches.

She breathed out. "Yessum, from far away, you'd swear they were a bunch of birds sitting there. But you get up close and you know they're not." She paused. "So, when I got close enough to Mr. Sosebee, I saw it wasn't really love."

"Oh," I said.

"Yep. You know the real thing when you get close."

"But, why? **Why** can't you just stay friends?" I finally asked.

"There's a lot of things you don't understand, Lou," she said, "A woman has needs for one thing. Then there's decency. A woman my age just can't go hanging around some man. . ."

I was too stunned to listen to the rest of it. I concentrated in-

stead on my purple stained fingers and the bloody scratch pulsing on my knuckle. I needed to get away from Imo. "You pick
'em," I said, that whole neck of the woods a wavery blur on account of the tears in my eyes.

I wasn't certain on how to begin my discussion with
Reverend Peddigrew.

"Loutishie," he said and leaned back in his chair. "What brings
you here today?"

In his overalls and a checkered shirt, Reverend Peddigrew
looked like he was ready to plow a field.

"Hasn't it been unseasonably hot lately?" I said.

"Yes indeed."

I looked at the wall of bookshelves behind him. "You read all
of those?"

"Most of them," he said, looking at me over the top of his bifocals. "How's school?"

"Okay," I said.

He offered me a ginger ale from the tiny refrigerator in the
corner. I accepted and he rose to get it, his big work boots out
of place on the polished oak floor. He sat back down and leaned
forward. "And your aunt? I hear she's getting married." He
pierced me with his understanding eyes.

"Yep," I said through clenched teeth.

"How do you feel about all this?"

"I don't know," I said.

"You don't want your aunt to marry again?" Reverend
Peddigrew shook his head.

"No. I don't know." I looked down.

"You feel like she's ill-advised in this union?"

"Right." I had a sip of my ginger ale. "I mean she says she loves him . . . he's not after her for money . . ." I paused for effect.

"Go on, child."

"Well, I mean it's not like he can get it up anymore. At his age, I mean."

Reverend Peddigrew's face turned as red as a turnip. "I see." He focused on a paper weight on his desk.

"So, you may ask," I went on, "what exactly is the problem?"

"I might ask that." His voice was meek.

"The problem, Reverend," I paused for effect, "is, if she satisfies this earthly desire, what's she going to do when she gets up to heaven and there's Uncle Silas? The man she spent forty-eight years married to? And here she is re-married?"

A car pulled up and stopped outside. Reverend Peddigrew rose up slightly.

"It's just Jeanette," I said. "She'll wait."

He mopped his brow. "You're basically worried that your aunt will get up to heaven and be married to Mr. Mabry, while your Uncle Silas looks on."

"Yessir!"

He breathed out a long sigh and interlaced his fingers into one of those churches with his forefingers as the steeple. He opened his Bible. "For in the Resurrection they neither marry, nor are given in marriage, but are as the angels of God in heaven. Mark 12, verse 25."

"What?" I looked at him.

He read this passage where the Sadducees were trying to trip Jesus up with a question about a woman who married seven brothers, one after another, when they kept dying on her. They asked Jesus whose wife was she going to be in the Resurrection, and he said none. Boy, the Bible was clear on that one.

Jeanette said, "About time, holy roller," when I got into the car, but it didn't bother me.

Imo was on the porch when we pulled up. She looked at me hard, and it was like she could see the change in my heart. She grabbed my shoulders and pulled me into her bosom for a hug. I squeezed her back and tried to think of something I could say, like "I'm sorry," but I couldn't find the words.

Dear God, I prayed silently, **let us all be safe and happy and keep me pure and holy and make Jeanette turn from the lusts of the flesh and thank you for Mr. Mabry making Imo so happy and please don't let the Rapture happen in my lifetime.**

CHAPTER SIXTEEN

No Stranger to the Rain

"*Gardeners! Be encouraged—Euharlee has set a
new record for rainfall this autumn.
While the soggy days may dampen our spirits, just
think of how easy they make it to put in our spring
bulbs. I have a wide selection of hardy bulbs:
Dutch iris, muscari, hyacinth, tulips,
crocus, daffodil, and lilies.*"
— MRS. KENNETH BEAL
advertisement in the *Euharlee Weekly Farm Bulletin,* page three

*I*t was late October before Euharlee really began to
cool down. Much to everyone's relief, temperatures
dropped below sixty degrees in the evenings. So far,
it had been the wettest fall in memory.

As depressing as the constantly overcast sky and the ever-
present puddles were, Imo managed to keep her thoughts
on December fourteenth. She stopped at the kitchen calendar with little Silas slung over one arm. "Six weeks," she
told him. Sometimes she couldn't believe it was actually
happening. Wedding clothes the color of a spring daffodil
hung in her closet.

That made her pause to consider the pasteboard boxes full of bulbs that she had waiting in the well-house. Daffodils, crocuses, and Dutch irises. She'd been waiting for the rain to let up before she put them in the ground.

But what if it went on like this? Imo had to remind herself that tomorrow never came and that if she wanted a beautiful yard come spring, she'd have to get on out there. She gathered her gloves, the mattock, and a digging fork.

Lou appeared on the back porch as Imo was stepping into her gardening shoes. "You sure you want to get out in this?" Lou asked.

Imo smiled. "I can't think of any other way to get my bulbs planted."

"Let me do it!"

"Aren't you sweet." Imo looked out at the back yard full of puddles with big drops plopping down into them. "I reckon I could use the time to clear out Silas's things from the closet and the chest of drawers."

Did she see Lou stiffen when she said that? It had seemed at last that the girl was accepting the upcoming marriage. "Why don't we do the bulbs together?" Imo said gently. "Then we can talk."

Imo waited while Lou hunted her boots. She had to remind herself that Lou was a *teenager*, prone to these mood swings. She would be back to herself soon. She adored Fenton.

Imo smiled her warmest smile and led Lou out into the overcast day. "I've got the permanent ink marker and some flat stones in my pocket," she said, as they stopped near the last of the cleomes and dahlias. "They're almost gone, aren't they?" she asked, pointing to the flowers.

"I guess," said Lou, leaning against a hoe.

"I'm thinking of making my own wedding cake this go-round." Imo pushed up her cuffs and surveyed the sodden ground.

"Who did your first cake?"

"Mrs. Scruggs. She's dead now."

"You could just not have a cake at all this time." Lou narrowed her eyes as Imo swung the mattock.

"What?"

"Why don't you just go to a justice of the peace? Do it quick. Don't worry about cake. I don't even care if you invite me!" Lou cried, swiping tears mixed with rain from her cheeks.

"Oh, Lou," Imo said, laying down the mattock, "I thought you were happy about all this."

"I did too," said Lou.

Imo thought quickly. "When we get done, let's look at my wedding album together. I had bridesmaids then, and Silas looked so handsome! I had a beautiful white dress Mama sewed. This wedding certainly won't compare to that one!"

That should do the trick. She simply would prove to Lou that she was not forgetting Silas. Wasn't replacing him.

Now, clothes plastered to them, they set in the bulbs. It was satisfying work. She lost track when she was out here in the dirt. Time and troubles ceased to exist. When they were finished, Imo knelt and slid a hand into her pocket, pulled out three stones, and hovered over them like an umbrella. She wrote daffodil, crocus, and iris, and instructed Lou on where to place them on top of the freshly mounded earth.

"What for?" Lou asked, blinking raindrops from her lashes.

"This," Imo said, "is like a little insurance policy."

"Looks like a graveyard to me," said Lou, shaking her head.

"It's to help us mind where the bulbs are down there," Imo said, nodding her head. "You cannot imagine the sick feeling you get when you slice into one of your bulbs by accident."

When they got inside and dried off, Imo hurried to the china cabinet and slid out her wedding album, eager to touch the yellowed satin cover. She knew each picture by heart. There were only five. Money had been tight, and all they got was one of the whole wedding party, one with both sets of parents, and three of the bride and groom.

She pointed out the one of her cutting the cake and feeding a bite to a grinning Silas. "See there, Lou? Big fancy three-layer cake. These roses here were deep pink."

The girl looked at the photo, unblinking. "I'm tired," she said and left Imo with the memories.

Silas. She touched his face. Their image had begun to fade a little, and a panic seized her. Could a photo fade completely away? Her hands trembled as she closed the album. She remembered the first time she laid eyes on him. Sweet, sweet Silas. For a moment, she let herself wallow in the past, and she was a bride again, looking eagerly forward to a life with Silas Lavender.

"*Is this me? Imogene Lavender, getting married again?*" She touched her chest, dragged herself into the bedroom and fell across the bed. Tears fell like the rain outside.

The next day, Halloween, turned out to be another soppy day. Imo summoned up the gumption to sort through Silas's things. She would not allow herself to even think as she worked.

That afternoon, Jeanette dressed little Silas up like a ghost. She held him up to Imo and sang the words, "twick or tweat."

Imo was glad for the distraction. She stood up and patted his head. "Aren't you precious? About time for us to get busy on supper, isn't it sweetie?"

Shadows were long as Imo browned ground beef for chili. Soon it would be pitch dark. She looked at little Silas in his swing, his costume flapping behind him with every forward motion. They never had any trick-or-treaters out this far. But still, she'd bought a bag of Mary Janes for her and Fenton to share.

Imo emptied a packet of Chili-O seasoning into the pot. "We'll eat when Fenton gets here, girls," she called. Jeanette had the TV on. An anchorwoman was warning all the ghosts and goblins to trick or treat with an adult and to wear light-reflective clothing.

"Lou!" she hollered down the hallway as she stirred the simmering chili. She set out the salad and a box of saltines. Mr. Mabry should be there any second. She walked down the dark hall, Lou's door was pulled to, outlined in light. She tapped gently.

"Who is it?" Lou called.

"Me. Can I come in?"

"Yes."

Imo went in. The girl was sitting on the floor, using a tablespoon to scoop out bird seed onto squares of netting, which she was tying with ribbons. She knew this was Lou's way of showing acceptance.

"He here yet?" Lou looked up from her work.

"No." Imo glanced at her watch. "He's never been late before, has he? You keep an ear out, I'm going to carry some things out to the barn."

Imo scurried back and forth through the rain with bags, checking her watch every few minutes.

At seven, she was getting concerned. Finished and resting in her bedroom, she decided Fenton had gotten cold feet about marrying her. It could happen. She closed her weary eyes. It was pure dark outside, and now he was one hour late. She drifted off to sleep.

Imo jumped when there was a knock at the door. She groped the air above her bedside table for her lamp and heard Lou laughing. It was eight o'clock. The first thing she thought was she'd burned the chili.

Imo raced down the hallway. When she hit the bright

lights of the den she saw Lou pouring candy into a hat held out by Fenton.

"Our first trick-or-treater!" Lou turned to Imo, beaming. "Mr. Mabry's dressed up like a park ranger!"

"I see that." Imo took in his khaki pants and shirt with a clip-on photo-badge at the pocket. With a twinkle in his eye he unwrapped a Mary Jane.

"Smells mighty good in here," he said.

She resisted the urge to ask him why he was late.

"Chili's ready," Lou said.

"Great," he said.

As they ate, Imo peered at the photo on his badge. It really was him. "I didn't know you were a park ranger," she said.

"Actually, I'm just a honorary one. Or you might say, an ornery one tonight. The boys gave me these," he gestured to his hat and shirt, "when I cut that deal with them."

Then he told them he was late because he'd had to attend to some hooligans. "Yep, bunch of boys drinking beer. Setting up a deer stand."

"Really?" Lou asked.

"Yep. They was just a laughing and carrying on. Playing loud music, honking horns. Had rocking chairs set up in the back of two pickups." He shook his head. "Had on them fake rubber faces. Let's see, there was a Ronald Reagan and a Elvis and what's that old fellers' name? One who plays the piana and wears all them glittery costumes?"

"Liberace," Imo said.

"Him. Some others I didn't recognize. Drunk as skunks. Building a deer stand."

Lou took in a sharp breath. "What'd you say to them?"

"Said it was private property. Then I preached at 'em some. Told 'em drunkards and trespassers weren't going to inherit the kingdom."

"Wow." Lou's eyes were huge. "They leave?"

He grinned. "Not till I put on my o-fficial get-up here. Figgered if they was going to be dressed up, I was too."

After supper was over and cleaned up, and little Silas was tucked in for the night, the three of them played Scrabble and chewed on Mary Janes.

"You still got all your own teeth, Fenton?" Imo unwrapped a piece of candy.

He gave her a wide smile. "Enough of 'em."

She laughed.

Loutishie's Notebook

In November, women streamed in and out of the house with wedding gifts. One evening there was a knock at the door. "I'll get it!" I hollered. Wanda stood there with a present in her hands.

"Hello, Lou. Imo here?"

"Just a minute." I ushered Wanda into the dining room where all the gifts were displayed.

"Sure is racking up the loot, isn't she? For a second wedding?" Wanda was looking at two little blue glass birds nestled in tissue paper. "I hear he's loaded with money."

"He's a truck farmer."

"What?"

"He sells what he grows from the back of his pickup."

"I see." She frowned. "Well, what does he look like then?"

"*Gorgeous*," I said.

Imo hurried in. "Hello, Wanda. How nice to see you."

"Hi hon'. I just had to drop by and bring you a little something." Imo had hardly gotten her breath when Wanda put the gift in her hands and said, "Open it! I can't wait."

I lurked behind the recliner, watching Imo carefully slit the tape. "How lovely!" she said, peering underneath tissue paper.

The best I could tell it was a white nightgown.

"Now, I knew you would need a new gown darlin'." Wanda winked at me. "For your wedding night. Go on, take it out. I fancied it up a little bit."

"What?" Imo was puzzled. She pinched it at the shoulder seams and whipped it out with a flourish. Slinky white clouds dripped to the floor. The funny thing was, there was a pink feather boa awkwardly stitched around the hem of the gown.

"How interesting," Imo said, fingering the pink froth.

Wanda giggled. "Like it?"

"Yes, dear. It's mighty fancy." Imo smiled. I could tell she was just being polite.

"Now, listen. I sewed that fur on there for a reason."

"Well, you certainly made it pretty. Did a fine job."

"I sewed that fur on the hem so you could keep your neck warm at night!" Wanda's big red lips screeched with laughter. I saw Imo blush.

The next evening was a Thursday and when Mr. Mabry walked into the dining room, he got all excited. "Never had so many purty things," he said, fingering stacks of tablecloths, towels, and nightgowns. "I reckon I **am** rich now."

It was dusk the following Sunday, and we were in the kitchen making pineapple sandwiches.

The phone rang.

"I'll get it," I said, setting the mayonnaise knife on a napkin.

"May I speak to Imogene Lavender, please," a crackly elderly lady's voice said. I would have thought it was a relative or a friend, but the woman asked for "M-O-Jean", like there was no I at the front of her name. I held my hand over the receiver. "For you, Imo. I think it's long-distance."

Imo carefully placed the jagged-edged lid of the pineapple can into the trash, wiped her fingers, and picked up the receiver. "This is she." Her voice was bright and perky.

I bit into the soft white bread of my sandwich and looked through the window at the last of the sun sinking down behind the barn. Imo's eyes rested on me as she listened.

Then, out of nowhere, she gave a gutteral "uhhn!", and her eyes became vacant and uncomprehending. I watched as she swayed to one side, groping at a shelf of ceramic chickens before she collapsed with a sickening thud.

Immobilized by shock for a moment, I tasted the metallic can of the pineapple. My scalp tightened, and my neck hairs flew up, and like a crazy dream, I flung my sandwich to the floor and leapt over to her. Her feet were splayed apart on the cool linoleum, and she was crying out, "Help us, Jesus, my Lord God in Heaven!"

Too terrified to even breathe, I knelt and held her by her shoulders. Jeanette stared with enormous eyes as Imo babbled about mules and deer hunters and guns. Finally I found my voice.

"Imo, Imo," I pled, "what's wrong? You're not making a lick of sense." Fear kept me from swallowing the slick, gummy ball of bread stuck in my throat.

Imo struggled to tell us something, but the effort made her limp, and her eyes closed. Purple veins jutted out on her temples. Jeanette plunked little Silas on the floor, sank to her knees and shuffled over right beside me.

"Oh my God!" she screamed into my ear, "Mama's having a heart attack! Oh my God. Oh my God. Oh my God." Then she fell forward onto Imo's chest, sobbing. Little Silas began to shriek at the top of his lungs, and out of the phone, which was hanging down and scraping the floor, was the voice of that old lady squawking away.

It was bedlam, the entire world was flying apart.

EPILOGUE

*T*he days right after that are hazy. All I really see clearly inside the house is the way someone, probably Martha, packed up all the wedding presents, put them on top of the sideboard, and draped a sheet over them. And how the kitchen table was loaded with pies and cakes that nobody was interested in.

Fenton's funeral was held at the Church of God in Rockmart, Georgia, which met in a vacant mattress warehouse with folding chairs for pews.

Fenton's daughters and their families flew in from Louisiana for the funeral, and they told us how the park rangers said they found him. No one could rightly figure how it all happened, but the deer hunters must have mistook Ruby Jane for a deer and shot her clear through the head. Then the bullet must have passed into Fenton's heart and killed him instantly. He didn't suffer at all, they said.

Before the funeral commenced, Imo sat on a burgundy velvet sofa right inside the double glass doors saying, hi, to folks. Fenton's daughters said to Imo: "You made him happy. He talked about you on the phone all the time. And your girls, too."

The preacher was a man in his early thirties named Montgomery Pike, and he had tattoos and scars and piercings all over his body. Martha told Imo that he traveled around the country giving his testimony to youth groups and telling them not to try drugs, but to try God. He'd been a singer in a band called Greasy Cheese Sluts before he got hooked on hymns.

He preached right to the faces of Fenton's daughters. They were seated along the front row.

"We can't control life," he started out. He reminded me of Elvis a little, the way he strutted up and down a strip of orange carpeting and shook his head around.

"But Fenton Mabry knew how he wanted to leave this life on earth. And he left doing something that he loved. He loved farming. Getting his hands in God's rich soil. He loved sowing seeds and reaping a harvest." The minister pantomimed digging a hole and dropping a seed in.

"And on more than one occasion, after services, I stopped him, and I said to him, 'Fenton, I hope I'm as spry and active as you are when I'm in my eighties.' And he laughed and said to me how thankful he was to still be able to get around and have a sharp mind. He said to me that he wanted to leave this earth while he was still in his boots. Fenton didn't *want* to get feeble."

He rolled up his sleeves, and I saw a tattoo of a snake curled around his forearm. "So, people, this is an answer to prayer. We should rejoice that Fenton finished his earthly course, and we should praise our Maker for answering Fenton's prayer!" He cupped a hand behind his ear to elicit some "Amens."

I didn't feel too joyous. When we got home from the funeral, I ran down to the bottoms. I lay down on the cold, hard bank of the Etowah and cried my eyes out.

Imo was sitting in the dark, rocking little Silas, a couple of months after she got the call that told her Fenton was dead. "It doesn't make sense," I said to her, "the way this world works."

Imo said not to try and figure it all out. That some things were beyond comprehension. That some of God's finest gifts were unanswered prayers. She said it in a toneless voice that made me wonder if she really believed that.

But God *did* answer Fenton's prayer! At the same time I was praying for him and Imo's happiness together, he was beseeching God to let him cross on over before he got feeble.

Maybe all the criss-crossed, tangled-up prayers of folks on Earth, shooting upwards to God, made this life on Earth something you couldn't control.

That spring after Fenton's funeral, our daffodils, crocuses, and irises came up and spread their colors everywhere. Imo planted as big and fine a garden as she'd ever had. She practically lived out there, her brow wrinkled in thought and murmuring to herself. She didn't seem happy though. Even as we harvested and put by more tomatoes than all of Euharlee could eat, her face wore that same grim expression she had after Uncle Silas died. She looked as if she might never smile again.

That August, she sliced up Crimson Sweets that she'd grown from some of Fenton's seeds. We were all sitting on the porch with a lap full of newspaper and watermelon when, out of the blue, Imo slapped her knee and smiled. Then she laughed. "We had fun while it lasted!" she said, and neither Jeanette nor I knew who or what she was talking about.

That fall, people said Imo had finally made her peace and that she was happy.

I took Bingo with me when I left Euharlee right after high school. He was ten at that point, and he lived another four years and died in his sleep on my twenty-second birthday.

Jeanette finished high school and then she went on to beauty school. She got a job at a salon in Cartersville and she married Montgomery Pike, that Church of God minister who preached Fenton's funeral.

"I don't understand her one bit," Jeanette likes to tell me whenever I call and ask about Imo. "She stays out in that hot old garden."

I can understand. I know these are Imo's happiest times, her fingers deep in the Euharlee dirt. Something about the fact that SEEDS can turn into squash, or cucumbers, or tomatoes is a miracle, and there is nothing like the garden to make her feel a connection with heaven. To make her feel close to Uncle Silas, and to Fenton Mabry. Okay, so there's no marriage up there in heaven, but I'll bet they grow some pretty big tomatoes.

ACKNOWLEDGMENTS

One of the first feelings that comes to me when I think about the publication of this novel is gratitude, and I owe so many people for their support and generosity.

I especially want to thank my husband, Tom, for listening to ideas, for reading various drafts while the book was taking shape, and for encouraging me. Mostly I am indebted to him for his computer and tech support.

I am deeply grateful to my editor, Judy Long, for fine-tuning this book page by page, and to Tom Payton, publisher of Hill Street Press, for his far-reaching vision and enthusiasm.

I was also fortunate to have the keen and discerning eye of Lisa Knighton, who offered invaluable advice. For a tempting cover and gorgeous guts, I thank my dear friend, Anne Richmond Boston.

I acknowledge and praise the following books, each of whom augmented my gardening expertise: *The Great American Tomato Book* by Robert Hendrickson, *The Tomato Handbook* by Jennifer Bennett, *How To Grow World Record Tomatoes* by Charles H. Wilbur, *Terrific Tomatoes* by the editors of *Organic Gardening* and *Farming*, and *Putting Food By* by Ruth Hertzberg, Beatrice Vaughan, and Janet Greene.

Thanks also to Guy Clark, country troubadour, whose song entitled "Home Grown Tomatoes" echoes my sentiments exactly.

Finally, I am beholden to my family. Without the living witness of my grannies, I could not have understood the joy of growing things, and I would not be where I am today without the love and encouragement of my folks, Gloria and Bob Lowrey, who have answered innumerable questions about the practical aspects of growing things and about putting-by things from the garden.

Julie Cannon
October 2000
Athens, Georgia